"What Are You Thinking?"

"Your hair," Alana responded, slowly. "Like winter mink . . ." Her hand lingered as she allowed his hair to sift between her fingers.

"Good," Rafe murmured, "but you should take lessons from a furrier. They rub the pelt with their palms and fingertips, tease the fur with their breath, hold its softness to their lips, smell it, taste it, then gently slide the fur over their most sensitive skin."

"Do they really?" Alana asked, her breath catching.

"I don't know," Rafe admitted, his voice husky, "but that's what I'd do to you if you were a fur and I were a furrier."

Dear Reader:

There is an electricity between two people in love that makes everything they do magic, larger than life. This is what we bring you in SILHOUETTE INTIMATE MOMENTS.

SILHOUETTE INTIMATE MOMENTS are longer, more sensuous romance novels filled with adventure, suspense, glamor or melodrama. These books have an element no one else has tapped: excitement.

We are proud to present the very best romance has to offer from the very best romance writers. In the coming months look for some of your favorite authors such as Elizabeth Lowell, Nora Roberts, Erin St. Claire and Brooke Hastings.

SILHOUETTE INTIMATE MOMENTS are for the woman who wants more than she has ever had before. These books are for you.

Karen Solem
Editor-in-Chief
Silhouette Books

Forget Me Not

Elizabeth Lowell

Silhouette Intimate Moments
Published by Silhouette Books New York
America's Publisher of Contemporary Romance

Silhouette Books by Elizabeth Lowell

Summer Thunder (DES #77)
The Danvers Touch (IM #18)
Lover in the Rough (IM #34)
Summer Games (IM #57)
Forget Me Not (IM #72)

 SILHOUETTE BOOKS, A Division of Simon & Schuster, Inc.
1230 Avenue of the Americas, New York, N.Y. 10020

Copyright © 1984 by Ann Maxwell
Cover artwork copyright © 1984 Lisa Falkenstern

Distributed by Pocket Books

ISBN: 0-671-47541-X

First Silhouette Books printing October, 1984

10 9 8 7 6 5 4 3 2 1

America's Publisher of Contemporary Romance

Printed in the U.S.A

for my sister
Susan Mills
port in many storms

Chapter 1

THE NIGHTMARE BEGAN AS IT ALWAYS DID, WITH A feeling of climbing up mountain heights, the smell of pines and granite, ice and darkness closing around, clouds seething overhead, lightning lancing down, soundless thunder and an explosion of fear that shook Alana Jillian Reeves to her soul.

Cold.

She was too cold but there was no warmth, only fear hammering on her, leaving her weak. She tried to scream but no sound came. She tried to run but her feet weighed as much as mountains and were as deeply rooted in the earth. Each step took an eternity. She had to try harder, move faster or she would be caught. She was broken and bleeding, screaming down the night, running, stumbling, sprawling and then lifted high, she was falling, she spun and screamed, falling—

Alana sat up, her heart a drumroll of terror. Vaguely, she looked around, barely recognizing her surroundings despite the nightlight plugged into the wall socket near her bed. Even though she had lived in the condominium for three weeks, the room was neither comfortable nor familiar to her. It wasn't as real as the nightmare about Broken Mountain.

But then, nothing was.

Abruptly, Alana got out of bed. She stood by the wall of glass, trying to shake off the residue of nightmare and death, mistakes and a past that was beyond her ability to change or understand.

The Oregon dawn etched Alana's bedroom in shades of rose and vermilion, gold and translucent pink. The September sun was a gloaming warmth that caressed her as she stood in front of the sliding glass door that led to a private patio. She stared at her reflection in the glass as she often had since Broken Mountain, searching for some outer sign of the inexplicable six-day blank in her memory. Yet nothing showed on the outside. She looked the same as she had before she had gone up the mountain with her husband, Jack, and his futile hopes of a reconciliation.

No visible marks of the ordeal remained on Alana's five-foot-five-inch body. Her ankle had healed; it ached only when it was cold. The bruises and welts and cuts were gone, leaving no scars. She no longer had to diet in order to fit into the slender image demanded by the public. Since Broken Mountain, her appetite had gone. But it wasn't something that showed.

Alana leaned forward, staring intently at her nearly transparent reflection in the sliding glass door. Everything still looked the same. Long legs, strong from a childhood spent hiking and riding in Wyoming's high country. Breasts and waist and hips neither large nor small, skin a golden brown. Nothing unusual. Yet surely something must show. She couldn't just lose her husband and six days of her life and wonder about her sanity and not have any of it show.

But nothing did. Though her eyes were too dark, too large, too haunted, her mouth still looked as though it were curved around a secret inner smile. Her hair was still black and glossy, divided into two thick braids that fell to her waist.

Alana stared at the braids for a long moment, realizing for the first time that something about them made her . . . uneasy. She had never particularly liked having long hair but had accepted it as she had accepted the nickname Jilly, necessary parts of the childlike image that audiences loved to love. The image went with her voice, clear and innocent, as supple and pure as a mountain stream . . . *water rushing down, cold, and darkness waiting, lined with rocks.*

Alana's heart began to beat wildly again, responding to the fragment of nightmare turning in her mind.

"Stop it!" she told herself, seeing the reflection of her terror in dawn-tinted glass and sliding black shadows.

She took several deep breaths, bringing herself under control, telling herself that she had to stop treating her nightmare as though it were real. It wasn't. The nightmare was simply a creation of her mind as it dealt with the horror of Jack's death in a mountain storm, and her own near-death from exposure and the fall that had left her bruised and beaten.

That was what Dr. Gene had told her, and she had trusted his gravel voice for as long as she could remember. He had said that her amnesia, while unusual, was not pathological. It was a survival reflex. When her mind felt she was strong enough to remember the details of her husband's death and her own suffering as she clawed her way down Broken Mountain, then she would remember. And if she never remembered? That, too, was all right, he had assured her. She was young. She was healthy. She could go out and make a new life for herself.

Alana's lips twisted bitterly. It had been easy for Dr. Gene to say. He wasn't the one whose mind was turning six missing days into endless nightmares. It wasn't that she missed Jack. She and Jack had been two very separate people bound together by the accident of perfect harmony. That was enough for a successful singing career. It wasn't enough for a successful marriage. Maybe if she had done something different, tried harder or not so hard, been weaker or not so strong, cared for Jack more or pitied him less.

Or if she had never met Rafe, never loved and lost him. . . . Rafe with his laughter and his passion and his gentle, knowing hands. She had loved him since she was fifteen, had been engaged to him when she was nineteen. And they had become lovers when she was twenty. Rafael, dark hair and amber eyes glowing, watching her change as he touched her. Her fingers looked so slender against the male planes of his face, the sliding sinew and muscle of his arms. His strength always surprised her, as did his quickness, but she had never been afraid with him. Rafe could hold her, could surround her softness with his power and she felt no fear, only a consuming need to be closer still, to be held tighter, to give herself to him and to take him in return. With Rafe there had been only beauty.

Then, four years ago, the Pentagon had told Alana that Rafael Winter had died. They had told her nothing more than that. Not where her fiancé had died. Not how. Certainly not why. Just the simple fact of his death. It was a fact that had destroyed her. Never again would the lyric beauty of Rafe's harmonica call to her across the Western night. Never again would her voice blend with the chased silver instrument that sang so superbly in Rafe's hands. She had sung with Rafe for pleasure and had known no greater beauty except making love with him, bodies and minds sharing a harmony that surpassed everything, even song.

Alana had been empty, uncaring, after Rafe's death. When the minutes and hours without Rafe had piled up one by one, dragging her into darkness, she instinctively had turned to song as her only salvation, her only contact with the love she had lost.

Singing meant Jack Reeves, the man she had sung with in all the little cafés and fairs and roadhouses, the man for whom singing was a business rather than a pleasure. Jack had measured Alana's vulnerability, her desperation, and had calmly told her that there would be no more duets unless she married him and left the high plains for the high life in the city. Alana had resisted marriage, wanting no man but the one who was dead.

Then the hours without Rafe had heaped into the hundreds, a thousand, fifteen hundred . . . and she had agreed to become Jack's wife because she must sing or go insane. Rafe was dead. There was nothing left but the singing career that Jack had persistently badgered Alana for.

So Alana had left the high plains and mountains of Wyoming, hoping that in another part of the world she wouldn't hear Rafe in every summer silence, sense him in every moonrise. She had married Jack, but it was a marriage in name only. With Jack Reeves there had been nothing but an emptiness Alana had tried to fill with songs.

Now Jack was dead, killed four weeks ago by the country he had despised. She had been with him on Broken Mountain when he died. She didn't remember, though. Those six days were a blank wall. Behind that wall fear seethed and rippled, trying to break free.

And Rafe? A year ago Alana had been told that he was

alive. But it hadn't been Rafe who told her. She had found out by accident, from her brother. Rafe had never called her, never written, never in any way contacted the woman he once had said he loved.

Alana closed her eyes, unable to face their dark reflection in the glass door. Rafe dead and then not dead. Jack dead now and forever. Her love for Rafe, undying.

With a small sound, Alana turned sharply until she could no longer see her reflection. She had to get a grip on her emotions, stop living in the past, stop tearing at herself over things that were beyond her ability to change. At the very least, she had to learn to get up in the morning without going over the last three weeks and the missing six days like a litany of fear and despair.

The phone rang. Alana turned to it with a feeling of relief. It was too early for anyone she knew on the West Coast to be up. That meant it was probably her brother in Wyoming calling to see how she was.

"Hello," she said, keeping her voice steady, hoping it was Bob.

"Alana?"

She all but sighed in relief. "Hi, Bob. How's Merry?"

"Counting the weeks until February," said Bob. "If she gets much bigger, we'll have to put her in a stall with the rest of the broodmares."

Alana smiled at the thought of the petite blond Merry tucked into one of the heated stalls Bob kept for his prize mares. "Better not let Merry hear you say that."

"Hell, it was her idea." Bob paused, then, "Sis?"

Alana's hand tightened on the phone. She'd heard that tone before, little brother to big sister, a smile and affectionate wheedling.

"When are you coming home?" he asked.

Alana's heart began to beat too fast. She didn't know

how to tell Bob that she was frightened by the thought of returning to the ranch, to Broken Mountain, mantled in ice and darkness. Before Jack's death she had loved the ranch, the mountains, the silence, the heights and clouds swirling overhead. In time, even the memories of Rafe had comforted her—Rafe reflected in every lake, every fragrant forest, sunsets and sunrises sweeping across the land like fire, the wind's keening harmonies echoing the music Rafe had made. She had come to love the land even more because she and Rafe had been part of it, lovers suspended between sky and mountains, more beautiful than either, timeless, burning with the sun.

But now those mountains terrified Alana, and the memories were both an agony and an armor that she pulled around her like the colors of dawn, hoping to drive away the horror and darkness that crawled up out of the abyss of those six missing days.

"I've already talked to your agent," continued Bob. "He told me you've refused to accept any concerts and won't even look at the songs he's sent to you. So don't tell me how busy you are. If you're writing songs again, you can write them just as well here. Better. You always did your best work here."

With a conscious effort, Alana loosened her grip on the phone. She had no more excuses, so she said nothing.

"Sis? I need you here."

"Bob—"

"Don't say no, sis," he said urgently. "You don't even know what I want yet."

And you don't know what I want. You've never even asked if I want something. But the words went no farther than Alana's mind, a silent cry of need. Even as the cry echoed in her mind, she recognized its unfairness. What she needed Bob couldn't provide—warmth and reassurance, safety and a man's hard strength standing between her and the abyss, protecting her until she knew what had happened and could protect herself once more. Love waiting instead of terror. A dream to banish a nightmare.

Rafe.

But Rafe was just a dream. The nightmare was real. Death had taught her that. Her mother's death. Rafe's mistaken death. Jack's unmistakable death. That was the world she had to live in.

With a deep breath, Alana gathered herself and set about living in that world just as she always had, alone. She had done this many times before, the deep breath and the determination to do the best she could with what she had, no matter how little that seemed when nightmare descended like a storm.

"What do you want, Bob?" she asked softly.

"You know cash has always been a problem with the ranch," said Bob quickly. "Land-poor, as they say. Well, Merry and I had this idea for a classy—and I mean classy—dude operation. High-country fishing safaris for people who can pay high prices. We had it all planned, all lined up, all our ducks in a row. Our first two customers are very exclusive travel agents. Their clientele reads like *Who's Who*. Everything was going great for us. Then Merry got pregnant. I mean, we're both happy, we've been trying for two years, but . . ."

"But what?"

"Dr. Gene says Merry can't go on the pack trip. She was going to be our cook and entertainer and general soother, take the rough edges off, you know what I mean."

Alana knew exactly what her brother meant. It was the same role she had played since she was thirteen and her mother had died, leaving behind three boys, a devastated husband, and a daughter who had to grow up very quickly.

That was when Alana had learned about reaching down into herself for the smile and the touch and the comfort that the people around her had needed. She had rebuilt the shattered family as best she could; for she, too, needed the haven and the laughter and the warmth.

"It will really be more like a vacation than a job," coaxed Bob. His voice had a disturbing thread of urgency beneath the gentleness. "Riding and fishing and hiking in the high country just like we used to do. You'll love it, sis. I just know it. A real vacation for you."

Alana blocked the harsh laugh in her throat. *Vacation.* In the mountains that had nearly killed her and had killed her husband. Oh God, that was some vacation her little brother had planned for her!

"Sis," Bob said coaxingly, "I wouldn't ask if I didn't really need you. I don't have anywhere else to turn. The pack trip is all set and the two dudes are here. Please?"

Unbidden, the image of Rafe came to Alana. Late summer, a narrow mountain trail, a lame horse and a saddle that weighed nearly as much as she did. She had been leading the horse, dragging the saddle and watching the silent violence of clouds billowing toward a storm. At fifteen, she knew the dangers of being caught on an exposed ridge in a high-country cloudburst. Without warning, lightning had come down so close to her that she smelled the stink of scorched rock. Thunder came like the end of the world. Her horse had screamed and reared, tearing the reins from her hand. Then the horse's lameness had been overridden by terror, and the animal had bolted down the mountainside.

She, too, had been terrified, her nostrils filled with the smell of lightning and her ears deafened by thunder. Then she had heard someone calling her name. Rafe had come to her across the talus slope, riding his plunging, scrambling horse with the strength and grace she had always admired. He had lifted her into the saddle in front of him and spurred his horse back down the slope while lightning arced around. Sheltered in a thick growth of spruce, she had waited out the storm with Rafe, wearing his jacket and watching him with the eyes of a child-woman who was more woman and less child with every breath.

On Broken Mountain she had found first fear, then love, and finally horror. Was there another balance to be discovered on Broken Mountain, opposites joined in harmony, freeing her from nightmare?

"Sis? Say something," pleaded her brother.

Alana was appalled to hear herself take a deep breath and calmly say, "Of course I'll help you."

She didn't hear Bob's whoop of victory, his assurances that he wouldn't tell any of the dudes that she was Jilly, his gratitude that she was helping him out. She didn't hear anything but the echoes of her own agreement.

"I've got you booked on the afternoon flight to Salt Lake," said Bob quickly, as though he sensed the fragile nature of his sister's agreement. "From there, you're booked on a little feeder flight into the airport here. Got a pencil?"

Bemused, Alana stared at the phone. The simple fact that Bob had thought to take care of the details of her transportation was so unusual as to be overwhelming. It wasn't that Bob was thoughtless; he was very considerate of Merry, to the point that he was almost too protective. Alana, however, had always been taken for granted in the manner that parents and older siblings often are.

"Sis," patiently, "do you have a pencil? He'll skin me if I louse this up."

"Who will skin you?" asked Alana, as she went through

kitchen drawers looking for a pencil. She found one before Bob found his tongue.

There was a static-filled silence. Then, "The travel agent who made the arrangements," said Bob, laughing abruptly. "Ready?"

Alana grabbed a brown shopping bag, smoothed it out, and wrote down the flight numbers and times.

"Today?" she objected, as Bob's words finally penetrated her morning daze. "That's not much warning, little brother."

"That's the whole idea," he muttered.

"What?"

"Nothing, sis. Just be sure you're on that plane or my butt is grass. And thanks. You won't regret it. If anyone can pull it off, he can."

"The travel agent?" asked Alana, feeling as though she were missing half the conversation, and the most important half at that.

"Yeah, the travel agent. He's something else," said Bob dryly. "See you tonight, sis."

Numbly, Alana responded, all the while asking herself why she had agreed to do something that terrified her. She was a fool to let her warm memories of Rafe lure her back to the icy source of nightmare. She didn't even know if he was in Wyoming. In the past, Rafe's job had taken him all over the world; his time at the Winter ranch had been limited to a few weeks now and then. It had been enough, though. She had learned to love him and to accept his leaving. She had learned to live for the day when he would come home and marry her and she would never cry for him at night again.

And then Rafe had died. Or so the Pentagon had said.

Alana realized that the line was dead. She hung up and

stared at the phone. It was bright red, like the flowers in the Spanish tile that covered the kitchen counters. Red like the fireweed that was the first plant to grow after fire or avalanche devastated the mountain slopes. Red like blood.

Had she seen Jack die? Was that why her mind refused to remember?

With a shudder, Alana jerked away from the bright telephone. Rubbing her arms to chase away the chill that had been with her since Broken Mountain, she walked quickly to the closet and pulled on jeans and an old cotton blouse. From habit, she buttoned the blouse completely, concealing the delicate gold chain that Rafe had given to her. As always, her fingertip lingered on the tiny symbol of infinity, a graceful reclining figure 8, that was part of the chain. Love ever after, love without end. A dream.

Sunlight surrounded Alana as she opened the front door and retrieved the newspaper from a patch of grass. Her attention was caught by the headline in the entertainment section of the paper: *Jack 'n' Jilly's Last Song.* Slowly, she walked into the kitchen. With hands that wanted to tremble, she plugged in the coffee pot, scrambled two eggs and buttered a piece of toast. She forced herself to eat, knowing that she would have no appetite after she had read the article. But she would read it, just as she had read everything written about Jack's death, even the most scurrilous imaginings of the yellow press. She would read the article because she could not help herself. She hoped that after a month someone would know something that she didn't about Jack's death, that a word or a phrase would trigger something in her mind and the six days would spill through, freeing her from her nightmare.

Or sending her into a more terrifying one. There was always that possibility lurking in the twisting shadows of her mind. Dr. Gene had suggested that there could be horrors she didn't imagine even in nightmare. Amnesia could be looked at many ways. Gift of a kind God. Survival reflex. Fountainhead of horror. All of them and none of them. But fear was always there, pooled in shadows, waiting for night. Maybe Dr. Gene was right. Maybe she'd be better off not remembering.

Impatiently, Alana shoved the unwelcome thought into the back of her mind. Nothing could be worse than not trusting her own mind, her own courage, her own sanity. Since her mother had died, Alana had always been the strong one, the one who saw what had to be done and did it.

Then there had been Rafe. Alana had loved him and he had died. She had been destroyed. Music had been her only solace. With it she had woven glowing dreams of warmth, Rafe's laughter, and a love that could only be sung, not spoken. With song, she had survived even Rafe's death. She could do whatever she had to. She had proved that in the past. Somehow, she would prove it again. She would survive. Somehow.

Alana shook out the paper, folded it carefully and began to read.

The first part of the story was a review of the Jack 'n' Jilly album that had just been released. The rest of the article was a simple retelling of the facts of Jack's death. A month ago, Jack and Jilly Reeves had gone on a pack trip in the Wyoming back country. An early winter storm had caught them. They had tried to get out, but only Jilly had made it. Jack had been killed in a fall. Jilly had somehow managed to hobble down the mountain on a badly wrenched ankle until she had reached a fishing cabin and radioed for help. Even so, she had nearly died of exposure. The experience had been so traumatic that she had no memory of the time she had spent crawling down the mountain. Hysterical amnesia, said the doctor. Apparently Sheriff Mitchell had agreed, for an autopsy listed the cause of Jack's death as a broken neck sustained in a fall.

Alana reread the article, searching for the key to her amnesia. She didn't find it. She was neither surprised nor disappointed. Deliberately, she put away the paper and cleaned up the remnants of her breakfast. The morning stretched before her, featureless, bleak. She should read the stacks of song sheets her agent had sent over, new material, solo material for the sole survivor of the duo.

She should, but she wouldn't, for she no longer could sing.

That was the most bitter loss, the most unbearable pain. Before Broken Mountain, she had been able to draw songs around her like colors of love chasing away the gray of loneliness and the black of despair. She had taken her love for a man she believed was dead and had transformed that love into song. Singing had been her greatest pleasure, her reason for living after she was told that Rafe was dead. Jack hadn't loved her, but she had always known that. Nor had she loved him. It had been a business marriage. Jack had loved fame and Jilly had loved singing.

Now Jack was dead and Jilly could only sing in her dreams.

It wasn't that she was afraid of being in front of people now, afraid of the savage doggerel running through fans' minds:

> Jack 'n' Jilly
> Went up the hilly.
> Jack fell down
> And broke his crown,
> And Jilly lost her mind.

Alana had listened to it all before, read it in print a hundred times, heard it whispered. She could face that. But she couldn't face opening her lips and feeling her throat close with terrible finality, as though there were no more songs in her now and never would be again, nothing but screams and the silence of death.

"Stop it!" Alana said aloud, her voice harsh in the quiet room. "It isn't the end of the world if you can't sing for a while. You can still write songs. You can still talk. You can still walk and laugh and do everything everyone else does. So pull up your socks and quit whimpering and *do* something."

Out of the corner of her eye, Alana saw her reflected image in the glass door that opened onto another part of the patio. She looked like a mountain deer caught in the instant of stillness that precedes wild flight. Long brown limbs and brown eyes that were very dark, very wide, wild.

A black braid slid over her shoulder and swung against the glass as she leaned forward. She brought the other braid forward over her shoulder, too. It was a gesture that had become automatic; when her braids hung down her back she pulled them forward. That way if she had to run suddenly, they wouldn't fly out behind her, twin black ropes, perfect handles for something to grab and hold her and *lift her up, trapped, weightless, falling, she was falling—*

Alana throttled the scream clawing at her throat. Without looking away from her reflection, she groped in a kitchen drawer. Her fingers closed around the handle of a long carving knife. The honed blade glittered as she pulled it out of the drawer. She lifted the knife until the blunt side of the blade rested against her neck just below her chin. Calmly, deliberately, she began slicing through her left braid. The severed hair fell soundlessly to the floor. With no hesitation, she went to work on the right braid.

When Alana was finished she shook her head, making her hair fly. The loose natural curl that had been hidden beneath the weight of braids asserted itself. Wisps of hair curved around her face, framing it in soft, shiny black. Her brown eyes glowed darkly, haunted by dreams. Abruptly, Alana realized what she had done. She stared at the long black braids on the floor, the long steel knife in her hand, the reflection in the window that no longer looked like Jilly.

The knife dropped to the floor with a metallic clatter. Alana stared at herself and wondered if she had finally gone crazy.

She ran from the sun-filled kitchen to the bedroom. There, she pulled her few things out of drawers and off hangers, packing haphazardly. It didn't matter. Most of her clothes were still in L.A. or at the ranch, left there in anticipation of weeks spent with her brother and Merry. She had been too frightened to go back to the ranch and pack after she had fled the hospital. She had simply run to Portland, a city she had never been to, hoping to leave the nightmare behind.

As Alana packed, she kept looking at the bedroom telephone. She wanted to call Bob, to say that she had changed her mind and then hang up before he could object. Yet every time she reached for the phone, she thought of Rafael Winter, a dream to balance her nightmare. She used memories of Rafe like a talisman to draw the terror from her six missing days. The greatest pleasure and the greatest horror in her life had both taken place on Broken Mountain. Perhaps they would simply cancel out each other, leaving her free to go on with her life. Neutral, balanced. Neither memories of the man she had loved, nor of the husband she had not. Neither memories of the lover who had died and then come back, nor of the husband who had died and would never come back. Rafe, who came to her in dreams. Jack, who came to her in nightmares.

When Alana finally picked up the phone, it was to call a nearby beauty salon and make an appointment to have her hair styled. The utterly normal activity reassured her. By the time she got on the airplane, she felt more calm. Tonight she would be home. If nightmares stalked her, it would be down the familiar corridors of her childhood home rather than the strange hallways of a rented condominium. She held to that thought as she switched planes in Salt Lake City and settled in for the flight to Wyoming. Finally, surprisingly, she slept.

As the plane slid into its landing pattern, Alana sat up and nervously ran her fingers through her hair. Her head felt strange, light, no longer anchored by dense black braids. The stylist had transformed the remnants of her knife-cut hair into a gently curling cap that softened but didn't wholly conceal the taut lines of Alana's face. The result was arresting—glossy midnight silk framing an intelligent face haunted by sadness and dreams.

The small commercial plane touched down with a slight jerk. A few eager trout fishermen got off before Alana, trading stories of the past and bets for the first and biggest fish of the future. She stood up reluctantly and walked slowly down the narrow aisle. By the time she had descended the metal stair, her baggage had already been unloaded and placed neatly beside the bottom step. She picked up her light suitcase and turned toward the small building that was the only sign of habitation for miles around. Behind her the aircraft began retreating. It moved to the head of the runway, revved hard and accelerated, gathering speed quickly, preparing itself for a leap into the brilliant high-plains sky.

Alana reached the building as the plane's engines gave a full-throated cry. She set down her bag and turned in time to see the aircraft's wheels lift. It climbed steeply, a powerful silver bird flying free. She listened until the engines were no more than a fading echo and the plane only a molten silver dot flying between the ragged grandeur of the Wind River and Green Mountain ranges.

Alana closed her eyes for a moment, her head tilted toward the sky, feeling the tenuous warmth of the Wyoming sun. The wind was redolent of earth and sagebrush. Not the stunted, brittle sagebrush of the Southwestern desert, but the profuse lavender-gray high-country sage, bushes as high as her head, higher, slender shapes weaving dendritic patterns against the empty sky. A clean wind sweeping down from granite heights, carrying sweetness and the promise of rain. Blue-green rivers curling lazily between boulder-strewn banks, evergreens standing tall and fragrant against summer moons, coyotes calling from the ridgelines in harmonies older than man.

Home.

Alana breathed deeply, torn between pleasure and fear. She heard footsteps approaching across the cement. She spun around, her heart beating heavily. Since Broken Mountain, she was terrified if anything approached her unseen.

A man was walking toward Alana. The sun was at his back, reducing him to a black silhouette. As he walked closer, he seemed to condense into three dimensions. He was about seven inches taller than she was. He had the easy stride of someone who had spent as much time hiking as he had on horseback. His jeans were faded. His boots showed the scuff marks peculiar to riding. His Western shirt was the same pale blue as the sky. Hair that was a thick, rich brown showed beneath the rim of his black Stetson. His eyes were the color of whiskey, his lips a firm curve beneath a silky bar of moustache.

With a small sound, Alana closed her eyes. Her heart beat wildly, but it sent weakness rather than strength coursing through her. She was going crazy, hallucinating. *Storm and cold and terror, falling—*

"Alana," he said, his voice gentle, deep, reaching out to her like an immaterial caress.

"Rafael?" she breathed raggedly, afraid to open her eyes, torn between hope and nightmare. "Oh, Rafe, is it really you?"

Chapter 2

Rafe took Alana's arm, supporting her. Only then did she realize that she had been swaying as she stood. His warmth and strength went through her like a shock wave. For an instant she sagged against him. Then she realized that she was being touched, held, and she wrenched away. Since Broken Mountain she was terrified of being touched.

"It's really me, Alana," said Rafe, watching her intently.

"Rafael—" Alana's voice broke as emotions overwhelmed her.

She extended her fingers as though she would touch him, but did not. With an effort that left her aching, she fought down the tangle of emotions that were closing her throat. She was being torn apart by conflicting imperatives. Run to him. Run from his male presence. Be held by him. Fight not to be held by a man. Love him. Feel nothing at all because the only safety lay in numbness. Remember how it felt to be loved. Forget, forget everything, amnesia spreading outward like a black balm.

"Why are you here?" she asked in a ragged voice.

"I've come to take you home."

Inexplicably, the words all but destroyed Alana. With a small sound, she closed her eyes and struggled to control herself. Coming here had been a mistake. She had wanted a dream of love to balance a nightmare of terror. Yet Rafe was real, not a dream. And so was terror. She clung to the shreds of her control, wondering what had happened during those six missing days that left a black legacy of fear. And most of all she wondered if the nightmare would ever end, freeing her, letting her laugh and sing again . . . or would she simply break, amnesia claiming all of her mind, all of her?

Rafe watched Alana, his eyes intent. When he spoke, his voice was casual, soothing, utterly normal. "We'd better hurry. I'd like to beat the thundershower back to the ranch."

He bent to take Alana's suitcase from her nerveless fingers. With the easy movements of a mountain cat, he straightened and walked toward a Jeep parked a few hundred feet away. Alana watched, her hand resting on the high neck of her wine silk blouse. She took a deep breath, still feeling the warmth of Rafe's hand on her arm as he had supported her.

Motionless, her heart beating rapidly, her dark eyes wide, Alana watched Rafe turn back toward her. The slanting late-afternoon sun highlighted the strong bones of his face and made his amber-colored eyes glow. As he turned, his shirt stretched across his shoulders, emphasizing the strength and masculine grace of him. His jeans fit the muscular outline of his legs like a faded blue shadow, moving as he moved.

Alana closed her eyes, but still she could see Rafe. He was burned into her awareness with a thoroughness that would have shocked her if she had had any room left for new emotions. But she didn't. She was still caught up in the moment when he had turned back to her, light brown eyes burning, mouth curved in a gentle male smile. That was Rafe. Male. Totally. She had forgotten, even in her dreams.

Rafe hesitated as though he wanted to come back to Alana, to stand close to her again. But he didn't move. He simply watched her with whiskey-colored eyes that were both gentle and intent, consuming her softly, like a song.

"It's all right, Alana." Rafe's voice was as gentle as his smile. "I've come to take you home."

The words echoed and reechoed in Alana's mind. Cold and wind and snow, terror and screams clawing at her throat. Pain and terror and then . . . *It's all right. I've come to take you home.* She had heard words like those before, and something more, other words, incredible dream and nightmare intertwined. She whimpered without knowing it, swaying visibly, caught between hope and fear, dream and nightmare.

"What?" said Alana breathlessly, her heart beating faster, her voice urgent. "What did you say?"

Rafe watched Alana with a sudden intensity that was almost tangible. "I said, 'I've come to take you home.'" He waited, but Alana simply watched him with wide, very dark eyes. Rafe's expression shifted, gentle again. "Bob threatened to have my hide for a saddle blanket if I didn't get you home before Merry fell asleep. And," added Rafe with a smile, "since she falls asleep between coffee and dessert, we'd better hurry."

Alana watched Rafe with eyes that were dazed and more than a little wild. "That wasn't what you said before."

Alana's voice was as tight as the hand clutching her throat. Her eyes were blind, unfocused.

"Before?" asked Rafe, his voice intent, hard, his topaz eyes suddenly blazing like gems. "Before what, Alana?"

It was dark, so dark, black ice around her, a glacier grinding her down until she screamed and tried to run but she couldn't run because she was frozen and it was so cold.

Alana shuddered and swayed, her face utterly pale, drained of life by the voracious nightmare that came to her more and more often, stalking her even in the day, stealing what little sanity remained. Rafe came to her instantly, supporting her, his hands warm and strong. Even as she turned toward his warmth, fear exploded in her. She wrenched away with all her strength. Then she realized that it hadn't been necessary, Rafe hadn't tried to hold her, she was reacting to something that hadn't happened.

"I—" Alana watched Rafe with wild, dark eyes. "I don't—I'm—" She held out her hands helplessly, wondering how to explain to Rafe that she was drawn to him yet terrified of being touched, and that above all she thought she was losing her mind.

"You're tired, Alana," said Rafe easily, as though Alana's actions were as normal as the slanting afternoon light. "It was a long flight. Come on. Bob and Merry are waiting for you like kids waiting for Christmas morning."

Rafe turned back to the suitcase, picked it up and walked toward the Jeep. Before he arrived, a man got out of a Blazer and approached Rafe. As Alana walked closer, she recognized Dr. Gene. He smiled and held out his arms to her. She hesitated, fighting against being held, even by the man who had delivered her, who had attended to all her childhood ills and cried in frustration at her mother's deathbed. Dr. Gene, who was as much a member of her family as her father or brothers.

With an effort of will that made her tremble, Alana submitted to Dr. Gene's brief hug. Over her head, the doctor looked a question at Rafe, who answered with a tiny negative movement of his head.

"Well, it's good to have you back," said Dr. Gene. "No limp, now. You look as pretty as ever, Trout."

"And you lie very badly," said Alana, smiling a little at the nickname from her childhood. She quickly stepped back from the doctor's hug. Her haste was almost rude, but she couldn't help herself. That was the worst part of the nightmare, not being able to help herself. "The only thing that was ever pretty about me was my voice."

"No pain?" persisted the doctor. "How's your appetite?"

"No pain," she said evenly, ignoring the question about her appetite. "I don't even use the elastic bandage any more." And then Alana waited in fear for the doctor to ask her about her memory. She didn't want to talk about that in front of Rafe.

She didn't want to talk about her memory at all.

"You cut your hair," said Dr. Gene.

Alana raised her hand nervously, feeling the short, silky tendrils that were all that remained of waist-length braids. "Yes." And then, because the doctor seemed to expect something more, "Today. I cut it today."

"Why?" said Dr. Gene, his voice as gentle as the question was blunt.

"I—" Alana stopped. "I was—I wanted to."

"Yes, but why?" persisted the doctor, his blue eyes very pale, very watchful beneath the shock of gray hair and weathered forehead.

"The braids made me . . . uneasy," said Alana, her voice tight, her eyes vague. "They kept . . . tangling in things." She made a sudden motion with her hands, as though she were warding off something. "I—" Her throat closed and she could say nothing more.

"Alana's tired," said Rafe, his voice quiet and very certain. "I'm going to take her home. Now. Excuse us, Dr. Gene."

Rafe and Dr. Gene exchanged a long look; then the doctor sighed.

"All right, Rafe. Tell Bob I'm trying to get some time off to go fishing."

"Good. The Broken Mountain camp always has a cabin for you."

"Even now?"

"Especially now," said Rafe sardonically. "We may disagree on means, but our goal is identical." Then, before Alana could say anything or ask any questions, Rafe said to her, "Just a little fishing expedition in the high country. The good doctor prefers to drown worms. I, on the other hand, prefer to devise my own lures."

Dr. Gene smiled briefly. "Bet I catch more trout than you, Winter."

"I'm only after one trout. A very special one."

Alana wondered at the currents of emotion running between the two men, then decided it was her own hypersensitivity. Since Broken Mountain, she had jumped at sighs and shadows and seen conspiracy and pursuit when there was nothing behind her but night and silence.

Dr. Gene turned to Alana. "If you need anything, Trout, I'll come running."

"Thanks, Dr. Gene."

"I mean it, now," he added.

"I know," she said softly.

He nodded, climbed back in his Blazer, and drove off. Rafe handed Alana into the Jeep and climbed in himself. She watched him covertly, matching memories with reality.

Rafe was older, much more controlled than her memories. When he wasn't smiling, his face was hard. Yet he still moved with the easy strength that had always fascinated her. His voice was still gentle, and his hands were . . . beautiful. An odd way to describe anything as strong and quick and callused as a man's hands, yet she could think of no better word. Not all hands affected her like that, though. Sometimes she saw hands and terror sleeted through her.

"We're lucky today," said Rafe as he guided the Jeep expertly over the rough field that passed as a parking lot.

"Lucky?" said Alana, hearing the thin thread of panic in her voice and hating it.

"No rain so far. Rained a lot the last few days."

Alana tried to conceal the shudder that went through her at the thought of lightning and thunder, mountains and slippery black ice. "Yes," she said, "I'm glad there isn't a storm."

"You used to love storms," said Rafe quietly.

Alana went very still, remembering one wild September afternoon when a storm had caught her and Rafe while they were out riding. They had arrived at the fishing cabin, soaked and breathless. He had peeled her wet jacket off her, then her blouse, and his hands had trembled when he touched her.

Alana closed her eyes and tried to forget. The thought of being touched like that by Rafe made her weak with desire—and all but crazy with fear, dream and nightmare tangled together inextricably.

"We had a good frost above five thousand feet last week," continued Rafe, as though he hadn't remembered the September storm. "The aspen leaves turned. Now they look like pieces of sunlight dancing in the wind." He looked quickly at Alana, seeing the lines of inner conflict on her face. "You still like aspen, don't you?"

Alana nodded her head, afraid to trust her voice. Mountain aspen with its white bark and quivering, silver-backed leaves was her favorite tree. In fall, aspens turned a yellow as pure as—sunlight dancing in the wind. She glanced sideways, saw Rafe watching her with whiskey-colored eyes.

"I still like aspen," said Alana, trying to keep her voice normal, grateful for the safe topic. The present, not the past. The past was more than she could handle. The future was unthinkable. Just one day at a time. One hour. A minute. She could handle anything, one minute at a time. "Even in winter," she added, her voice little more than a whisper, "when the branches are black and the trunks are like ghosts in the snow."

Rafe accelerated down the narrow, two-lane blacktop road. "Be a while before there's real snow in the high country," he said, glancing for a moment at the magnificent granite spine of the Wind River Mountains rising on his left. "The frost put down the insects, though. Then it turned warm again. Trout ought to be hungry as hell. That means good fishing for our dudes—guests," he corrected immediately, smiling to himself. "Nobody likes to be called a dude."

"*Our* dudes?" asked Alana slowly, watching Rafe with eyes so brown they were almost black.

Sunlight slanted through the windshield, intensifying the tan of Rafe's face and the richness of his dark brown moustache, making his eyes almost gold. His teeth showed in a sudden gleam of humor, but his expression said the joke was on him. He answered her question with another question.

"Didn't Bob mention me?"

"No," said Alana, her voice ragged. "You were a complete surprise."

Rafe's expression changed. For an instant Alana thought she saw pain, but it came and went so quickly that she decided she had been wrong. Hypersensitive again. Overreacting. Yet still she wanted to touch Rafe, to erase the instant when she sensed she had hurt him and didn't even know how. The thought of touching him didn't frighten her. Not like being touched. For an instant she wondered why, but all that came to her was . . . nothing. Blank. Like those six days.

"Looks like we'll have to do it the hard way," sighed Rafe, an odd blend of resignation and some much stronger emotion in his voice, something close to anger. Then, before Alana could say anything, Rafe did. "Bob and I are partners."

"Partners? In what?"

"The dude—*guest* ranch. The cottages and fishing water are on Lazy W land. My land. The horses and supplies belong to Bob. He's the wrangler, I'm the fishing guide and you're the cook. When Dr. Gene shows up," added Rafe with a crooked smile, "he'll be chief worm dunker."

Alana didn't know what to say. She would be going up Broken Mountain with Rafael Winter. Dream and nightmare running together, pouring over her, drowning her in freezing water. She sat without moving, letting the sunlight and landscape blur before her, trying to gather her fragmenting thoughts. No wonder Bob had said nothing about Rafael Winter. If she'd known that Bob had a partner she might have been tempted to let the partner bail Bob out of the mess.

Especially if she had known that the partner was Rafael Winter. It was all she could do to handle the recent past, amnesia and accident and death. Bob should have known that she couldn't handle a present that included Rafe. A year ago Bob had told her that Rafe was alive. Then Bob had taken her letter to Rafe's ranch. Bob had come back with the letter unopened, DECEASED written across the envelope's face—*written in Rafe's distinctive hand*. Bob had seen Alana's pain and anger, and then her despair.

"Alana—" began Rafe.

Somehow Alana was certain that Rafe was going to talk about the past, about dying but not quite, about surviving but not wholly, about her and Jack and an envelope with a "dead" man's handwriting across its face, tearing her apart. She wasn't strong enough for that. Not the past. Not anything but this minute. Now.

"Bob and Tom Sawyer have a lot in common," said Alana quickly, her voice as strained as it was determined. "Don't go near either of them if a fence needs painting. Unless you like painting fences, of course."

Rafe hesitated, visibly reluctant to give up whatever he had wanted to say. But Alana's taut, pale face and haunted eyes persuaded him as no conversational gambit could have. "Yes," he said slowly, "Bob could charm the needles off a pine tree."

Relieved, Alana sat back in the seat again. "The only thing that ever got even with Bob was the hen he poured jam on and then dumped in the middle of eight half-grown hounds. That hen pecked Bob's hands until she was too tired to lift her head."

Rafe's laughter was as rich as the slanting sunlight pouring over the land. Alana turned toward him involuntarily, drawn by his humor and strength, by the laugh that had haunted her dreams as pervasively as the scent of pines haunted the high country.

"So that's how Bob got those scars on his hands," said Rafe, still chuckling. "He told me it was chicken pox."

Alana's lips curved into a full smile, the first in a long time. "So it was, after a fashion." She glanced up at Rafe through her thick black lashes and caught the amber flash of his eyes as he looked away from her to the road. For an instant her heart stopped, then beat more quickly. He had been watching her. Was he comparing the past with the present? "And just how did Bob talk you into painting his fence?" she asked quickly, wanting to hear Rafe talk, his voice deep and smooth and confident, like his laughter.

"Easy. I'm a sucker for fishing. I spend a lot of my time in the high country chasing trout. Might as well make it pay."

"Land-poor," murmured Alana. "Rancher's lament."

"I've got it better than Bob," Rafe said, shrugging. "I'm not buying out two brothers."

Alana thought of Dave and Sam. Sam worked for a large corporation with branches around the world. Dave was a computer programmer in Texas. Neither brother had any intention of coming back to the ranch for anything other than occasional visits. Of the four Burdette children, only she and Bob had loved the ranching life. Jack hadn't loved it. He couldn't leave Wyoming fast enough. He had hungered for city streets and crowds applauding.

"Jack hated Wyoming." Startled, Alana heard the words echoing in the Jeep and realized she had spoken aloud. "He's dead."

"I know."

Alana stared at Rafe. Then she realized that of course he knew; Bob must have told him. They were partners. But how much had Bob told Rafe? Did he know about her amnesia? Did he know about the nightmares that lapped over into day, triggered by a word or a smell or the quality of the light? Did he know that she was afraid of going crazy? That she clung to her memories and dreams of Rafe as though they were a lifeline capable of pulling her beyond the reach of whatever terror stalked her?

As though Rafe sensed Alana's unease, he added quietly, "It was good of you to help Bob. It can't be easy for you so soon after your . . . husband's . . . death."

At the word "husband," Rafe's mouth turned down sourly, telling Alana that her marriage was not a subject that brought Rafe any pleasure. But then, Rafe had never liked Jack. Even before Rafe had "died," Jack had always been urging Alana to pack up and leave Wyoming, to build a career where artificial lights drowned out the cascading stars of the Western sky.

"Did Bob tell you how Jack died?" asked Alana, her voice tight, her hands clenched in her lap.

"No." Rafe's voice was hard and very certain.

Alana let out a long breath. Apparently Bob had told Rafe only the bare minimum: Jack had died recently. Nothing about the amnesia or the nightmares. She was glad Bob had told Rafe something, though. It would explain anything odd she might do. Jack was dead. Recently. She was a widow.

And when she slept, she was a frightened child.

The Jeep jolted off the pavement onto a gravel road. The miles unwound easily, silently; gently rolling sagebrush and a distant river that was pale silver against the land. Nothing moved but the Jeep and jackrabbits flushed by the sound of the car. There was neither fence nor sign to mark the beginning of the Broken Mountain Ranch. Like many Western ranchers, Alana's grandfather, father and brother had left the range open where possible. They fenced in the best of their breeding stock and let the beef cattle graze freely.

"Has Bob brought the cattle out of the high country yet?" asked Alana, searching the land for signs of Broken Mountain steers grazing the high plains.

"Most of them. He's leaving them in the middle elevations until late September. Later, if he can."

Alana nodded. The longer the cattle stayed in the high and middle elevations, the less money Bob would have to spend on winter feed. Every year was a gamble. If a rancher left his cattle too long in the high country, winter storms could close in, locking the cattle into certain starvation. If the rancher brought his cattle down too soon, though, the cost of buying hay to carry them through winter could mean bankruptcy.

"Grass looks thick," she said, keeping to the neutral conversational territory of ranching, afraid that if the silence went on too long Rafe might bring up the recent past and Jack's death or, even worse, the far past, Rafe's death and resurrection, a bureaucratic error that had cost her . . . everything. "I'll bet Indian Seep is still flowing. The hay crop must have been good."

Alana's dark eyes catalogued every feature of the land, the texture of the soil in road cuts, the presence or absence of water in the ravines, the smoky lavender sheen of living growth on the gnarled sagebrush, the presence or absence of wildlife, all the indicators that told an educated eye whether the land was being used or abused, husbanded or squandered.

And in between, when she thought Rafe wasn't looking, she watched his profile, the sensuous sheen of his hair and lips, the male line of his nose and jaw. Rafe was too powerful, too hard to be called handsome. He was compelling—a man made for mountains, strength and endurance, mystery and silence, and sudden laughter like a river curling lazily beneath the sun.

"Am I so different from your memories?" asked Rafe.

Alana drew in her breath sharply. "No. But there are times when I can't tell my memories from my dreams."

Alana looked away, unable to meet Rafe's eyes, regretting her honesty and at the same time knowing she had no choice. She had enough trouble sorting out truth from nightmare. She hadn't the energy to keep track of lies, too.

When the truck rounded the shoulder of a small ridge, Alana leaned forward intently, staring into the condensing twilight. A long, narrow valley opened up before her. A few evergreens grew in the first creases of land, which soon became foothills and then finally pinnacles clothed in ice and distance. But it wasn't the savage splendor of the peaks that held Alana's attention. She had eyes only for the valley. It was empty of cattle.

Alana sat back with an audible sigh of relief. "Good for you, little brother," she murmured.

"Bob's a good rancher," said Rafe quietly. "Not an inch of overgrazed land on Broken Mountain's range."

"I know. I was just afraid that—" Her hands moved, describing vague fears. "The beef market has been so bad and feed is so high now and he has to pay Sam and Dave. I was afraid Bob would gamble on the land being able to carry more cattle than it should."

"Since when do people on the West Coast notice feed prices and the carrying capacity of Wyoming ranchland?" asked Rafe, glancing aside with the lightning intensity that she remembered from her dreams.

"They don't. I do." Alana made a wry face. "People in cities think beef grows between styrofoam and plastic wrap, like mushrooms in the cracks of a log."

Rafe laughed again, softly. Alana watched him, feeling the pull of his laughter. Above his pale collar, sleek neck muscles moved. She felt again the moment of warmth at the airport, the texture of Rafe's skin on hers before she had snatched back her arm. He was strong. It showed in his movements, in his laughter, in the clean male lines of his face. He was strong and she was not. She should be terrified of him. Yet when he laughed, it was all she could do to keep herself from crawling over and huddling next to him as though he were a fire burning in the midst of a freezing storm.

The thought of being close to Rafe both fascinated and frightened Alana. The fascination she understood; Rafe was the only man she had ever loved. She had no reason to fear him. Yet she did. He was a man, and she was terrified of men. The fear baffled her. At no time in her life, not even during the most vicious arguments with Jack, had she been afraid.

Was she afraid of Rafe simply because he was strong?

Alana turned the thought over in her mind, testing it as she had tested so many things in the weeks since Jack had died and she had awakened alone in a hospital, six days and a husband lost. It couldn't be something as simple as physical strength that frightened her. Jack had been six foot five, very thick in the shoulders and neck and legs. He hadn't used his strength, though, or even seemed to care about it. He had done only what was needed to get by.

Jack had been born with a clear tenor voice that he'd accepted as casually as his size, and disliked working with almost as much as he'd disliked physical labor. She had been the one who'd insisted on rehearsing each song again and again, searching for just the right combination of phrasing and harmony that would bring out the levels of meaning in the lyrics. Jack had tolerated her ''fanaticism'' with the same easygoing indifference that he'd tolerated crummy motels and being on the road three hundred and fifty-two nights a year. Until Jack 'n' Jilly had become successful, that is. Then Jack would rehearse a new country or folk song only as long as it took him to learn the words and melody. Anything beyond that was Jilly's problem.

A year ago she had left Jack and come to Broken Mountain Ranch to think about her life and her sad sham of a marriage. When word of her leaving had leaked to the press, record and concert ticket sales had plummeted. Their agent had called Alana and quietly, cynically suggested that she continue to present a happily married front to the world. Fame was transient. Obscurity was forever. That same afternoon, Bob had come back from a trip to the high country babbling about seeing Rafe Winter. She had written the letter to Rafe, seen Rafe's rejection condensed into a single harsh word: DECEASED. She had wept, and then she had gone back to L.A. to appear as one half of Country's Perfect Couple.

Until six weeks ago, when she had told Jack that it was over. He had pleaded with her to think again, to take a trip with him to the high country she loved and there they would work out a reconciliation. But Jack had died, instead.

"Did you miss the ranch?" asked Rafe quietly.

Alana heard Rafe's question as though from a great distance, calling her out of a past that was another kind of nightmare waiting to drag her down. She reached for the question, pulling it eagerly around her. "I missed the ranch more than . . . more than I knew."

And she had. It had been like having her eyes put out, hungering for the sight of aspen's green and silver shimmer but seeing only dusty palm trees; searching for the primal blue of alpine lakes set among the chiseled spires of mountains older than man, but finding only concrete freeways and the metallic flash of cars; always looking for the intense green silences of the wilderness forest, but discovering only docile squares of grass laid down amid hot stucco houses.

All that had saved her was singing. Working with a song. Tasting it, feeling it, seeing it grow and change as it became a part of her and she of it. Jack had never understood that. He had loved only the applause and worked just hard enough to get it. She loved the singing and would work to exhaustion until she and the song were one.

"If you missed the ranch that much, why did you leave after Jack died?"

Alana realized that she had heard the question before. Rafe had asked it at least twice and she hadn't answered, lost in her own thoughts.

"Jack died there," she whispered. "On Broken Mountain."

She looked to the right, where the Green Mountains lifted seamed granite faces toward the gloaming sky. High-flying clouds burned silver above the peaks, and over all arched an immense indigo bowl, twilight changing into night.

"You must have unhappy memories," said Rafe quietly.

"Yes, I suppose I must."

Alana heard her own words, heard their ambiguity, heard the fear tight in her voice. She looked up and saw that Rafe had been watching her. But he said nothing, asked no more questions, simply drove her closer and closer to the ramparts of stone and ice where her husband had died and she had lost her mind.

Chapter 3

IT WAS DARK BY THE TIME RAFE TURNED ONTO THE FORK of the road that led to the Broken Mountain ranch house. An autumn moon was up, huge and flat and ghostly, balanced on the edge of the world. Clouds raced and seethed, veiled in moonlight and mystery, veiling the moon in turn. The mountains were invisible, yet Alana could sense them rising black and massive before her, comforting and frightening her at the same time, childhood memories and recent fear setting her on an emotional seesaw that made her dizzy.

She knew she had been here just four weeks ago. She knew she and Jack had ridden into the high country. She knew Jack was dead. She knew—*but she didn't.*

She had awakened in the hospital, bruised and cut, iceburned and aching. And frightened. Every shadow, every sound had sent her heart racing. It had taken an effort of will to allow Dr. Gene to examine her. He had tried to explain the inexplicable in ordinary words, telling her that her fear was normal, the overreaction of someone who had never known physical danger, much less death. In time, her mind and body would adjust to the presence of danger, the nearness of death in everyday life. Then she would be calm again. Until then, Dr. Gene could prescribe something to help her.

Alana had refused the tranquilizers. She had seen too many musicians dependent on drugs. For her, chemical solutions were no solution at all. But it had been tempting, especially at first. The presence of Dr. Gene had unnerved her to the point of tears. Even Bob, her favorite brother, had seen Alana withdraw from any kind of physical touch, any gesture of affection he made. Bob had been hurt and very worried about her, his brown eyes clouded with conflicting feelings.

Then, on the third morning after the mountain, Alana had quietly walked out of the hospital, boarded a plane and flown to Portland, a city she had never before seen. She hadn't waited for Sheriff Mitchell to come back down off the mountain with Jack's body. She hadn't stopped to think, to consider, to reason. She had simply run from the black gap in her mind.

Portland was big enough to lose herself in but not big enough to remind her of L.A. and her life with Jack. There were mountains in Portland, but only in the distance. Yet fear had run with her anyway. Though she had never before been afraid of flying, of heights, there had been a horrible moment of terror as the plane had left the ground.

Earth falling away and her body twisting, weightless, she was falling, falling, black rushing up to meet her and when it did she would be torn from life like an aspen leaf from its stem, spinning away helplessly over the void—

"It's all right, Alana. You're safe. It's all right. I've come to take you home."

Vaguely, Alana realized that Rafe had parked the jeep at the side of the road. She heard Rafe's soothing murmur, sensed the warmth of his hand over her clenched fingers, the gentle pressure of his other hand stroking her hair. She felt the shudders wracking her body, the ache of teeth clenched against a futile scream. Rafe continued speaking quietly, repeating his words, words warming her, words as undemanding as sunlight, driving away the darkness that gripped her.

Alana turned her head suddenly, pressing her cheek against the hard strength of Rafe's hand. But when he would have drawn her closer, she moved away with a jerk.

"I—" Alana stopped, drew a deep breath. "I'm sorry. Something—" Her hands moved restlessly. "Sometimes I—since Jack—" Alana closed her eyes, despairing of making Rafe understand what she herself had no words to describe.

"Seeing death is always hard," said Rafe quietly. "The more sheltered you've been, the harder it is."

Rafe's hand stroked Alana's hair, his touch as gentle as his words, as his presence, his warmth. Alana let out a long sigh, feeling tentacles of terror loosen, slide away, the nightmare withdrawing. She turned her head and looked at Rafe with eyes that were no longer black with fear.

"Thank you," she said simply.

Rafe's only answer was a light caress across Alana's cheek as his hand withdrew from her hair. He started the Jeep again and pulled back onto the narrow gravel road leading to the Burdette family house. Beneath the truck, the country began to roll subtly, gathering itself for the sudden leap into mountain heights. The ranch house was on the last

piece of land that could be described as high plains. Behind
the ranch buildings, the country rose endlessly, becoming
black peaks wearing brilliant crowns of stars.

Gradually, squares of yellow light condensed out of the
blackness as the ranch house competed with and finally
outshone the brightness of stars. Black fences paralleled the
road, corrals and pastures where broodmares grazed and
champion bulls moved with ponderous grace. A paved loop
of road curved in front of the house before veering off
toward the barns.

As Rafe braked to a stop by the walkway, the front door
of the house opened, sending a thick rectangle of gold light
into the yard like a soundless cry of welcome. Three
quicksilver dogs bounded off the porch, barking and baying
and dancing as though the dewy grass were made of icicles
too sharp to stand on.

Rafe climbed out of the truck and waded into the hounds
with good-natured curses, pummeling them gently until
they had worked off the first exuberance of their greeting.
Then they stood and watched him with bright eyes, nudging
his hands with cold noses until each silky ear had been
scratched at least once. In the moonlight the hounds' coats
shone like liquid silver, rippling and changing with each
movement of their muscular bodies.

Alana slid out of the Jeep with a smile on her lips and the
hounds' welcoming song echoing in her ears. She stood
quietly, watching the dogs greet Rafe, feeling the cool
breeze tug at her hair. One of the hounds lifted its head
sharply, scenting Alana. It gave an eager whine and
scrambled toward her. Automatically Alana bent over to
greet the animal, rubbing its ears and thumping lightly on
its muscular barrel, enjoying the warm rasp of a tongue
over her hands.

"You're a beauty," Alana said, admiring the dog's lithe lines and strength.

The dog nosed her hand, then the pocket of her black slacks, then her hand again.

"What do you want?" asked Alana, her voice carrying clearly in the quiet air.

"The crackers you spoiled Vamp with the last time you were here," called Bob as he stepped out onto the porch, laughter and resignation competing in his voice.

Alana looked up blankly. "Crackers?" She looked down at the dog.

The dog watched her, dancing from foot to foot, obviously waiting for something.

"Crackers," said Bob, holding one out to Alana as he walked toward her. "I figured you'd forgotten—I mean, that you wouldn't have any crackers on you—so I brought one."

"Vamp?" said Alana, taking the cracker and looking at the pale square as though she'd never seen one before. She held it out. The dog took the tidbit with the delicate mouth of a well-trained bird dog.

"Vampire," said Bob, gesturing to the dog at Alana's feet. "You know, for all the sharp teeth she had as a pup."

The look on Alana's face made it clear that she didn't know the story behind the dog's name. Yet it was equally clear that Bob had told her the story before.

"Hell," said Bob underneath his breath. Then, hugging Alana, speaking so softly that only she could hear, "Sorry, sis. It's hard for me to keep track of all the things you've forgotten."

Alana stiffened for an instant as her brother's arms held her; then she forced herself to relax. She had to get over her irrational fear of human contact. The source of fear was in her nightmares only, a figment of her mind that had nothing to do with here, now, reality. Withdrawing would hurt Bob badly, just as she had hurt him at the hospital. She returned the hug a little fiercely, holding on too tightly, releasing him too quickly. Bob gave her a troubled look but said nothing.

Then, "What in God's name did you do to your hair!" Bob yelped.

"I cut it." Alana shook her head, making moonlight run like ghostly fingers through the loose black curves of her hair.

"Why?" demanded Bob.

"It seemed like a good idea at the time," she said, wishing everyone wouldn't make such a fuss over a perfectly normal thing. Other women got haircuts and no one objected. "Does it matter?"

"But you've always had long hair," said Bob in a voice that was surprisingly plaintive for a man who was just over six and a half feet tall and nearly twenty-three years old.

"Things change, little brother," said Alana tightly.

"Not you, sis," he said confidently. "You're like the mountains. You never change."

Alana stood without moving, not knowing what to say. In that moment she realized how much like a mother she was to Bob, how fixed in his mind as a port for every storm. Somehow she had given a continuity of love and caring to him that she hadn't ever found for herself after their mother died. And Rafe, who had died and then not died. But he had come back too late. Like now. Too late. How could she tell Bob that there were no ports any more, only storms?

"You're forgetting something, Bob," said Rafe, his voice easy yet somehow commanding. His eyes and smile reflected the light pouring out of the ranch house. "Sisters are women, too. Some''—amber eyes flashed briefly as Rafe looked at Alana—"are even beautiful women.''

Bob cocked his head and looked at Alana as though she were a stranger. "A matter of taste, I suppose,'' he deadpanned. "Looks like a stray fence post to me. Didn't they have any food in Portland?''

Rafe looked from the graceful curve of Alana's neck to the feminine swell of breasts, the small waist, the firm curve of hips, legs long and graceful. "Burdette,'' said Rafe, "you're as blind as a stone rolling down a mountain.''

Alana felt herself flush under Rafe's frankly approving glance. Yet she was smiling, too. She was used to being told that she had a beautiful voice. As for the rest, she had never felt especially attractive. Except when she had been with Rafe and he looked at her the way he was looking at her now, smiling.

"I guess Rafe told *you*, baby brother,'' Alana said, glad that the words came out light, teasing. She smiled at Rafe. "I'll bet you ride a white horse and rescue maidens in distress, too.''

Rafe's face changed, intent, watching Alana as though he were willing her to do . . . something. The look passed so quickly that Alana thought she'd imagined it.

"Wrong, sis,'' said Bob triumphantly, yanking her suitcase out of the back of the Jeep. "The horse Rafe rides is as spotted as his past.''

Alana looked from Bob to Rafe, wondering what her brother had meant. What had Rafe done in the years before, and after, he had been declared dead in Central America?

"Bob, you need a bridle for that tongue of yours,'' said Rafe. His smile was narrow, his voice flat.

Bob winced. "Stepped in it again. Sorry. I'm not very

good at forgetting. Or''—he looked at Alana apologetically —''remembering, either.''

She sighed. ''You couldn't even keep secrets at Christmas time, could you?''

''Nope,'' agreed Bob cheerfully. ''Not a one. In one ear and out the mouth.''

Rafe made a sound between disgust and amusement. ''There are times when I can't believe you're Sam's brother.''

Alana looked quickly at Rafe. Something in his voice told her that Rafe had seen Sam more recently than the times when Sam had hero-worshiped the older Rafe from afar. ''Have you seen Sam? I mean, lately?'' she asked Rafe.

''We met in Central America, when he was drilling a few dry holes.'' When Bob would have spoken, Rafe gave him a quelling look. ''I haven't seen Sam for a while, though.''

Alana's lips turned down. ''Neither have I. Years. I was in Florida doing a concert the last time he came to the States.''

''My brother the spook,'' said Bob. ''Now you see him, now you don't.''

''What?'' said Alana.

''Oops,'' said Bob.

What Rafe said was mercifully blurred by Merry's voice calling out threats to the husband who had let her sleep through Alana's homecoming.

''Honey,'' said Bob, dropping Alana's suitcase and racing toward the steps, ''be careful!''

The dogs ran after Bob, yipping and yapping with excitement. Alana couldn't help laughing as Bob swept Merry off her tiny feet and carried her across the grass, swearing at the dogs every step of the way. Merry was laughing too, her face buried against Bob's neck as she squealed and ducked away from the long-tongued, leaping hounds. Rafe put his fists on his hips and shook his head, smiling. He turned to Alana and held out his hand.

"Welcome to Broken Mountain Dude Ranch," he said wryly. "Peace and quiet await you. Somewhere. It says so in fine print on the brochure."

"I'll hold you to that," murmured Alana.

Smiling, she lightly rested her hand on Rafe's, feeling the heat and texture of his palm as his fingers curled around hers. The touch sent both pleasure and fear coursing through her.

The instant before Alana would have withdrawn, Rafe released her hand and picked up her luggage. She went ahead quickly, opening the screen door for Rafe and for Bob, who was still carrying a giggling Merry. The dogs stopped short at the threshold and begged silently, their yellow wolf eyes pale and hopeful. Alana looked toward Bob.

"No," he said firmly. "No weimaraners allowed."

"Not even Vamp?" Alana said coaxingly.

"Sis," Bob said in an exasperated tone, "I told you the last time that I don't want to take a chance of Merry tripping over a dog." Bob stopped abruptly, remembering too late that Alana had no memory of her last trip to the ranch.

"Sorry," Alana said tightly, closing the door. "I forgot."

"So did I. Again. *Damn.*" Bob ran his fingers through his thick black hair in a gesture sister and brother had learned from their father.

"Oh, Alana," said Merry softly, her pretty face stricken as she looked at her sister-in-law. "Bob didn't mean to hurt you."

"I know." Alana closed her eyes and unclenched her hands.

"Where do you want the suitcase?" said Rafe into the silence, his voice easy, ignoring the undercurrents of emotion.

"The upstairs bedroom on the east corner," said Merry, wriggling in Bob's arms. "Put me down, you big moose. There's nothing wrong with my feet."

"Never mind," said Rafe. "I know where the room is. Don't climb any more stairs than you have to."

"Not you, too!" Merry rolled her blue eyes and pulled on her long blond hair in mock despair. "Why me, Lord? Why am I stuck with men who think pregnancy is an exotic kind of broken leg?"

Rafe smiled crookedly as he watched the tiny woman's halfhearted struggle in Bob's thick arms. "Enjoy it, Merry. Comes diaper time, Bob will develop an exotic kind of broken arm."

"Slander," muttered Bob to Merry, nuzzling her cheek. "Don't believe a word of it."

"Believe it," said Alana. "Every time there were grubby chores to be done, Bob evaporated."

"Hey, no fair," Bob said, a wounded look on his face.

"Not fair or not true?" asked Alana wryly.

"I grew up after that carniverous hen ate half my hands."

"Chicken pox," called Rafe, just before he disappeared down the hall at the top of the stairway. "Remember?"

Bob groaned. "He's worse than Sam when it comes to keeping track of life's little lies. Mind like a steel trap. No fun at all."

Privately, Alana thought it would be wonderful to have a mind that forgot nothing, held everything. If she knew about those six days, her nightmares would be gone. Or

would they just move in and take over her days, too? Maybe
Dr. Gene was right. Maybe she wasn't ready to accept what
had happened, at least not all of it, every little detail.

Height and ice and falling . . .

"You look tired, sis," said Bob, setting Merry on her
feet with exaggerated care and watching her as she yawned,
waved good night, and went back to the downstairs bedroom. He turned back to Alana. "Want to go right to bed?"
Bob waited, but there was no answer. "Sis?"

Alana came out of her thoughts with a start. Her hand
was against her neck, as though holding back a scream.

"Sis? What is it? Are you remembering?"

Alana forced herself not to flinch when Bob's big hand
came down on her shoulder. "No," she said, hearing the
harshness of her voice but unable to make it softer. "I'm
trying, but I'm not remembering anything."

"Where does your memory stop?" asked Bob hesitantly.

"California. I was packing to come here."

"Where does it begin again?"

"When I woke up in the hospital."

"Six days."

"Nice counting, baby brother," Alana said sardonically.
Then, "I'm sorry. It's just . . . not easy. I don't know why
I forgot, and I'm . . . afraid."

Bob patted Alana's shoulder clumsily, not knowing how
to comfort the older sister who had always been the one to
comfort him. "I love you, sis."

Tears burned behind Alana's eyes. She looked up into the
face that was as familiar to her as her own. Familiar, yet
different. Bob was a man now, but in her memories he was
so often a boy. "Thanks," she whispered. "I love you,
too."

Bob smiled almost shyly and squeezed Alana's shoulder.
A frown passed over his face as he felt her slight body

beneath his big hand. "You're nearly as small as Merry," said Bob, surprise clear in his voice.

Alana almost laughed. "I'm three inches taller."

Bob dismissed the inches with a wave of his hand. "That's not what I meant. I've always thought of you as . . . bigger. You know. Physically."

"And I've always thought of you as smaller. Guess we both have some new thinking to do."

"Yeah, guess so." Bob ran his thick fingers through his hair. "I've been thinking a lot since Merry got pregnant. It's kind of scary." Then he grinned. "It's kind of fantastic, too."

Alana smiled despite her trembling lips. "You'll be a good father, Bob. Just like you're a good rancher."

Bob's eyes widened slightly, showing clear brown depths. "You mean that, sis? About being a good rancher, too?"

"You've been good to the land. It shows. Rafe thinks so too," she added.

Bob smiled with pleasure. "High marks from both of you, huh? That means a lot to me. I know how much you love the ranch. And Rafe, well, he's a hard son of a bitch but he's working miracles with the Lazy W. It had really gone to hell by the time his father had that last stroke."

"How long has Rafe lived there?"

"A couple of years." Bob looked uncomfortable, obviously remembering the time Alana had come for a visit and he had told her that Rafael Winter was alive.

"All the time?" asked Alana. Before, when she had known Rafe, loved him, been engaged to him, his work had taken him on long trips to unexpected places. "He used to travel."

"Yeah. About four years ago he was, uh, he had some kind of accident in some godforsaken place. And then his father died. Rafe's stayed on the Lazy W the whole time since then. Guess he's here for good. Unless something goes to hell overseas or Sam gets in trouble again and needs Rafe to pull his tail out of a crack.''

"Sam? In trouble? How? And what could Rafe do about it?''

Bob laughed wryly. "Sis, Rafe would—"

"Bring him a toothbrush," said Rafe from the stairway.

Alana looked up. Rafe was leaning against the wall, his hands in his pockets, his shirt tight across bunched shoulder muscles. For all his casual pose, she sensed that Rafe was angry about something.

Bob breathed a curse and an apology. "I warned you, Rafe. I'm no damn good at—"

"Burdette." Rafe's voice cracked with authority. "Shut up. If you can't do that, talk about the weather."

There was a charged silence for a moment. Alana looked from Bob to Rafe and back again. Although her brother had five inches and fifty pounds on Rafe, Rafe didn't seem the least bit intimidated by the prospect of a brawl.

"Storm coming on," said Bob finally. "Should be thunder in the high country by midnight, rain down here before dawn. It's supposed to clear up at sunrise, though. Part of a cold front that's moving across the Rockies. Now, if you ask me, I think we should roust those sleeping dudes upstairs and leave for your lodge at dawn or as soon afterward as it stops raining."

"That," said Rafe distinctly, "is one hell of an idea. Do you suppose you can keep your feet out of your mouth long enough to sit a horse all the way to the Five Lakes Lodge?"

"Didn't you know? I'm a trick rider," said Bob, his smile wide and forgiving.

"Who had chicken pox," retorted Rafe, but he was smiling too.

"Now you got it," said Bob approvingly. "Hold that good thought till morning."

Whistling softly, Bob moved toward the downstairs bedroom where Merry waited.

"How did you hold your own?" said Rafe, shaking his head. "Sam and Bob. My God. And Dave. Boggles the mind." Rafe laughed silently.

"What did Bob mean about your 'spotted past'?" asked Alana.

"Terrible work record," said Rafe laconically. "Moved around a lot. Remember?"

"And Sam being in trouble?"

"He's not in trouble now."

"But he was?" persisted Alana.

"Everyone gets in trouble now and again."

Alana made an exasperated sound. "Am I permitted to ask about the dudes?"

Rafe's glance narrowed. "Sure. Ask away."

"But will I get any answers?"

"Now I remember how you held your own with your brothers," Rafe said, smiling. "Stubborn."

"I prefer to think of it as determined."

"Good thing, determination."

Alana looked at Rafe's carefully bland expression, at the intelligence and humor that gave depth to his whiskey eyes, at the clean line of his lips beneath his moustache. He had taken off his hat, revealing the rich depths of color and texture in his hair. Very dark brown, surprising gleams of gold, clean and thick and lustrous. No shadow of a beard lay beneath his skin, which meant that he must have shaved before he picked her up at the airport. The open collar of his shirt revealed hair darker than his moustache, curly, springy. Her glance went back to his forehead, where the rich brown hair had been combed back by his fingers. Was it only a memory/dream, or had his hair once felt like winter mink between her fingers?

"What are you thinking?" said Rafe casually, as though he were asking the time.

Reflexively, Alana responded to the casual tone, answering before she realized what Rafe had asked or what her answer would reveal. "Your hair, like winter mink . . . ?" she murmured.

"Want to find out?"

"Find out what?" asked Alana, off-balance.

"If my hair feels like mink," said Rafe, as though it were a perfectly normal thing for her to do. Then, very softly, "Don't worry, Alana, I won't touch you at all. I know you don't want to be touched." His voice was low, murmurous, as soothing as it had been in the Jeep when nightmare had overtaken her without warning. "Go ahead and touch me. I promise I won't do anything but stand here. You're safe with me, Alana. Always. I'm the man who came to take you home."

Alana looked at the amber eyes and gentle smile while Rafe's voice surrounded her like an immaterial caress. His hands were still in his pockets, his body relaxed, every aspect of him telling her that he understood and accepted her fear of being touched, held.

"How did you know?" she asked, her voice trembling.

"That you didn't want to be touched?"

"Yes."

"Every time I touch you, you freeze. That's as good as words for me. Better."

"It isn't anything personal," Alana said quickly, caught by the emotion she sensed sliding beneath Rafe's surface calm. He had sent back her letter, but had he dreamed of her, too? Was her coldness cutting him, making him bleed as she had bled when her letter came back unopened? But that was the past. This was not. Today, Rafe had shown her only kindness, and she had hurt him. She wanted to hold on to him, comforting both of them, but the thought of being held in return made her body tense to fight or flee.

"Are you sure it isn't something I've done?" asked Rafe.

Alana looked at him. His eyes were as clear as a high-country stream. Glints of gold and topaz mixed with the predominant amber color, radiating outward from the black pupil. He was watching her with strange intensity. "I'm sure," she sighed.

"Then what is it?" Rafe asked, his voice gentle.

"I—I don't know. Since Jack died, I just don't like people touching me."

"Do you like touching people?"

"I—" Alana stopped, a puzzled expression bringing her black brows together. "I hadn't thought about it that way."

Rafe waited, watching her.

And she watched him, his silence and his restraint, the pulse beating slowly in his neck, the slide and coil of muscles across his chest as he breathed in the even rhythms of relaxation, waiting for her. Slowly, her hand came up. He bent down to make it easier for her to touch him. Her fingers brushed over his hair lightly, hesitated, then retreated quickly.

"Well?" Rafe asked as he straightened, smiling. "Is someone going to skin me for a fancy coat?"

Alana laughed a little breathlessly. "I'm not sure," she admitted.

"Try again," he offered, as casually as he would have offered to pass her the salt.

Alana climbed the stairs until she was on the same step as Rafe. This time her hand lingered as she allowed his hair to sift between the sensitive skin between her fingers.

"Better, but you should take lessons from a professional

furrier. They rub the pelt with their palms and fingertips,'' said Rafe, his glance moving from Alana's mouth to her glossy black hair, ''and they tease the fur with their breath, hold its softness to their lips, smell it, taste it, then gently slide the fur over their most sensitive skin.''

''Do they really?'' asked Alana, her breath catching.

''I don't know,'' Rafe admitted, his voice husky as he smiled down at her, ''but that's what I'd do to you if you were a fur and I were a furrier.''

Though Rafe hadn't moved any closer, Alana felt surrounded by him, by sensual possibilities that sent warmth showering through her. Suddenly, vividly, memories from the time they had made love went through her body like liquid lightning. She had spent so long trying to forget. Or were her memories of Rafe's exquisite touch merely hunger and dream entangled so thoroughly that truth was lost? Another kind of amnesia, kinder, but just as fraught with pitfalls in the present.

Yet she had just touched Rafe, and he had felt better than her memories.

Rafe smiled as though he knew exactly what Alana was feeling. Before she could retreat, he pushed away from the wall and passed her on the narrow stairway without touching her.

''Get some sleep, Alana,'' Rafe said, his voice pitched to a normal tone again. ''Bob and I weren't kidding about leaving at dawn. If you need anything, I'm in the room next to yours. Don't worry about making noise. The dudes are still on Virginia time. Sleeping like babes all in a row.''

She stared at Rafe as he walked toward the living room.

''And Alana . . .'' Rafe turned back toward her, his face half in light, half in shadow, his eyes the lambent gold of sunset rain.

''Yes?''

"Don't be afraid. Whatever happens, I'm here."

Rafe vanished into the living room before Alana could answer. Slowly, she walked upstairs to her room. The exhaustion of sleepless nights combined with the familiar background sounds of the ranch to send Alana into a deep sleep. She slept undisturbed until clouds gathered and thickened, stitched together by lightning and torn apart by thunder. She began to sleep restlessly, her head moving from side to side, her limbs shifting unpredictably, her throat clenched over unspoken words.

Riding next to Jack. He was angry and the clouds were angry and the mountains loomed over her like thunder. Spruce and fir and aspens bent double by the cruel wind. Wind tearing off leaves, spinning them like bright coins into the black void, and the horses were gone, screaming but no one could hear, she was a single bright leaf spinning endlessly down and down and down—

Cold, sweating, Alana woke up, her heart hammering against her ribs, her breath ragged. She looked at the bedside clock. Three-forty. Too soon to get up, even if they were leaving at dawn. Lightning bleached the room, leaving intense darkness behind, trailing an avalanche of thunder.

Suddenly, Alana felt trapped. She leaped out of bed, yanked open the door and ran into the hallway. She raced down the stairs and out onto the front porch. Incandescent lightning skidded over the land, separated by split seconds of darkness that were almost dizzying. Frightened, disoriented, a broken scream tearing at her throat, Alana turned back to the front door.

A man came out, walking toward her. At first Alana thought it was Rafe; then she realized that the man was too tall. But it wasn't Bob. The walk was different. Lightning came again, outlining the man, revealing his pale hair, long sideburns, blunt nose, narrow mouth and eyes so blue they were almost black.

Jack.

Alana scrambled backward, hands flailing frantically, falling, she was falling, and this time she could hear the screams tearing apart her throat. But it wasn't Jack's name she screamed as she spun toward the void.

It was Rafe's.

Chapter 4

Running, scrambling, falling and everywhere ice and lightning, thunder and darkness and screaming—

Past and present, nightmare and reality fused into seamless horror. Helpless, terrified, shaken by thunder and her own screaming, Alana called Rafe's name again and again. The front door burst open and slammed back against the wall. Abruptly, Jack disappeared between one stroke of lightning and the next. At first Alana thought that Jack had been a product of her imagination, a waking nightmare from which she would soon be freed. Then she saw Jack laid out on the porch, Rafe astride him, Rafe's forearm like an iron bar across Jack's throat.

For an instant panic exploded inside Alana, shards of ice ripping through her, paralyzing her. Jack was so much bigger than Rafe, as big as Bob, bigger, and Jack could be so cruel in his strength. Then paralysis melted, sliding away into darkness and lightning as she realized that Rafe was in control, that it was Jack who was down and was going to stay that way until Rafe decided to let him up again.

Bob ran out onto the front porch, flashlight in one hand and shotgun in the other. He saw Rafe and the man beneath him. "What in hell—?" Then, as Bob saw Alana backed up against the porch railing, terror in every line of her face, her hands clenched around her throat, "Sis? Oh, God—!" He started for her, holding out his arms.

Alana screamed.

Rafe came to his feet in a single powerful lunge. He stood between Bob and Alana. "Don't touch her," said Rafe coldly.

"But—" began Bob.

Lightning flared again and Bob saw Rafe's face, hard and utterly savage. Bob backed up without further argument. Rafe turned with the same fluid grace that he had used to come up off the porch floor. He looked at Alana with eyes that burned with rage and regret. He ached to gather her into his arms, to hold her, to feel her melt and flow along his body as she accepted his embrace. And he knew that was a dream, and she lived in nightmare. Broken Mountain was destroying their future as surely as his "death" once had.

"It's all right, Wildflower," said Rafe quietly. "I won't let anyone touch you. Do you understand? No one will touch you, not even me."

Numbly, Alana nodded her head, hearing the word *Wildflower* echo and reecho in her mind, a name from the deep past, before Rafe had died and been reborn, killing her without knowing it. Wildflower. A name out of dreams. A name out of nightmares.

"Bob," said Rafe without turning around, "pick up Stan and get the hell out of Alana's sight."

Bob had no desire to argue with that whiplike voice, the poised fighting stance, muscles visibly coiled across Rafe's

naked back, ready to unleash violence. Bob bent over,
levered the man called Stan to his feet, and dragged him
into the living room. The screen door banged shut behind
them, a sound like a small crack of thunder.

Distant lightning came, revealing Rafe's face, harshness
and yearning. Alana blinked, but he stayed before her,
inscribed on her eyes by forked lightning, a man both lean
and powerful, wearing only jeans, regret a dark veil across
his features. She swayed toward him, instinctively seeking
comfort. Rafe stood without moving, looking at her slender
body shaken by shudders of cold and fear, his own private
nightmare come true. He would have put his arms around
her but he knew that she would only scream again, tearing
both of them apart.

In the end, Rafe could not help holding out his hand to
Alana. It was a gesture that asked nothing, offered everything.

"Hold on to me, Wildflower," he said softly. "If you
want to."

With a small sound, Alana took Rafe's hand between her
own. She held on to him with bruising intensity, but he
didn't object. Nor did he so much as curl his fingers around
hers. She took a shuddering breath, then another, fighting to
control herself.

"I thought—" Alana's voice broke. She bent over,
touching her forehead to the back of Rafe's hand. She
swallowed and tried again. "I thought he was J-Jack."

Rafe's left hand hovered over Alana's bent head, as
though he would stroke her hair soothingly. Then his hand
dropped to his side and remained there, clenched into a fist.
He was afraid to touch her, to frighten her and rend the
fragile fabric of trust being woven between them.

"Stan is one of the dudes," said Rafe quietly, but

emotions turned beneath the smooth surface of his voice, testing his control. "Stan is big, like Jack was. And blond. If I had known that the first time you saw Stan it would be in lightning and darkness, a storm, like Broken Mountain—" Rafe didn't finish. "I'm sorry, Alana. For so many things."

But the last was said so softly that she wasn't sure she had heard the words at all. For a moment longer she clung to Rafe's hand, drawing strength and warmth from him, nightmare draining away, fading like thunder into the distance. Her head came up as she drew more deep breaths, sending oxygen through a body that had been starved for it, paralyzed by fear to the point that she had forgotten to breathe.

Gradually the shuddering left Alana's body, only to return as shivers of cold rather than fear. Windblown rain had lashed over her as she crouched against the porch railing, terrified. For the first time, she realized that she was wearing only a thin silk nightshirt which icy rain had plastered across her body. The vivid orange cloth looked nearly black where water had touched it, as dark as her eyes looking up at Rafe.

Alana shivered again, and for a moment Rafe held his warm hand against her cheek. A single fingertip traced the black wing of her eyebrow with such exquisite gentleness that she forgot to be afraid. Tears stood in her eyes, magnifying them. Tears flowed silently down, tears as warm as Rafe's hand. With dreamlike slowness, she turned her face until her lips rested against his palm.

"Thank you for understanding," whispered Alana, her breath another caress flowing over his skin.

Rafe's body tensed visibly as he fought his impulse to hold Alana, to turn her lips to his own, to taste again the warmth of her, to feel her respond. He knew if he reached for her she would retreat, terrified. And that knowledge was a knife turning inside him.

Slowly, Alana released Rafe's hand. For an instant he held his palm against her cheek, then he withdrew.

"I feel like such a fool," said Alana, closing her eyes. "What must that poor man think of me?"

"Stan thinks he was a real horse's ass to come barging outside after you in a storm, scaring you half to death," said Rafe, his voice like a whip once more. "He's lucky I didn't take him apart."

Alana made a sound of protest. "It was my fault, not his. I'll have to apologize."

"Like hell. Stan will apologize to you, in good light, when you can see him clearly. And then he will stay away from you."

Rafe's words were clear and hard, like glacier ice. Alana realized that he was furious, but not with her. With Stan, because Stan had frightened her. And Rafe was also furious with himself, because he hadn't prevented Alana from being frightened.

"It wasn't your fault," whispered Alana.

Rafe's eyes narrowed. "Wasn't it?" Then, before she could respond, he said, "You're shivering. Are you ready to go back inside?"

Alana hesitated. The thought of seeing the man who looked so much like Jack disturbed her deeply. But she had no choice. She refused to spend the rest of her life at the mercy of her own fears. She clenched her hands at her sides, took a deep breath and lifted her chin. "Yes, I'm ready."

"You don't have to," said Rafe quietly. "I'll go in and tell Bob you'd rather not meet Stan right now."

"No. I've got to stop being so . . . fragile."

"Alana, you've been through too much, too recently," said Rafe, his voice gentle. "More than anyone should have to bear. Don't be so hard on yourself. Ease up. Give yourself a chance to heal."

She shook her head. She wasn't healing. The nightmare was getting worse, taking over more and more of her waking hours. "Life goes on, Rafe. The biggest cliché, and the one with the most truth. I have to go on, too. I have to leave those six days behind me. *I have to.*"

"Just like a wildflower," said Rafe, his voice soft and deep. "Delicate and tough, growing in the most difficult places." Then, "Will you let me help you?" he asked, holding out his hand to Alana.

After a moment's hesitation, Alana put her hand on Rafe's. The warmth of his skin was like fire, telling her how cold her own body was. He opened the door and led her back into the living room.

Bob and Stan were sitting inside, talking about storms and high-country trout. Both men looked up, then away, clearly not wanting to intrude if Alana needed privacy. Rafe plucked a flannel shirt off a rack near the door, draped the colorful plaid folds over Alana, and turned toward the two men. Instantly, Stan stood up. Alana took a quick breath and stepped backward until she came up hard against Rafe's chest.

"Alana Reeves, meet Stan Wilson," said Rafe, smiling coldly as he looked at the blond, muscular giant who was every bit as tall as Bob. "Stan, you'll understand if Alana doesn't want to shake hands," continued Rafe. "You have an unnerving resemblance to her recently deceased husband."

For a long moment, Rafe and Stan measured each other. Then Stan nodded, a slight incline of his head that was almost an apology. He turned and looked toward Alana. At

the sight of Stan's cobalt blue eyes, Alana made a small
sound. Like Jack. Just like Jack. Only the solid warmth of
Rafe at her back kept her from falling into nightmare again.

"I'm sorry, Mrs. Reeves," said Stan. "I sure didn't
mean to frighten you like that."

Alana felt relief uncurl deep inside her. The voice was
different, entirely different, deeper, permeated by the subtle
rhythms of the Southwest. "Please, call me Alana," she
said. "And I'm sorry for—"

"You have nothing to apologize for," said Rafe, cutting
across Alana's words. "Now that Stan is aware of the
situation, I'm sure he won't take you by surprise again."

Rafe's voice was smooth and polished, steel hard, having
no soft surfaces that might admit to argument. His eyes
were narrowed, watching Stan with the intensity of a
cougar stalking deer. Again, Stan hesitated. Again, Stan
nodded slightly, though his expression was as hard as
Rafe's.

Alana looked from one man to the other, and then to Bob,
who she feared would be worried about the fate of his
dreams for a dude ranch. If Stan Wilson had an awful
vacation at the Broken Mountain Dude Ranch, he would
hardly recommend it to his wealthy clients. Yet Bob didn't
look upset. He looked more like a man making bets with
himself, and winning. When Bob realized that Alana was
watching him, he smiled at her.

"Some homecoming, sis," said Bob, shaking his head.
He yawned and looked at the wristwatch he always wore.
"Well, there's not much point in me going back to sleep,"
he said, stretching. "I'll start working on the pack string.
Stan, you said you wanted to watch a real cowboy. Still
game?"

The faint challenge in Bob's voice brought a smile to

Stan's face. Alana looked away. The smile was like an echo of Jack, charming and boyish. Stan was a very handsome man . . . and her skin crawled every time she looked at him. It wasn't rational or fair to Stan, but it wasn't something she could control, either.

"I'll be glad to help you, Bob," drawled Stan, "seeing as how you're such a puny thing."

Bob looked startled, then laughed aloud. He clapped Stan on the shoulder and led him toward the kitchen. "Merry left some coffee warming. We'll need it. And," Bob's voice drifted back as the two huge men left the room, "I've got a jacket that I think will fit you, seeing as how you're such a puny thing, too."

Listening, Alana realized that her brother liked Stan. That was different from before, from Jack. Bob hadn't liked Jack at all. None of the Burdettes had. She heard Stan's laughter trailing back into the room, laughter as charming as his smile. Yet, unlike the smile, it didn't remind Alana of Jack. Jack had rarely laughed, and never at himself.

Even so, she was glad that Stan was out of sight. It was unnerving to catch a glimpse of him out of the corner of her eye, blond shades of Jack stalking behind her. She let out a long sigh as the kitchen door slammed, telling her that the two men were on the way to the barn.

"Okay?" asked Rafe, feeling the deep breath Alana had taken and let out, for her back was still pressed against his chest.

Alana nodded. "He—he's nice, isn't he?"

Rafe grunted, a sound that told her nothing.

"Bob likes him," said Alana.

"They're a lot alike," said Rafe dryly. "Muscle and impulse in equal amounts and places."

"Between their ears?" suggested Alana.

"Sometimes," sighed Rafe. "Just sometimes."

Alana shifted her weight slightly. The movement reminded her that she was standing very close to Rafe, all but leaning on him. The contact didn't bother her, though. He wasn't touching her. She was touching him. The difference was both subtle and infinitely reassuring. The warmth of his bare chest radiated through the flannel shirt and her damp silk nightshirt, a fire as natural as the embers glowing in the living room hearth. For an instant she wanted to turn and wrap herself in his warmth, chasing away the chill that had come the day they'd told her that Rafe was dead.

She shivered again, but not from cold.

"You should try to sleep a little more," said Rafe. "You're still on West Coast time."

Rafe was so close that Alana felt the vibration of his chest as he spoke, the subtle movement of his muscles as he bent slightly toward her, the brush of his breath over her ear. She closed her eyes, savoring the tactile intimacy that demanded nothing from her.

"I feel safer here with you," she said simply.

Alana felt Rafe's quick, subdued breath and realized what she had said. She tensed, knowing that if Rafe accepted her unintended invitation and put his arms around her, she had only herself to blame. The worst of it was that part of her very much wanted his arms around her; and part of her panicked at the thought of being held.

Suddenly she wondered if Jack had been holding her when they fell. Was that why she froze at a man's touch? Had her mind equated the act of being embraced with falling and terror and death?

Alana stiffened, listening intently, hoping to hear an inner voice say *yes* or *no*, hoping to tear the veil of amnesia and look upon just a few minutes of those six missing days. The only answer, if answer it was, came in the sudden coldness of her skin, nausea turning in her stomach, her heart beating quickly, erratically.

"What's wrong?" asked Rafe, sensing the change in her. Then, sadly, "Does being close to me frighten you?"

"No," said Alana, "it's not that. I was thinking of Jack."

Behind her, Rafe's expression changed, tightening, anger and defeat. But his voice was neutral when he spoke. "Did you love him?"

Alana closed her eyes. "No."

"Then why did you marry him so fast? Not even two months after—" Abruptly, Rafe stopped speaking.

"They told me you were dead," said Alana, her voice ragged. "Music was all that was left to me. And that meant Jack, a voice to make angels weep."

"I'm sorry," said Rafe, stepping backward. "I had no right to ask."

Rafe's voice was neutral, distant, and Alana's back felt cold without his warmth. She spun around, suddenly angry, remembering the letter that had come back, Rafe's own handwriting telling her that he didn't want to say anything to her, not even good-bye. "That's correct. You have no right. You didn't even open my letter."

"You were another man's woman." Rafe's voice was as opaque as his eyes, his mouth a thin line of remembered anger beneath his dark moustache.

"I never belonged to Jack. Not like that."

"You were his wife. Didn't that mean anything to you?"

"Yes," she said harshly. *"It meant you were dead!"*

Tears spilled suddenly down Alana's cheeks. She spun away, wanting only to be alone, not to be torn between a past she couldn't change and a present that was trying to destroy her.

"Alana, please don't turn away."

Rafe's voice was gentle, coaxing, making subtle music out of her name. She knew without turning around that he was holding his hand out to her, asking her for something she could not give. Trust. Caring. Warmth. Passion. Love. All the things she needed but no longer believed in. Not really. She had had them taken away from her once too often. She had survived her mother's death. She had survived her lover's death. She had survived her husband's death. Now she was trying to survive a different kind of death, a shattering loss of belief in her own strength, her own mind, her music. Now she was trying not to ask herself if it was worth it, any of it, if there was no end to fear and loss and death.

"Alana, I'm sorry. I shouldn't have brought up the past. It's too soon. You're too close to what happened on Broken Mountain."

Rafe walked to her, not stopping until he felt the cool, rough flannel he had draped around her shoulders rubbing against his chest. Alana sensed his arm moving and held her breath, anticipating his touch, not knowing whether she would run or scream or stand quietly. It was agony not to know, not to be able to trust anything, most of all herself.

"No," said Alana hoarsely, stepping away. "I can't take any more. Leave me alone, Rafe."

"Is it the letter, Alana? Is that what you can't forgive me for?" Rafe asked sadly.

"No. It's worse than the letter, although that was bad enough, losing you a second time. . . ." Her voice died.

"If not the letter," said Rafe softly, urgently, "what? What have I done? *What are your memories?*"

At first Alana thought she wasn't going to tell him. Then words rushed out of her in a bittersweet torrent. "After you, I couldn't bear another man's touch. God, how Jack hated you! You ruined me for any other man."

Rafe's face changed, all anger and urgency gone, only hunger remaining. He reached for Alana and could not help protesting when she flinched away.

"Alana. Don't. Please."

She turned and looked at Rafe with eyes that were wild and dark, shadows as deep as despair.

"Jack got even with me, though," she whispered. "Somehow he ruined me for any man at all. Even you."

Alana turned and fled up the stairs, not stopping even when Rafe called her name in a voice hoarse with emotion, a cry out of her dreams and nightmares. She locked the bedroom door behind her and stared out the window until dawn came, bringing color and life to the black land. She watched the world change, born anew out of the empty night.

Just as the last star faded, she heard Bob's voice.

"Sis? You awake?"

Alana realized she was shivering, her skin icy, roughened by gooseflesh. Every muscle ached with the tension that hadn't left her since Broken Mountain as she faced another day like all the other days. But not quite. This day would bring the exquisite torture of being close to the only man she had ever loved. So close and yet so very, very far away. Dream and nightmare and nothing in between, no safety, no port in the unending storm.

"Alana?"

"Yes," she said tiredly. "I'm awake."

"Don't sound so happy about it," teased Bob.

Alana tugged the flannel shirt more firmly around her, opened the door and pulled her mouth into the semblance of a smile. "Morning, little brother," she said, grateful that her voice sounded better than she felt. "Is it time for me to cook breakfast?"

"Nope. Merry's doing the food this morning. I just came up to get your gear."

Alana gestured to the small duffel bag on the bed. "Have at it."

"That's all?" said Bob, raising a black eyebrow.

"This is a pack trip, right? I don't think the trees will care how I'm dressed," Alana said, shrugging.

"Er, right." Bob gave her a sidelong glance, then asked softly, "Are you sure you're up to this?"

"What does that have to do with it?" asked Alana sardonically. "Ready or not, here life comes." She smiled to take the sting out of her words but could tell from Bob's worried look that she hadn't been very convincing. "It's okay, Bob. Not to worry. I'm doing fine. Just fine."

He hesitated, then nodded. "Like Dr. Gene says, Burdettes are survivors. And you're the toughest Burdette of all, sis. You taught the rest of us how to survive after Mom died."

Alana blinked back sudden tears. "Would you mind very much if I hugged you?" she asked.

Bob looked startled, then pleased. Remembering Rafe's blunt instructions, Bob kept his arms at his sides while Alana gave him a hard hug.

"You're stronger than you feel," said Bob, patting her slender shoulder.

Alana laughed strangely and shook her head. "I hope so, baby brother. I hope so."

"Are you—are you remembering anything now that you're home?" asked Bob in a rush. Then, "Damn, there I go! Rafe will nail my dumb hide to the barn if he finds out."

Alana stiffened at Rafe's name. "What happens between me and my brother is none of Rafe's business."

Bob laughed. "Don't you believe it, sis. That is one

determined man. Makes a pack mule look positively wishy-washy.''

She looked narrowly at her brother. ''You don't resent him, though, do you?''

Surprised, Bob stared down at Alana. His dark eyes, so like her own, narrowed as he measured the emotion on her face. ''Rafe is quite a man. I don't resent learning from him. Granted,'' said Bob with a smile, ''he's a jealous s.o.b. I thought he was going to field-strip Stan and feed him to the coyotes.''

Alana blinked, seeing the previous night from another perspective. ''Jealous?''

Bob snapped his fingers and waved his hands in front of her face. ''Wake up, sis. Stan wouldn't have minded, er, soothing you. And Rafe has made it pretty plain that—'' Bob shrugged and shut up, his caution for once getting the better of his tongue. ''Rafe cares about you, and Stan is bigger, stronger, and better looking than Rafe. No surprise that Rafe's jealous.''

''Stan's bigger,'' agreed Alana, ''but it was Stan who ended up flat on his back. And there's more to looks than blond hair, bulging muscles and a big smile. A lot more.''

Bob grinned. ''Does that mean you've forgiven Rafe for not opening your letter?'' Bob watched her face change and swore again. ''Sorry. I'll never learn when to keep my big mouth shut.''

''Sure you will,'' said Rafe's voice from the doorway, ''even if I have to pound the lessons into your thick skull one by one with a sledgehammer.''

Alana spun and saw Rafe lounging against the door-frame, his rich brown hair alive with light, his mouth hard yet oddly sensual, his face expressionless except for the whiskey eyes burning with suppressed emotion. She wondered how Bob could think that Stan was better looking than the utterly male Rafe. And then she wondered how much of the conversation Rafe had overheard.

"Morning, Rafe," said Bob with a cheerful grin. He turned and grabbed Alana's duffel off the bed.

Rafe looked at Alana. The flannel shirt she still wore was in shades of russet and orange and chocolate brown. The long tails came nearly to her knees, and the sleeve cuffs lapped over her fingertips, making her look very small, very fragile. Only in her face and in her movements did her strength show, a woman's strength made of grace and endurance. A wildflower with pale cheeks and haunted eyes, watching him.

The sound of Bob unzipping Alana's duffel bag seemed very loud in the silence. He rummaged for a few seconds, muttered under his breath and went to the closet where she had left her clothes from the last, disastrous visit. Bob ran a critical eye over the contents of the closet, then began pulling bright blouses and slacks off hangers. He hesitated between a scarlet jumpsuit and a floor-length, indigo wraparound that was shot through with metallic gold threads.

"Which one of these travels best?" asked Bob, looking over his shoulder at Alana.

With a start, Alana pulled her attention away from Rafe. She saw Bob in front of her closet, his arms overflowing with color and silk. In his large hands, the clothes looked exquisitely feminine, as intimate as French lingerie.

"What are you doing?" asked Alana.

"Packing for my big sister," said Bob patiently. "As cute as you look in Rafe's flannel shirt, that wasn't what I had in mind when I told the dudes we dressed for dinner. This is a classy operation, remember?"

Alana looked down at the big flannel shirt folded around

her like a warm blanket. Rafe's shirt. The thought disturbed her. She had assumed that the shirt belonged to Bob.

"Sis? Anybody home?"

"Oh. Er, the dark blue one packs best."

Bob nodded and began folding the wraparound with more determination than expertise. Alana started to object, then shrugged. Whatever Bob did to the silk could be steamed out at the other end. But when he went back to the closet for more clothes, and then more, she finally protested.

"How long are we staying on Broken Mountain?" she asked.

"As long as it takes," said Bob laconically, folding bright clothes.

"As long as what takes?"

Rafe's voice cut across whatever Bob had been going to say. "As long as it takes to convince the dudes that Broken Mountain is a good place to send clients. Right, Burdette?"

Bob swallowed. "Right," he said, folding clothes industriously. "I'm counting on your cooking to win them over, sis."

"But—" began Alana.

"But nothing," Bob said suddenly, his dark eyes looking at Alana with a combination of affection and maturity that was new to him. "You signed on for the duration. Get used to the idea. No running out this time, no matter what happens. We'll come after you if you do. Right, Rafe?"

"Right," said Rafe, looking narrowly at Bob. "You're learning, Burdette."

"And not a sledgehammer in sight," pointed out Bob, smiling widely.

Rafe glanced at Alana and saw her baffled look. "Better get dressed," he said, as he went back into the hallway. "Breakfast is getting cold."

Bob zipped up Alana's duffel bag and left her standing in the room with a bemused look on her face. "Hurry up, sis. Like Dad always used to say, 'You can't keep the mountain waiting.' "

The phrase from her childhood gave Alana a dizzying sense of déjà vu. She remembered her first pack trip up Broken Mountain. She had been only nine and wild with pride that her father was taking her on a fishing expedition, just the two of them. It had been a wonderful time, campfires and long conversations while stars moved in slow motion overhead like a silent, glittering symphony.

It hadn't been like that the last time, when she and Jack had gone to the mountain. Six days. Six blank days poisoning past memories, poisoning each day, poisoning her, Broken Mountain looming over her with inhuman patience, waiting, waiting. For what? For her to die, too?

You can't keep the mountain waiting.

With a shudder, Alana turned away from her thoughts and dressed quickly. The thought of food didn't appeal to her. She avoided the dining room, where she heard laughter and strange voices, Stan's and the woman whom Alana hadn't officially met. She didn't feel up to meeting Janice Simpson right now, either. Alana let herself quietly out of the front door, then circled around to the barn where the pack mules waited patiently.

There were five horses lined up at the hitching posts. One horse was a magnificent Appaloosa stallion. Two were good-looking bays, their brown hides glossy in the sun. Of the two remaining horses, one was as black as midnight and one was a big dapple-gray gelding.

Alana went to the black mare and stood for a moment, letting the velvet muzzle whuff over her to drink her scent. When the mare returned to a relaxed posture, accepting

Alana's presence, she ran her hand down the mare's muscular legs and picked up each hoof, checking for stones or loose nails in the shoes.

"Well, Sid," said Alana, straightening up from the last hoof, "are you ready for that long climb and that rotten talus slope at the end?"

Sid snorted. Alana checked the cinch and stirrup length, talking softly all the while, not hearing Rafe approach behind her.

"Good-looking mare," said Rafe, his voice neutral.

Alana checked the bridle, then stepped back to admire the horse. "Sid's a beauty, all right, but the best thing about her is the way she moves. She just flattens out those mountain trails."

"Sid?" asked Rafe, his voice tight.

"Short for Obsidian," explained Alana, returning to the bridle. "You know, that shiny black volcanic glass."

"Yes, I know," he said softly. "You say she has a good trail gait?"

"Yes," answered Alana absently, her attention more on loosening the strap beneath the bit than on the conversation. "Riding her is like riding a smooth black wind. A real joy. Not a mean hair on her shiny hide."

"She didn't mind the talus slope?" continued Rafe in a voice that was restrained, tight with emotion.

"No. The gray didn't like it much, though," said Alana, rearranging the mare's forelock so that it wouldn't be pulled by leather straps.

"The gray?"

"Jack's horse," she said casually, gesturing toward the big dapple-gray gelding. "It—" Alana blinked. Suddenly her hands began to shake. She spun and faced Rafe. "It balked. The horse balked. And then Jack—Jack—" She closed her eyes, willing the memories to come. All that came was the thunder of her own heartbeat. She made an anguished sound. "It's gone! I can't remember anything!"

"You remembered something," said Rafe, his whiskey eyes intent, appraising her. "That's a start."

"Jack's horse balked," said Alana harshly. "Six seconds out of six days." Her hands clenched until her fingernails dug deeply into her palms. "Six lousy seconds!"

"That's not all you remembered."

"What do you mean?"

"Sid. You walked out here today and picked her out of a row of horses without any hesitation at all."

"Of course. I've always ridden—" Alana stopped, a startled look on her face. "I can't remember the first time I rode Sid."

"Bob bought her two months ago. He hadn't named her by the time you and Jack came. You named her. And then you rode her up Broken Mountain."

Chapter 5

THE FIRST HALF OF THE EIGHT-HOUR RIDE WASN'T STRENU-
ous. The trail wound through evergreens and along a small,
boulder-strewn river that drained the series of lakes higher
up the mountain. The air was vibrant with light and
fragrance. The horses' hooves provided a soothing, subtly
syncopated beat that permeated Alana's subconscious,
setting up tiny earthquakes of remembrance beneath amnesia's opaque mantle.

Little things. Simple things. Sunlight fanning through a
pine branch, stilettos of gold and quivering green needles.
The ring of a horse's steel-shod hoof against stone. The
liquid crystal of a brook sliding through shadows. The
dazzling burst of silver as water poured through sunlight.
The creak of a saddle beneath a man's shifting weight. The
pale flash of blond hair just off her shoulder when Jack's
gray horse crowded against Sid's side.

No, not Jack's horse. Stan's horse. Jack was dead and the sky over Broken Mountain was clear, no clouds, no thunder, no ice storm poised to flay her unprotected skin and make walking a treacherous joke. There was sunlight now, hot and pouring, blazing over her, warming her all the way to her bones. She was hot, not cold. Her hands were flexible, not numbed to uselessness. Her throat wasn't a raw sore from too many screams. It was just rigid with the effort of not screaming now.

Deliberately, Alana swallowed and unclenched her hands from the reins. She wiped her forehead, beaded with cold sweat despite the heat of the day. She didn't notice Bob's concerned looks or the grim line of Rafe's mouth. When Rafe called for an early lunch, she thought nothing of it, other than that she would have a few minutes of surcease, a few minutes longer before she had to face Broken Mountain's savage heights.

Alana dismounted and automatically loosened the cinch. She was a little stiff from the ride, but it wasn't anything that a bit of walking wouldn't cure. Janice, however, didn't appear to be as resilient. She groaned loudly and leaned against her patient horse. Rafe came up and offered his arm. Janice took it and walked a few painful steps. Alana watched the woman's chestnut hair gleam in the sun and heard her feminine, rueful laughter joined by the deep, male sound of Rafe's amusement. Slowly, the two of them walked back down the line of horses on the opposite side of the trail, coming closer to Alana, who was all but invisible as she leaned on Sid.

Envy turned in Alana as she watched Janice with Rafe. To be able to accept touch so casually. To laugh. To feel Rafe's strength and warmth so close and not be afraid. To remember everything. Did Janice know how lucky she was? And did she have to cling so closely to Rafe that her breasts pressed against his arm?

Alana closed her eyes and choked off her uncharitable thoughts. Obviously, Janice wasn't at all accustomed to riding. Her legs must feel like cooked spaghetti. Yet she hadn't complained once in the four hours since they had left the ranch. Bob had demanded a brisk pace, wanting to reach Five Lakes Lodge on Broken Mountain before the late-afternoon thundershowers materialized. It hadn't been easy on the two dudes, who weren't accustomed either to riding or to the increasingly thin air as the trail climbed toward timberline.

But no one had objected to the pace. Not even Stan, who had good reason to be feeling irritable. Stan, who had been first screamed at and then attacked with no warning, laid out flat, choking beneath Rafe's hard arm. Blood rose in Alana's cheeks as she remembered last night's fiasco. She put her face against the smooth leather of the saddle, cooling her hot skin.

Stan came up on the other side of Janice and took her arm, supporting her. She smiled up at him in rueful thanks. The smile was vivid, inviting, a perfect foil for Janice's clear blue eyes. Stan smiled back with obvious male appreciation.

"I'll leave you in Stan's capable hands," said Rafe, withdrawing. "But don't go too far. We have to be back on the trail within half an hour."

"Which trail?" asked Stan, looking at the meadow just beyond the trees, where several trails snaked off in various directions.

"That one," said Rafe, pointing toward the rugged shoulder of Broken Mountain looming at the end of the meadow.

Janice groaned and rolled her eyes. "Only for you, Rafe Winter, would I get on that damned horse again and ride up that god-awful trail."

Alana lifted her head and looked over Sid's back with sudden, intense curiosity. Janice's words, her ease with Rafe, everything about the two of them together added up to people who had known each other longer than a few hours. Stan, too, seemed familiar with Rafe, more like an old friend than a new client for Broken Mountain Dude Ranch. As Janice and Stan hobbled off down the trail, Rafe smiled after them with a combination of affection and amusement. Alana watched both the smile and the man, and wondered how well Rafe knew Stan and Janice. Especially Janice.

As though Rafe sensed Alana's scrutiny, he looked up and saw the black of her hair blending perfectly with Sid's shiny hide. Other than her eyes and hair, Alana was hidden behind the horse's bulk.

"You know them," said Alana when she saw the whiskey eyes watching her. Her voice sounded accusing.

Rafe waited for a long moment, then shrugged. "I used to travel a lot. The two of them were my favorite agents." He smiled swiftly, amused by a private joke. "We've done a lot of business together, one way or another."

"She's very attractive," said Alana, a question mark in her eyes if not her voice.

Rafe glanced in the direction of Janice, now well down the trail, leaning on Stan. "Yes, I suppose she is," said Rafe, his voice indifferent. Then he turned suddenly, pinning Alana with amber eyes. "So is Stan."

"Not to me."

"Because he reminds you of Jack?"

Alana thought of lying, then decided it was too much trouble. It was hard enough to keep dream separate from nightmare. If she started lying to herself and to Rafe, it would become impossible to separate threads of reality from the snarl of amnesia and unreality. "Stan isn't attractive to me because he isn't you."

Rafe's nostrils flared with the sudden intake of his breath. Before he could speak, Alana did, her voice both haunted and unflinching.

"But it doesn't matter that you're attractive and other men aren't," she said, her voice low, "because it's too late."

"No." Rafe said nothing more. He didn't have to. Every line of his taut body rejected what she said.

Slowly, Alana shook her head, making sunlight slide and burn in her black hair. "I can't handle any more, Rafe," she said, a thread of desperation in her voice. "I can't handle you and the past and today, what was and what wasn't, what is and what isn't. Just getting through the days is hard enough, and the nights—"

Alana took a sharp breath, fighting to control herself. It was harder each hour, each minute, for her mind was screaming at her that with every moment, every foot up the trail to Broken Mountain she came closer to death. Her death. It was irrational. She knew it. But knowing didn't stop the fear.

"Seeing you and then remembering the days before and knowing that it will never be again—" said Alana in a rush. Her breath came in raggedly, almost a sob. She closed her dark eyes, not wanting to reveal the hunger and fear and helplessness seething inside her. "I just can't!"

"No, Alana," countered Rafe, his voice both soft and certain. "I lost you once. I won't lose you again. Unless" —his face changed, tight and hard and whiskey eyes burning—"unless you don't want me?"

Alana made a sound that was halfway between a laugh and a sob. "I've never wanted anyone else, for all the good that does either one of us. It wasn't enough in the past, was it? And it isn't enough now. Even you can't touch me."

"It's only been three weeks, Alana," he said reasonably. "Give yourself time to heal."

"I'm getting worse, not better," she said, her voice husky with the effort it took to speak rationally about the panic that was turning her strength to water and then draining even that away. "I'm starting to hate myself. Coward. Hiding behind amnesia." She looked at Rafe, an unattainable dream. "I shouldn't have come back."

Rafe's face showed an instant of pain that made Alana catch her breath. "Was it better for you in Portland?" he asked, his voice quiet, almost uninflected.

Slowly, Alana shook her head. "No. When I slept the nightmares came, more each time, and worse. I'd wake up and fight myself. Hate myself. That's why I'm here. I thought—"

Rafe waited, but when she didn't say any more, he asked, "What did you think?"

She took a deep, shuddering breath, then another. "I thought there was something here for me, something that would help me to be strong again. Something that would—" Her voice broke but she went on, forcing herself to tell Rafe what she had told no one else. "Something that would let me sing again," she whispered.

"What do you mean?" asked Rafe, wondering if he had heard correctly, her voice was so soft, so frayed.

"I haven't sung since Broken Mountain," she said. "I can't. Every time I try, my throat just closes." Alana looked at Rafe desperately, wondering if he knew how much singing meant to her. "Singing was all I had after you died. And now I can't sing. Not one note. Nothing. You're alive now, and I can't bear to be touched. *And I can't sing.''*

Rafe's eyes closed, remembering the sliding, supple beauty of Alana's voice soaring with his harmonica's swirling notes, Alana's face radiant with music and love as she sang to him. He wanted to reassure her, protect her, love her, give her back song and laughter, all that the past had taken from her and from him. Yet everything he did brought Alana more pain, more fear.

She could not sing.

He could not hold her.

Rafe swore softly, viciously. When his eyes opened they were clear and hard, and pain was a darkness pooling in their depths. ''I'll take you back down the mountain, Alana. And then I'll leave you alone if that's what you want. I can't bear hurting you like this.''

''Rafe,'' she said, catching her breath, touching his cheek with fingers that trembled, ''don't. None of this is your fault.''

''Yes, it is,'' he said harshly. ''I leaned on Bob to get you back here. Now you're here and everything I do hurts you.''

''That isn't true,'' said Alana, unable to bear knowing that she had hurt Rafe. She had never wanted that, even in the worst times after her letter had come back unopened.

''Isn't it?'' Rafe looked at her with narrow amber eyes. His anger at himself showed in his lips, sensual curves flattened into a hard line.

''No, it isn't true,'' she whispered.

But words weren't enough to convince Rafe. Alana could see the disbelief in his grim expression. If she could have sung her emotions to him, he would have believed her, but she couldn't sing. Hesitantly, she lifted her hand to Rafe's face, the face that had smiled and laughed and loved her in her memories, in her dreams. He had always been a song inside her, even in the worst of times, especially then, when nightmare and ice avalanched around her, smothering her. He had given her so much, reality and dream and hope. Surely she could give something of that back to him now, when his eyes were dark with pain and anger at himself.

Alana's fingertips pushed beneath the brim of Rafe's Western hat until it tipped back on his head and slid unnoticed to the ground. Fingers spread wide, she eased into the rich warmth of his hair. "You do feel like winter mink, Rafael," she murmured, giving his name its liquid Spanish pronunciation, making a love song of the three syllables. "Rafael . . . Rafael. You feel better than my dreams of you. And my dreams of you are good. They're all that has kept me sane since Broken Mountain."

Alana felt the fine trembling that went through Rafe, the outrush of his breath that was her name. For an instant she was afraid he would touch her, breaking the spell, but he didn't. Instead, he moved his head slowly, rubbing against her hand like a big cat, closing his eyes and concentrating on the feel of her fingers sliding deeply through his hair. His sensual intensity sent a new kind of weakness through Alana, fire licking down her fingers and radiating through her body, fire deep inside her, burning.

Rafe's dense brown lashes shifted as he looked at Alana, held her focused in the hungry amber depths of his eyes.

"I've dreamed of you," he murmured. "Of this."

Alana said nothing, for she could not. Her fingers tightened in his hair, searching deeply, as though she would find something in that thick male pelt that she had lost and had all but given up hope of ever finding again. Even when the sound of Janice and Stan walking back up the row of horses reminded Alana that she and Rafe weren't alone, even then she couldn't bring herself to withdraw from the rich sensation of his hair sliding between her fingers.

Bob's voice cut through Alana's trance. "Twenty minutes to trail time, everyone," he called from the front of the line of pack mules. "If you haven't eaten lunch, you'll regret it."

Slowly, reluctantly, Alana released the silk and warmth of Rafe's hair. Just before her hand would have dropped to her side again, her fingertips paused to smooth the crisp hairs of his moustache, a caress as light as sunshine. He moved his head slowly, sliding his lips over the sensitive pads of her fingers. When her hand no longer touched him, he bent swiftly and retrieved his hat.

"Bob's right about food," said Rafe, his voice husky and warm as he settled his hat into place with an easy tug. "You didn't have breakfast."

Alana shook her head, though it hadn't been a question. "I forgot to pack lunch," she admitted.

"Merry packed enough for twenty in my saddlebag." Then, smiling, Rafe added in a coaxing voice, "Share it with me, Alana. Even wildflowers have to eat something." Beneath his teasing was real concern. Alana was thinner than he had ever seen her. Too thin, too finely drawn, like an animal that had been hunted too long. "Roast beef, apples, homemade bread, chocolate chip cookies . . ."

Alana's mouth watered. She licked her lips with unconscious hunger. "Sold," she said breathlessly.

She and Rafe ate in the shifting shade of a windblown pine. They sat side by side, almost touching, sharing his canteen. The mint-flavored tea Merry had made for him tasted extraordinary in the clean mountain air. Alana ate hungrily, enjoying food for the first time in weeks. Rafe watched her, smiling. This, too, had been part of his dreams. Alana and the mountains and him. When everything else in his life had reeked of death and betrayal, he had dreamed of her.

"Saddle up," called Bob.

Alana stopped, her hand halfway into the paper bag of cookies. Rafe scooped up the bag and handed it to her.

"Take them," he said, smiling.

"Are you sure?" she asked. "I don't want you to be hungry just because I was too stupid to remember my own lunch."

"There's another bag of cookies in here," Rafe assured her, gesturing to the saddlebags draped across his leg. "Apples, too." He dug into a supple leather pouch. "Here. One for you and one for Sid." Rafe stood and pulled Alana to her feet with one hand, releasing her before she had time to be afraid. "I'd better help Janice," he said. "She's going to be sore."

Alana winced slightly. "She's not the only one. Although," added Alana, flexing her legs, "considering that it's been more than a year since I rode this hard, I'm not very sore at all." Then she heard the echo of her own words. Her face changed, tension coming back in a rush. "That's not true, is it?" she whispered. "It hasn't been a year. It's been less than a month." She closed her eyes and shuddered with the effort to remember. "Why can't I remember?" she asked, her voice raw.

"Alana," said Rafe urgently, bending over her, so close that he could see the pulse beating in her throat, smell the mint sweetness of her breath. Close, but not touching her, afraid to touch her and bring back nightmares in place of dreams. "Alana, don't. Clawing at yourself won't help you to heal."

She drew several long, ragged breaths. Her eyes opened again, very dark but not as wild. She nodded almost curtly, then turned and went back to her horse, clutching a bag of cookies in one hand and two forgotten apples in the other.

The rest of the ride became a waking nightmare for Alana. It began with the first of the five Paternoster lakes, so named because they were strung out like beads on a rosary, shining circles of blue water joined by silver cascades. The lowest lake was at six thousand feet and the highest was just above eight thousand. Pines grew down to the shores of the lower lakes, making dark green exclamation points against the silver-gray boulders that embraced the transparent water.

The first lake was beautiful, reflecting the sky in endless shades of blue, serene and quiet; and after one look, Alana felt fear rise and begin to prowl the corridors of her mind. She heard thunder belling from a cloudless sky, saw violent lightning in every golden shaft of sunshine, heard Jack's voice when nothing but ravens spoke.

Gradually, without realizing it, Alana's hands tightened on the reins until Sid fretted, tossing her sleek black head. After a time, Alana's nervousness was reflected in Sid's actions. A line of foam grew around the steel bit. The horse's long, easy stride became a mincing walk. Streaks of sweat radiated out from Sid's flanks despite the coolness of the air. The pressure of Alana's hands on the bit increased by subtle increments until finally Sid stopped. But even then the pressure didn't decrease. Sid shook her head, seeking freedom from the bit.

"Alana."

Rafe's voice was soft, undemanding despite the harshness of his expression as he watched Alana's blank, unfocused eyes. He leaned over and pulled slowly on the

reins, easing them out of her rigid fingers. Gradually, the
thin leather strips slid free, ending the relentless pressure of
the bit.

"It's all right, Wildflower," murmured Rafe. "I've
come to take you home."

Alana blinked and looked around with eyes that were still
caught between nightmare and reality.

"Rafael . . . ?"

"I'm here," he said quietly.

Alana sighed and flexed hands that were cramped from
the tension of hanging on to reins as though they were a
rope pulling her up out of a nightmare. She started to
speak, couldn't, and swallowed. The second time she
tried, her throat no longer closed around her dead husband's name. "Jack and I rode this way."

Beneath the shadow of the hat brim, Rafe's narrowed
eyes looked like brilliant lines of topaz. He knew that the
trail they were on was only one of three trails to the Five
Lakes Lodge. If Alana recognized this particular trail, she
must be remembering at least parts of the six lost days.

"You're sure," said Rafe, no question in his voice.

She nodded stiffly. "The first storm began here."

"The first?"

"There were several, I think. Or"—she frowned
suddenly—"was it just one long storm?" Her voice died.
"I don't remember!" Then, more calmly, "I don't remember." Alana closed her eyes, hiding the shadows that
haunted her. When she opened her eyes again, she saw only
the present. Rafe and the two horses standing patiently,
waiting for a command from their riders. "Where is
everyone?" she asked.

"Over the next ridge. I told them we'd catch up later, if
you felt well enough."

Alana wondered distantly what the two dudes thought of her. A woman with strange moods, hysterical. Crazy. The word kept ringing in her mind, an interior thunder drowning out the rational words she kept trying to think of, to cling to.

"Am I crazy?" she wondered aloud, not realizing she had spoken. "Crazy. Or does it matter? If sanity is terror, is there peace in madness? Or," she shuddered, "is there only greater terror?"

"You aren't crazy," said Rafe, his voice gentle and angry and sad. "Do you hear me, Alana? You aren't crazy. You've been beaten and terrified. You've seen your husband killed and you damn near died yourself. And then you were out of your head with shock and exposure. You've hardly eaten at all and slept even less since Broken Mountain. You aren't crazy, you're just at the end of your physical resources, driven right up to the edge of hallucinations just to keep reality at bay until you decide there's no choice but to face it."

Alana listened, heard the certainty in Rafe's voice, heard the state of her mind and body described so precisely in Rafe's deep tones. "How did you know?" she whispered.

"It happens to people when they're pushed too hard, too long."

Slowly, she shook her head. "Not to strong people. Like you. I used to think I was strong."

Rafe laughed, a harsh sound, almost cruel. "Anyone can be broken, Alana. Anyone. I know. I saw it happen in Central America time and time again. They said that I died. For a long time I believed them. It was like dying, only worse. There was no end to it. And then it happened again, here."

"What—what happened in Central America?" asked

Alana, searching Rafe's eyes and finding emotions she had never seen in him before. Violence and hatred and a rage so deep it went all the way to his soul.

Rafe's expression changed, becoming remote, shutting down, shutting her out. The muscles in his jaw flexed and he spoke slowly, with a reluctance that told Alana more than his words. "I've never told anyone. But I'll tell you. On Broken Mountain, I'll tell you. Unless . . ." He looked at her swiftly, concerned again. "Unless you want to turn back. I'll take you back, Alana. If that's what you want. Is that what you want?"

"I want to trust myself again, to trust my mind and my memory and my emotions," she said in a rush. "I want to be *me* again. And I want . . ."

Rafe waited, an expression of restraint and longing drawing his face into taut planes and angular shadows. "What do you want?" he asked softly.

"You," said Alana simply. "I was never more myself than when I was with you." But even as she spoke, she was shaking her head, not believing that what she wanted was possible.

Rafe held out his hand, palm up, not touching Alana but asking that she touch him. She put her palm lightly on his.

"I'm yours, Wildflower," said Rafe. "I have been since I saw you on that exposed trail with a lame horse and lightning all around. You were brave then. You're even more brave now."

"I don't feel brave," she whispered.

"You came back to Broken Mountain. You're honest with yourself, and with me. If that isn't courage, I don't know what is."

Rafe's voice was deep and sure, conviction reflected in every syllable and in the amber clarity of his eyes as he watched her. With fingers that shook slightly, Alana brushed away the tears that starred her eyelashes. Teardrops gleamed on her fingertips as she almost smiled at him.

"Thank you," she said.

"For telling the truth?" Rafe smiled sadly. "I have a lot more truths for you, Alana." At her quick look, he added, "But not now. My truths wouldn't help you now. And that's what I want. To help you, and me. We'll heal each other and then the past will stay where it belongs—in the past. Memories, not nightmares."

Rafe held out his other hand, palm up. Alana put her hand in his, felt the strong pulse in his wrist beneath her touch, saw the glitter of tears transferred from her fingertips to his smooth, tanned skin. Unerringly, he found the pulse points of her wrists and rested lightly against them, savoring the strong flow of her life against his fingertips.

"Are you ready for the mountain?" asked Rafe softly.

Alana nodded. Slowly, she withdrew her palms, letting his touch caress her from wrists to fingertips.

For the rest of the trip they rode side by side when the trail permitted. When it didn't, Alana rode first. As pieces of the nightmare condensed around her, she looked over her shoulder to reassure herself that it was Rafe rather than Jack who followed her. The pieces came unexpectedly, out of sequence, tormenting her because she couldn't be sure whether it was true memory or false nightmare that stalked her. Jack's voice raised in anger: Was it from the far past, the recent past, or were the words a creation of her own mind trying to fill in the missing six days?

Sometimes, there was no doubt. The sound of wind through the aspens, the shiver of yellow leaves, the song sticking in her throat. Those were real. Those she had heard before, seen before, felt before, and remembered only now. She and Jack had rested by the second lake, there, down by the glacier-polished boulder. They had drunk coffee from their individual canteens and watched trout fingerlings rise in the turquoise shallows. Then the wind had come again, moving like a melancholy hand over the lake, stirring reflections into chaos, bringing the scent of height and storms boiling down.

Jack had watched the clouds seething around the lonely ridges. He had smiled. And he'd said— What had he said? Something about the land. Something. Yes, that was it: *I always knew this country was good for something. I just never knew what.* And then he'd laughed.

Alana shivered and drew an imaginary jacket around her shoulders. Sid stumbled slightly, jarring her into the present. Alana loosened the reins, giving the horse more freedom. She looked over her shoulder. Rafe was there, riding the big Appaloosa stallion, his hat pulled low against the restless wind. She sensed his quick regard, his concern for her. She waved slightly, reassuring him that she was all right.

Other fragments of memory returned, hoofbeats following, wind twisting and booming between ridges, ice-tipped rain. An argument. They had argued over something. The storm. And the fishing camp. She had wanted to stay at the Five Lakes Lodge until the storm passed. Jack had refused, even though the fishing camp's five buildings were deserted, looked as though they had been deserted for years.

In the end Jack had won, but only because Alana couldn't bear to see the site of her greatest happiness standing blank eyed and empty, cabin doors ajar and porches heaped with dead needles and random debris. Everywhere she turned she had seen shadows of Rafe. Every breath she drew had reminded her of the first time Rafe had made love to her, in the loft of the main cabin with a storm coming down, surrounding them. But she hadn't been afraid then. She had been an aspen shivering, and he a mountain wind caressing her.

Sid snorted and shied as she came around the shoulder of an old landslide. Bob was waiting there, riding the big bay mare that was his favorite.

"Everything okay?" asked Bob, his dark glance roaming his sister's face, looking for and finding signs of strain.

"Yes," said Alana tightly.

"You don't look it," he said, blunt as only a brother can be.

"I'm remembering a few things. Little things."

"That's great!" said Bob, excitement lighting his eyes.

"Is it?" she countered quickly. Then, "Sorry. Of course it is."

"Have you told Rafe about remembering?" asked Bob, then rushed on before she could answer. "He was right," crowed Bob, delight in every word. "He said you'd remember once you were here and knew it was safe. And neither doctor would let him go to Portland because—"

"Burdette!" Rafe's whiplash voice stopped Bob's tumbling words.

Bob looked startled, then stricken. "Oh God, I really stepped in it this time. Damn my big mouth anyway."

Alana looked from Rafe to Bob, a question in her eyes.

"I told you I leaned on people to get you here," said Rafe, giving Bob a narrow glance that spoke volumes on the subject of loose lips and secrets. "When Merry couldn't be chief cook and tour guide, I thought of you. I thought it would be a perfect opportunity to get you back home, where you belonged." Rafe looked at Bob challengingly. "Is that how you remember it, Burdette?" asked Rafe, his voice soft and cold.

"Rafe leaned like hell," agreed Bob, looking relieved.

Then, to Alana, "You aren't mad, are you? I mean, about coming home. We just want what's right for you."

Alana sighed, caught as always by her affection for the brother who rarely had an unspoken thought. "No, little brother, I'm not mad. Maybe," she added, smiling crookedly, "I'm not even crazy."

Bob drew in his breath sharply. "Alana, what in hell gave you the idea that you were crazy?" he demanded.

"What would you call it when someone runs scared for six missing days?" she retorted.

"I'd call it shock," cut in Rafe smoothly. "Survival reflex. In a word, sanity." He looked from Alana to Bob. "Let's get to the camp. That storm won't hold off forever."

There was an urgency in Rafe's voice that allowed no argument. He didn't want Alana to be caught in the open in a storm. Not now. She was off-balance, easily startled, too tired, too fragile. She needed rest now, not a resurgence of nightmare and violence. It was enough that she had begun to remember. More than enough.

He didn't want the past to rise up and rend the delicate fabric of trust binding her to him. He didn't want her to remember too much, too soon; to lose her again only this time without hope, irrevocably.

Don't remember all of it, Wildflower, Rafe prayed silently. *Not yet. Give us time to learn to love again.*

Chapter 6

AFTER DINNER, ALANA AND RAFE HAD THE LODGE TO themselves. Bob and Stan had gone to Janice's cabin for a round of poker and conversation. Alana had refused as politely as possible. Even so, Rafe had given her a swift glance of understanding. He knew that Stan's resemblance to Jack still disturbed Alana. Rafe, too, had turned down the offer of cards, saying that he had some flies to tie before tomorrow's fishing.

As Alana finished setting the table for tomorrow's breakfast, Rafe came back from turning off the generator for the night. He shrugged out of a yellow slicker that sparkled with rain. So far, the evening storm consisted mainly of fat water drops randomly sprayed and distant mutters of thunder stalking elusive lightning.

"Hope the dudes don't mind kerosene lamps," said Alana, adjusting the wick on the kitchen light until it burned with a clear, steady glow.

"So long as they can see the cards, they'll do just fine," said Rafe, hanging the slicker on a hook by the back door. "Besides, it will nudge them into bed at a decent hour. Trout rise early. If you want to catch them, you'd better rise early, too." Whiskey-colored eyes measured Alana. "You should think about going to bed."

"It's hardly even dark," she protested, despite the tiredness welling up in her. She didn't want to be alone. Not yet. Not with lightning and thunder loose among the peaks.

"It won't be completely dark until nearly ten," said Rafe reasonably. "That's too late for you, if you're going to get up at five to cook breakfast. Tell you what, I'll do breakfast tomorrow. You sleep in."

"No," said Alana quickly. "You look like you haven't been sleeping too well either. Besides, I came here to cook and that's what I'm going to do. If I get too tired, I'll take a nap tomorrow afternoon."

Rafe looked as though he were going to protest, but all he said was, "Will the light bother you if I work down here for a while?"

Alana looked at the loft bedroom that was simply a partial second story. One "wall" of the room was a polished railing that prevented anyone from wandering out of bed and taking a fall to the living room floor. Curtains could be drawn across the opening of the loft, but that cut off the welcome currents of warmth rising from the hearth. Even though it was only the first week of September, the nights at sixty-three hundred feet could crackle with the promise of winter.

"You won't bother me," said Alana. "I always sleep with light now."

Again, Rafe paused. Again, he said nothing, merely looked at Alana with eyes that saw everything, accepted everything, even her fear. Knowing that he didn't withdraw from or judge her gave Alana a small measure of acceptance of her own irrational feelings.

"Go to sleep, Alana. If you need anything, I'll be in the downstairs bedroom. So will Bob, unless he plays cards all night like a young fool." As Rafe turned toward the dining room, he added, "There's plenty of hot water for a bath."

The thought of a tub full of steaming water made Alana close her eyes and all but groan with pleasure. "This is my idea of roughing it," she said emphatically.

Rafe turned and leaned against the door between the living room and dining room. "From what Dad told me, my mother and grandmother felt the same way. And to tell the truth, I'm not all that upset by having hot water. Only thing that bothers me is that damn noisy generator. As for the rest . . . this is home for me. It took me a lot of years and pain to realize it," he added softly, "but it was worth it."

Rafe looked around the lodge slowly, enjoying the vivid Indian blankets and brass camp lamps, the suede furniture and a fireplace big enough to stand in. Luxury and simplicity combined. The generator provided electricity for the refrigerator, the water pump and the lights. The kitchen stove, which also heated water for the cabin, burned wood. All that was lacking was telephone service. His father had taken care of that by adding a shortwave radio and a repeater on the nearby ridge. By tradition, though, the radio was reserved for emergencies.

Alana watched Rafe quietly, sensing his pleasure in his surroundings, a pleasure she shared. She had loved the Lazy W's lodge and cabins from the first time she saw them, when she and Rafe had raced a storm and lost. They had been drenched and laughing when they arrived. They would have been cold, too, but the bright currents of passion that radiated through them had made a mockery of cold. He had started a fire in the hearth to dry their clothes.

Then he had led her up to the loft and taught her about other kinds of fire, and the beauty that a man and a woman in love can bring to each other.

"I laid out your things in the bathroom," said Rafe, watching Alana hungrily, as though he knew what she was thinking. Or perhaps it was simply that he, too, was remembering a storm and a loft and the woman he loved burning in his arms.

"Thank you," Alana said, her voice almost husky.

Rafe nodded and turned away, leaving her alone.

The bath relaxed Alana, taking the soreness from her body and the tightness from her mind. When she buttoned the long, soft cotton nightgown and went up to the loft bedroom, Rafe was nowhere in sight. The hearth fire was blazing hotly, ensuring that she wouldn't be chilled by the trip from bathroom to bed. The bed itself had also been warmed. The metal warmer was still hot to the touch, the coals from the fireplace still glowing when she opened the lid. The covers had been turned down, inviting her to slide in and sleep deeply.

"Rafael," said Alana softly, though she knew he couldn't hear her. "Oh, Rafe, why does it have to be too late for us?"

There was no answer, unless the bed itself was an answer, a bridge between past and present, a promise of warmth and safety. With a sigh, Alana discarded her robe and slid underneath the covers, pulling them up to her chin as she snuggled into the haven that Rafe had so carefully prepared for her.

Sleep came quickly. So did dreams. As the storm outside the cabin quickened, dreams twisted into nightmares called by thunder and wind screaming from the ridgelines. A lake condensed around Alana, *a landscape subtly blurred, like water pushed by wind. A glacier-polished boulder stood askance, laughing, Jack was laughing and the sound was colder than the wind. Rain swirled, laughing, showing clear ice teeth, stirring water and rocks and trees until another lake condensed. Small, perfect, utterly real but for the palpable shadows of terror flowing out of the trees. Jack's arms reaching for her, his words telling her of desire and his eyes telling her of death. Jack holding her despite her struggles and then pain came, pain and terror and her screams tearing apart the world.*

Alana woke with her heart pounding and her skin clammy. She was breathing in short, shallow bursts. She had recognized the third lake in her nightmare, but not the other lake, the beautiful lake surrounded by horror. Jack, too, was new, unrecognizable, desire and death inextricably mixed. A raw nightmare, a horrible compound of today's memories and—what? Truth? Imagination? Both? Neither? Jack had wanted her, yes, but only as the other half of Jack 'n' Jilly. He hadn't wanted her as a woman; and if he had, it wouldn't have mattered. She didn't want him. She hadn't wanted any man but the one she loved and couldn't have. Rafael Winter. Jack had finally accepted that, after she told him she'd leave him if he touched her again.

So long ago, all of it, on the far side of a six-day gap in her mind that might as well be eternity. So far away and so futile. Jack was dead and she was not, not quite. She couldn't sing, she couldn't be touched, she couldn't love. But she was alive.

And so was Rafael Winter.

Lightning burst silently into the room, bleaching everything into shades of gray and a white so pure her eyes winced away from it. Thunder came, but only slowly, telling of a storm retreating down the mountainside. Taking a deep breath, Alana lay back, trying to sleep. Even as her head touched the pillow, she knew that it was futile. Her body was too loaded with adrenaline and the aftermath of nightmare for her to go back to sleep right away.

She got up, barely feeling the chill. Her deep green nightgown settled around her ankles. The soft T-shirt material clung and flared as she walked to the edge of the loft. The tiny silver buttons that went from her neck to her thighs winked like raindrops in the muted light from the living room. Below her, engrossed in the multicolored materials spread before him on a table, Rafe worked quietly. His back was to her, so she couldn't see precisely what he was doing. Alana hesitated long enough to be startled by another burst of lightning. Then she went quickly down the stairs. The battery-powered clock over the mantel told her it was just after eleven.

Though Alana would have sworn that she'd made no noise, Rafe knew she was there.

"Take the chair that's closest to the fire," said Rafe without looking up from the small vise in front of him.

Alana pulled out a chair and sat, careful not to come between Rafe and the light radiating out of the kerosene lantern. He was focused on a tiny hook held in a small vise just in front of him. Silently, delicately, he tied an iridescent bit of feather to the hook's shank using gossamer thread. In the warm light Rafe's eyes were almost gold, his lashes and hair almost black. Horn-rimmed half-glasses sat partway down his nose, magnifying the work in front of him. Deft, tapered fingers handled special tweezers and dots of glue no bigger than the tip of a needle. He wound the thread once more around the shank of the hook, made a half-hitch, tugged gently and cut the thread.

"There are two schools of thought about fly fishing," said Rafe as he picked up a delicate shaft of iridescent black feather. "One school is that you attract a trout by presenting it with something flashy but not frightening, something that it's never seen before. Like this.''

Rafe opened a small metal box. Inside were neat rows of flies, their sharp hooks buried in the wool fleece that lined the box. The fly that Rafe selected was nearly as long as his thumb. The colors were bright, a whimsical combination of blue, yellow and rose that culminated in graceful silver streamers reminiscent of lacy wings.

"Now, Bob swears by that Lively Lady," said Rafe, neatly replacing the fly in its box. "And," smiling, "I admit to using it a time or two, when the fishing was so bad I'd tried everything but a DuPont spinner."

"What's a DuPont spinner?"

"Dynamite," Rafe said dryly. "The Lively Lady is outrageous, but it's more sporting than shock waves."

"Does it work?" asked Alana, watching the play of light over the hair on the back of Rafe's hand.

"Only for Bob," sighed Rafe. "The times I used it you could hear the fish snickering all up and down the canyon."

Alana smiled and almost forgot to jump when lightning flicked again, washing the room with shards of white light. "What's the other kind of fly-fishing?" she asked, wanting to hear Rafe's deep, calm voice smooth off the jagged edges of the night.

"The kind that imitates natural conditions so exactly that the trout can't tell the difference," said Rafe, his voice casual yet reassuring, as though he sensed the fear that had driven Alana out of bed and downstairs to the table where he worked. He set aside the fly he had just tied and picked up a hook that already had been wound around with mink brown thread. "Usually at this time of year, all you have left are larger, darker flying insects. Most of the smaller bugs have all been killed off in the same frosts that turned the aspens pure gold. I'm a little short on the autumn flies, so I decided to do a few tonight.''

As Rafe talked, his fingers searched delicately among the boxes. There were feathers and tiny, shimmering drifts of fur, as well as nylon and tinsel and Mylar threads of various thicknesses. It was as though he looked with his touch as well as his eyes, savoring the subtle differences in texture with skilled, sensitive fingertips. There was no sense of hurry or frustration in his actions. If the thread he chose was stubborn or slippery, refusing to wrap neatly around the hook's shank, Rafe didn't show any impatience. He simply smoothed everything into place and began again, his fingers sure, his expression calm, his mouth relaxed.

With eyes darker than night, Alana watched Rafe's every movement. He had rolled the sleeves of his navy blue flannel shirt past his elbow. Dark hair shimmered and burned with gold highlights as his arms moved. Muscles tightened and relaxed, making light slide over his skin with each supple movement of his body. Beneath the skin, veins showed like dark velvet, inviting her fingers to trace the branching network of life.

''It's important to match environments precisely if you hope to lure a trout out of the depths of a lake or a river,'' said Rafe, tying a tiny slip of deep red feather to the body of the hook. ''It's so quiet down where they hide, safe and deepest blue. But being safe isn't enough for living things. They need more. They need to touch the sun. At least,'' he added, smiling crookedly, ''the special ones do.''

Alana watched Rafe's face, her eyes wide and intent, feeling his words slide past the fear in her, sinking down into her core, promising her something for which she had no words, only a song which couldn't be sung.

''So my job is to tempt a special trout out of those safe, sterile depths,'' continued Rafe, deftly tying a radiant filament of black to the shank. "To do that, I have to know what's happening around the fish. If dun-colored Mayflies are flying, then a black gnat will be ignored by my special trout no matter how beautifully the fly is tied or presented. You see, my special trout is neither stupid nor foolish. It is unique and strong and wary. Yet it's hungry for the sun."

Tiny shafts of color shimmered as Rafe worked, feathers as fragile as they were beautiful. He handled them so gently that not a single filament was crushed or broken. When he had taken what tiny contribution he needed for the fly, his fingers smoothed the feather, joining each iridescent shaft into a graceful arch again. Tufts of color curled and clung to his fingertips as though thanking him for understanding their delicacy and beauty.

Alana closed her eyes and let memories rise. Rafe had touched her like that the first time, his strength balanced with his understanding of her innocence. And she had responded, sighing and curling around him, clinging to his fingertips as his lips feathered across her breasts until she sang a love song that was his name. He had called to her in return, the exquisite beauty of his hands caressing her until she knew nothing but him, felt nothing but ecstasy shivering through her as she sang his name. Then he had come to her like gentle lightning, moving deeply until she had known what it was to die and be reborn in the arms of the man she loved.

To be touched like that again, exquisitely . . .

Alana shivered deep inside herself, a tiny ripple that was reflected in the subtle color high in her cheeks. Rafe glanced up and saw the faint flush and rapid pulse beating just above the soft emerald neckline of her nightgown. For an instant his fingers tightened and the color of his eyes became a smoky amber fire. Then he concentrated again on his work, knowing it wasn't time yet. He must be patient or he would frighten her back into the bleak safety of withdrawal from memory, from life, from him.

Alana's small, ragged breath sounded like fire flickering inside the glass cage of the kerosene lamp. She opened her eyes and watched Rafe, wanting to touch him, to savor the textures of his hair and skin as delicately as he was savoring the materials with which he tied flies. Yet if she did, he would touch her in return and she would be afraid; and then she would despise herself for her fears.

"Dad never used flies," said Alana, her voice husky as she searched for a safe topic. "Worms or metal lures only. Spinning rods. That's what I was raised with."

"A lot of people prefer them," said Rafe, his voice calm and neutral, demanding nothing of her.

"But you don't?"

He smiled slightly as he tied another tiny piece of feather onto the mink brown body of the fly. "I prefer the special fish, the shy and elusive one hiding deep in the secret places known only to trout," he said, turning a feather in the light as he spoke, admiring the play of color. "To tempt that trout out of the depths and into the sunlight will require all my skill and patience and respect."

"But wouldn't it be easier to fish down deep rather than to try to lure the trout to the surface?" asked Alana, watching Rafe intently.

"Easier, yes. But easy things have so little value." Rafe looked up at Alana over the dark rims of his glasses. His eyes were gold, as hot as the flame burning in the camp lamp. "The trout should want the fisherman. Otherwise it's a simple exercise in meat hunting. I want to create a lure so perfect that only a very special trout will rise to it."

"And die," said Alana, her voice sounding harsh in the golden silence.

"No," he said very softly. "My hooks have no barbs."

Alana's eyes widened. She looked at the hooks set out on the table, flies finished and half-finished and barely begun. Each hook was a clean, uncluttered curve, not a single barb to tear at the flesh. She looked back up into Rafe's amber eyes and felt the breath stop in her throat.

"Would you like to learn how to fly-fish?" he asked, absently turning a golden pheasant feather in the lamplight, letting color run unnoticed in iridescent waves over the shaft.

"I'd be all thumbs," said Alana, holding her hands out as though to convince him of her awkwardness.

Rafe shook his head. "Never," he murmured. Slowly he ran the feather from her wrists to her palms to fingertips. As the delicate softness stroked her, he said, "Your hands are just right, graceful and long and very, very sensitive."

Alana's breath came in raggedly as she saw Rafe's expression. She knew that he was remembering being touched by her, the sensual contrast of her hands against the male contours of his body, the heat and pleasure she had brought to him.

"You'll enjoy it," continued Rafe softly. "I promise you."

"I—all right. After breakfast?" she asked quickly, before she could change her mind and be afraid again.

"After breakfast." Rafe turned his attention to the hook in his vise. He released the hook and carefully buried the sharp tip in the foam-lined box. "Can you sleep now," he asked in a casual voice, "or would you like me to sit next to your bed for a while?" He looked up, catching and holding Alana's glance with his own. "I wouldn't touch you unless you asked me to. And," very softly, "I don't expect you to ask."

"I know," she said, her voice low. And she did. The realization sent a quiver of light through the dark pool of fear that amnesia had made in the depths of her mind. "Would you mind staying with me? Just for a few minutes? I know it's childish—"

"Then we're both children," said Rafe easily, cutting across her words, "because I'd rather sit with you than be alone."

Alana brushed his moustache with her fingertips. "Thank you," she breathed.

The touch was so light it was almost more imagined than real. Yet she felt it all the way to her knees. And so did he.

"My pleasure," said Rafe, his eyes tawny, reflecting the dance of flame from the lamp. "Go upstairs before you get cold," he said, looking away from Alana, not wanting her to see his hunger. "I'll clean up here."

"Can I help?"

"No. It will just take a minute."

Alana hesitated, then turned away as Rafe began deftly sorting materials and stacking small boxes onto a tray. But as soon as she no longer watched him, Rafe looked up, ignoring the brilliant materials at his fingertips. Motionless, entirely focused on Alana, he watched as she climbed up the narrow stairs to the loft. The glossy black of her hair caught and held lamplight like stars reflected in a wind-ruffled midnight lake. The green of her nightgown clung and shifted, revealing and then concealing the womanly curves beneath. Her bare feet looked small, graceful, oddly vulnerable beneath the swirling folds of cloth.

Silently, savagely, Rafe cursed Jack Reeves.

Alana opened the cast iron stove door, using a potholder that had been crocheted by Rafe's grandmother. Inside the belly of the stove, a neat pattern of wood burned brightly, vivid orange flames licking at the thick iron griddle above.

Alana closed the door, adjusted the vent, dipped her fingers into a saucer of water and flicked water drops onto the griddle. Water hissed and danced whitely across the griddle's searing black surface.

"Perfect," muttered Alana.

The kitchen was washed in the golden warmth of a kerosene lamp, for it was at least a half hour until dawn. The smell of bacon and coffee permeated the lodge and spread through the crisp air to the other cabins, prodding everyone out of bed. From just outside the kitchen door came the clean, sharp sound of Rafe splitting wood for the stove. It was a strangely peaceful sound, a promise of warmth and a reminder that Rafe wasn't far away. The rhythm of a song began to sift through Alana's mind, working its way down to her throat. She hummed almost silently, not knowing what she did, making only the barest thread of sound, more a hope of song than song itself.

Alana picked up the pitcher of pancake batter and poured out creamy circles. When the bubbles burst and batter didn't run in to fill the hollows, she flipped each pancake neatly. Soon she had several stacks warming at the back of the stove next to the thick slices of bacon she had already cooked and set aside. As she poured more batter onto the griddle, she sensed someone walking up behind her.

"I don't need more wood yet, Rafe," she said, setting aside the pitcher as she turned around. "Not until I—oh!"

It was Stan, not Rafe, who had come up behind Alana. Reflexively, she took a step backward, forgetting about the hot stove.

"Watch out!" said Stan, reaching toward her automatically, trying to prevent her from being burned.

Alana flinched away, bringing the back of her hand into contact with the cast iron stove. She made a sound of pain and twisted aside, evading Stan's touch at the cost of burning herself again. Again, he reached for her, trying to help.

"Don't touch her."

Rafe's voice was so cold, so angry, that Alana almost didn't recognize it. Stan did, though. He stepped back instantly. His blue eyes assessed the fear on Alana's face and he stepped back even more, giving her all the room she needed.

"What in hell do you think you're doing?" demanded Rafe. His voice was flat and low, promising violence. The stovewood he had carried inside fell into the woodbox with a crash that was startling in the charged silence.

Though Rafe hadn't made a move toward Stan, the blond man backed up all the way to the door between the dining room and the kitchen before he spoke.

"Sorry," muttered Stan. "Bob and I thought Alana might need help with . . . whatever."

"Bob and you? Christ," snarled Rafe. "That's an idiot's duet if ever there was one."

Stan flushed. "Now look, Winter."

"Go tell Bob that if Alana needs the kind of *help* you had in mind, I'll be the first to suggest it. Got that?"

Stan hesitated, then nodded.

"Good," said Rafe grimly.

Rafe turned his back on Stan and went to Alana. He held out his hand. "Let me see your burn," he said softly. The change in his voice was almost shocking. Warm, gentle, reassuring, it seemed impossible that the words came from the same man who had flayed Stan to the bone with a few razor phrases. "It's all right," murmured Rafe. "I won't hurt you."

With a long, shuddering release of breath, Alana held out her burned hand to Rafe. He looked at the two red bars where her skin had touched the stove and felt rage like raw lightning scoring his nerves. He turned on his heel, went to the refrigerator and pulled out a handful of ice. He dampened a kitchen towel, wrapped the ice and held it out to Alana.

"Put this over the burns. It will take away the pain."

Numbly, Alana did as he said. Within a few seconds, the pain from the seared flesh was gone. "Thank you," she sighed. Then, "It seems that I'm always thanking you."

"And it seems that I'm always hurting you," muttered Rafe as he took the spatula and flipped the pancakes that had begun to burn into the trash.

"Rafe, it wasn't your fault. It wasn't Stan's, either. It was my own foolishness," said Alana, self-recrimination clear in her tone and expression.

"You wouldn't be here if it weren't for me," said Rafe in a clipped voice, scraping charred batter off the griddle with short, vicious strokes. "And neither would Stan." With a disgusted sound, Rafe threw the spatula onto the counter. "Forgive me?" he asked, turning to Alana, his voice urgent and his eyes almost dark.

"There's nothing to forgive," she said helplessly.

"I wish to hell that were true." Abruptly, Rafe turned back to the stove. As he greased the griddle, he said, "I'll finish cooking breakfast."

"But—"

"Sit down and keep those burns covered. They aren't bad, but they'll hurt unless you leave on the ice."

Alana sat on the kitchen stool and watched Rafe covertly. He cooked as he did everything else, with clean motions, nothing wasted, everything smooth and sure. The stacks of pancakes grew. By the time everyone was seated in the dining room, there were enough pancakes to feed twice as many people as were around the table. At least, it seemed

like that until everyone began to eat. The altitude and crisp
air combined to double everyone's appetite. Even Alana ate
enough to make her groan. At Rafe's pointed suggestion,
Bob did the dishes. Stan insisted on helping, as did Janice.
Rafe set out fishing gear while Alana packed lunches.

There were still a few stars out when Rafe led the two
dudes to a stretch of fishing water and gave advice on the
most effective lures and techniques to use in the extraordi-
narily clear water. When Bob turned to follow Rafe and
Alana back up the trail, Rafe gave him a long look.

"I promised to teach Alana how to fly-fish," said Rafe.
"For that, she definitely doesn't need an audience."

"I won't laugh—much," said Bob, his lips quirked
around a smile.

"You won't laugh at all," said Rafe smoothly, "because
you're not going to be around."

Bob looked quickly at Alana, but she shook her head.
"Oh well, I promised Stan I'd show him how to use the
Lively Lady," said Bob. "Bet we catch more than you
do."

"You'd better," retorted Alana. "Rafe uses barbless
hooks. If we're going to eat trout, it's up to you, baby
brother."

"Barbless?" said Bob, giving Rafe a swift look. "Since
when?"

"Since I was old enough to shave."

"Hell of a way to fish," Bob said, turning away. "A man
could starve."

"Fishing is more than a way to feed your rumbling gut,"
pointed out Rafe.

"Depends on how hungry you are, doesn't it?" retorted
Bob over his shoulder as he walked down the trail.

"Or what you're hungry for," added Rafe softly. He
turned to Alana. "Ready? I've got a spot picked out by the

lake. Lots of room and nothing to tangle your line on the backstroke.''

"You're assuming that I'll get enough line out to tangle," she said, smiling wryly.

Rafe's soft laughter mixed perfectly with the sound of the stream flowing along the trail. Though the sun hadn't yet cleared the ridges, predawn light sent a cool radiance through the land, illuminating the path and making boulders look as though they had been wrapped in silver velvet. In the deep pools where water didn't seethe over rocks, trout rose, leaving behind expanding, luminous rings.

Without talking, letting the serenity of the land and the moment seep into Alana, Rafe led her to a narrow finger of glacier-polished granite that almost divided the lake into two unequal parts. As she stepped out onto the rock shelf, Rafe touched Alana's shoulder and pointed across the lake. A doe and two half-grown fawns moved gracefully to the water. While the fawns drank, the doe stood watch. Beyond them the granite face of Broken Mountain flushed pink beneath the gentle onslaught of dawn. The sky was utterly clear, a magic crystal bell ready to ring with exquisite music at the first touch of sunlight.

The doe and fawns retreated, breaking the spell. Alana let out her breath in a long sigh. Rafe watched her for an instant longer, then began assembling his fishing rod.

"Have you ever used a fly rod before?" he asked as he worked.

"No." She watched intently as the long, flexible rod took shape before her eyes. "I've always wondered how a fly rod works," she admitted.

"With spinning rods, the weight of the lure is used to pull line off the reel," Rafe said, tying a nearly weightless fly onto the thin, transparent leader. "With fly rods, the weight of the line is what counts. The leader and the lure barely weigh anything. They can't. Otherwise they'd land with a plop and a splash and scare away any fish worth catching," he added, pulling a length of the thick fly line off the reel. "Handled correctly, fly line will carry the fly and set it down on the water as lightly as if the fly really had wings. The point is to mimic reality as perfectly as possible. The leader is transparent and long enough that the fish doesn't associate the heavy fly line lying on the surface with the tasty insect floating fifteen feet away."

Alana looked at the opaque, thick fly line. "If you say so," she said dubiously.

"See that fish rising at about two o'clock?" asked Rafe.

She looked beyond Rafe's hand to an expanding ring. The ring was at least fifty feet out in the lake. "Yes, I see it."

"Watch."

With his right hand, Rafe held the butt of the fly rod near the point where the reel was clamped on. With his left hand, he stripped line off the reel. As he did so, his right hand began to move the rod forward and back in a smooth, powerful arc. Kinetic energy traveled up the rod's supple length, bending it with easy whiplike motions, pulling line through the guides. With each coordinated movement of Rafe's arm, line leaped out from the tip of the rod, more line and then more until it described fluid curves across the luminous sky.

Silently, smoothly, powerfully, Rafe balanced the forces of line and rod, strength and timing, gravity and flight, until an impossibly long curve of line hung suspended between sky and water. Then he allowed the curve to uncurl in front of him into a straight line with the fly at its tip. Gently, gently, the fly settled onto the water precisely in the center of the expanding ring left by the feeding trout. Not so much as a ripple disturbed the surface. It was as though the fly had condensed out of air to float on the dawn-tinted mirror of the lake.

And then there was a silver swirl and water boiling as the trout rose to the fly. The rod tip lashed down at the same instant that Rafe began pulling line in through the guides with his left hand. The supple rod danced and shivered as the trout tail-walked across the dawn like a flashing silver exclamation point. Line slid through Rafe's fingers, drawn by the trout's power. But slowly, gently, the line returned, drawn by Rafe's sensitive fingers, until finally the trout swam in short curves just off the granite shelf, tethered to Rafe by an invisibly fine length of leader.

Just as the first rays of sunlight poured over the lake, the trout leaped again. Colors ran down its sleek side, forming an iridescent rainbow that gave the fish its name. In reverent silence, Rafe and Alana admired the beauty swimming at their feet. It would have been a simple matter for Rafe to unhook the net at his belt, guide the fish into the green mesh and lift it from the water. Instead, Rafe gave an expert flick of his wrist that removed the hook from the cartilage that lined the trout's mouth. There was a moment of startled stillness, then water swirled as the trout flashed away.

"See how easy it is?" murmured Rafe, watching Alana with eyes as luminous as dawn. "It's your turn now."

Chapter 7

FOR WHAT SEEMED LIKE THE HUNDREDTH TIME, ALANA stripped line from the fat reel, positioned her left hand so that it could feed line from reel to rod, lifted her right arm and began the forward and back motion that was supposed to send line shooting up through the guides on the rod. As she stroked the rod forward and back, line inched up through the guides and started to form the lovely, fluid curve that was the signature of fly-fishing . . . and then the curve collapsed into an ungainly pile of line on the rock shelf behind her.

"I waited too long on the forward stroke, didn't I?" sighed Alana. "All the energy that was supposed to hold up the line went *fffft*."

"But you got out nearly twice as much line," pointed out Rafe, his voice and smile encouraging her.

"And before that, I broke three hooks on the rock, hooked myself on the backstroke, hooked you on the backstroke, lashed the water to a froth on the forward stroke, tied ruinous little knots in your beautiful leader, and in general did everything but strangle myself on the fly line.''

Alana shook her head, torn between frustration and rueful laughter. Rafe had been incredibly patient. No matter how many times she had done it wrong, no matter how many times the line or the leader snarled hopelessly, he had neither laughed at her nor gotten angry. He had been gentle, reassuring and encouraging. He had praised her and told funny stories about the monumental tangles he used to make when he was learning how to fly-fish.

''Alana,'' Rafe said softly, capturing her attention. ''You're doing better than I did the first time I had eight feet of limber rod and fifty feet of fly line in my hands.''

She grimaced. ''I don't believe it. I feel so damn clumsy.''

''You aren't. You're as graceful as that doe was.''

''Outrageous flattery,'' she said smiling, ''will get more knots tied in your line.'' She positioned the rod again. ''Here goes nothing.''

Not quite nothing. A rather impressive snarl ensued. Rafe untangled it with the same patience he had displayed for the last hour.

As he turned the rod over to Alana once more, he hesitated, then suggested quietly, ''If it wouldn't bother you, I could stand behind you, hold on to your wrist, and let you get the feel of the timing. And that's all it is. Timing. There's no real strength involved. Fly-fishing is a matter of finesse, not biceps.''

Alana nibbled on her lower lip as she eyed the deceptively simple appearance of fly rod and reel. ''All right. Let's give your way a try. Mine sure hasn't done much.''

Rafe stepped into position behind Alana. Less than an

inch separated them, for he had to be able to reach around
her and guide the rod. He stood for several moments
without touching her, letting her get used to the fact of
someone standing very close behind her.

"Okay so far?" he asked casually.

"Yes." Then, "Just knowing that you understand how I
feel makes it easier," Alana admitted in a low voice.

She took a deep breath. The mixed scents of high-country
air and sun and Rafe swept over her. His warmth was a
tingling sensation from her shoulders to her knees. She felt
his breath stir against the nape of her neck, sensed the subtle
movements of his chest as he breathed, the slight catch of
his flannel shirt against hers.

"Ready?" asked Rafe.

She nodded, afraid to trust her voice. The breathlessness
she felt had little to do with her fear of being touched.

"Take up the rod," he said.

Alana lifted the fly rod into position.

"I'm going to put my hand around your wrist and the rod
at the same time," said Rafe, reaching around Alana until
his hand covered hers and wrapped around the rod.

The contrast of his tanned skin against her hand was
arresting. It reminded Rafe of just how smooth Alana's skin
was, how pale where the sun had never touched it, how
incredibly soft when she had welcomed his most intimate
caresses. For an instant Rafe closed his eyes and thought of
nothing at all.

"All right so far?" he asked. His voice was too husky,
but there was nothing he could do about that any more than
he could wholly control the growing ache and heaviness of
his desire.

"Yes," said Alana, her breath drawing out the word until
it was almost a sigh. The warmth and strength of Rafe's

fingers curling around her hand riveted her. She wanted to bend her head and brush her lips over his fingers. Just the thought of feeling his skin beneath her mouth made liquid fire twist through her.

Rafe took a quiet breath and hoped that Alana had no idea of the havoc her closeness brought to his carefully imposed self-control. "Now, remember. The rod is only supposed to move in the arc between ten and two on our imaginary clock. That's where your greatest power and balance is. You get above or below that and you're going to get in trouble. Ready?"

Alana nodded.

Rafe guided her arm and the rod through the short arc between ten and two, counting softly as he did. "*One,* two, three, four. Now *forward,* two, three, four. And *back,* two, three, four."

Smoothly, easily, the rhythm flowed from Rafe to Alana and then to the rod. She felt the energy curl up the length of the rod, pulling line through the guides, bending the rod tip at the end of the arc, then the soft hiss of line shooting up and back over her shoulder just before the rod came forward smoothly, energy pouring up its length on the forward stroke, fly line shooting out magically, Rafe's voice murmuring, counting, energy and line pulsing along the rod.

Alana felt the rhythm take her until she forgot everything but Rafe's voice and his warmth and the line suspended in sinuous beauty above the silver lake. And still the rhythm continued, unvarying, serene and yet exciting, line pulsing out like a soundless song shimmering, lyrics sung in silence and written in liquid arcs curving across the dawn.

"Now," murmured Rafe, bringing the rod forward and stopping it precisely at ten o'clock, "let it go."

Line hissed out in a long, ecstatic surge. Gracefully,

delicately, the fly line, leader and fly became a part of the lake. Not so much as a ripple marred the perfect surface of the water at the joining.

Alana let out a long breath. "That was . . . incredible," she said, still enthralled by the beauty of the line uncurling, the sweeping blend of energy and rhythm, the timeless consummation of lure and silver water. "Thank you, Rafe," she said, her voice soft. "For your patience. For teaching and sharing this with me."

Rafe felt the shifting surface of Alana's body against his as she sighed. He wanted to close his arms around her, enfolding her. He wanted to feel her flow along his body as she fitted herself to him. At the very least he wanted to be able to trace the velvet edge of her hairline with the tip of his tongue, inhaling the sunlight and woman scent of her, testing the resilience of her flesh with gentle pressures of his teeth.

"You're a joy to teach," Rafe said in a quiet voice, ruthlessly suppressing the hunger that pulsed through him, tightening his body with each heartbeat. "You should take it easy for a while, though. You're using muscles you didn't know you had. Why don't we just sit in the sun and be lazy? There's a lovely patch of grass and wildflowers further up the lake."

"Sounds wonderful," said Alana, stretching the muscles in her shoulders by twisting from side to side. She didn't hear the subtle intake of Rafe's breath as she accidentally rubbed against him when she straightened again. "But aren't you supposed to be helping the dudes, too?"

"They know one end of a fishing rod from the other," said Rafe. He took the fly rod from Alana, removed the hook and wound in the line. He began breaking the rod into its component parts with quick movements of his hands. He worked with the economy and expertise of long familiarity.

"The dudes aren't what I expected," said Alana, watching Rafe's skilled fingers and the flex of tendons beneath the rolled-up sleeves of his navy flannel shirt.

Rafe looked up suddenly. His whiskey glance pinned her. "What do you mean?" he asked quietly, the intensity of his voice belying the softness of his tone.

"Stan's looks, for one thing," she said, shrugging. "I'm having a hard time getting used to seeing Jack's ghost. Poor Stan. He must think I'm more than a little unwrapped."

"He'll survive," said Rafe unsympathetically.

"I know. It's just a bit awkward," sighed Alana. "He and Janice have been such easy guests. They don't complain. They don't expect to be waited on. They're funny and smart and surprisingly fit. Not many people could have ridden the trail to Broken Mountain one day and popped out of bed the next morning ready to slay dragons—or even trout," added Alana dryly. "And no matter how strange I act, the two of them take it in stride. Even Stan, when I literally ran screaming from him, acted as though it was his fault, not mine." She laughed abruptly. "I guess the dudes are as unusual as the dude ranch."

"Luck of the draw," said Rafe tersely, breaking the rod down and slipping it into the carrying case.

"The fact that these good sports are your friends has more to do with it than luck," retorted Alana.

Rafe's eyes narrowed into topaz lines. "What are you hinting at?"

"I know what you're doing, Rafe."

"And what is that?" he asked softly.

"You're helping Bob get started. You know how much he needs a cash income to buy out Sam and Dave, and you know Bob doesn't want to destroy the land for a quick cash killing. So you beat the bushes for friends who could help Bob launch a dude ranch. Don't worry," added Alana quickly, resting her hand for an instant on Rafe's arm, "I won't say anything to Bob. I just wanted you to know that I appreciate what you're doing for him. He's got four left feet and he keeps them in his mouth most of the time, but he's a good man and I love him."

With a long, soundless sigh, Rafe let out the breath he had been holding. He smiled ruefully at Alana as he packed away the last of the fishing gear. He said nothing about Bob, neither confirming nor denying her conclusions.

In a companionable silence, Alana and Rafe walked along the margin of the lake, skirting boulders and gnarled spruces. Spring and summer had come late to the high country this year. Wildflowers still bloomed in the sheltered places, making windrows of color against the pale outcroppings of granite. Delicate, tenacious, radiant with life, drifts of wildflowers softened the harsh edges of rock and cerulean sky.

At the head of the third lake, a broad cascade seethed over slick rocks into the shallows. The cascade drained the second, higher lake in the chain. That lake was invisible behind the rocky shoulder of Broken Mountain. The cascade itself was a pale, shiny ribbon that descended the granite slope in a breathtaking series of leaps. The sun was more than halfway to noon, pouring transparent warmth and light over the bowl where the third lake lay.

Rafe stopped in a small hollow that was a hundred feet from the cascade. Evergreens so dark they were almost black formed a natural windbreak. Topaz aspens burned in the sunlight and quivered at the least movement of air, as though the trees were alive and breathing with tiny, swift breaths. Rafe pulled a waterproof tarp from his pack. Silver on one side, deepest indigo on the other, the tarp could gather or scatter heat, whichever was required. Rafe put the dark, heat-absorbent side up, knowing that despite the sun, the ground itself was cool. Spread out, the tarp made an inviting surface that two people could eat or sleep comfortably on.

"Hungry?" asked Rafe, lifting Alana's pack off her shoulders.

Alana was about to say no, when her stomach growled its own answer. With an almost soundless chuckle, Rafe went to his backpack and pulled out apples, hard-boiled eggs, and chocolate raisins. Alana's stomach made insistent noises. She looked chagrined.

"It's the air," said Rafe reassuringly, concealing a smile.

"If I do everything my stomach tells me to, I won't be able to fit into my clothes," she grumbled.

"Then buy new ones," he suggested, uncapping a canteen full of cold tea. "A few more pounds would look good on you."

"You think so?" she asked dubiously.

"I know so."

"My costume designer is always telling me to lose more weight."

"Your costume designer is as full of crap as a Christmas goose," said Rafe as he divided the food between Alana and himself.

She smiled blissfully. "In that case, I'll have another handful of chocolate raisins."

"What about me?" asked Rafe, his voice plaintive and his eyes brilliant with amusement.

"You," she said with a sideways glance, "can have my hard-boiled egg."

Rafe laughed aloud and pushed his pile of chocolate raisins over to Alana's side of the tarp. He left her egg in place. When Alana reached for the new pile of sweets, however, he covered it swiftly.

"Nope," he said, smiling at her. "Not until you eat the egg and the apple."

"Slave driver."

"Count on it," said Rafe, biting into his own apple with a hearty crunching sound.

They ate slowly, enjoying flavors heightened by clean air and healthy appetites. When she had eaten the last bit of chocolate and raisin, Alana sighed and stretched luxuriously. The exuberant splash of the cascade formed a soothing layer of sound between her and the rest of the world. Nothing penetrated but Rafe's occasional, low-voiced comments about fly-fishing and ranching and the silky feel of high-country sunshine.

"Why don't you take a nap?" he suggested finally.

Alana caught herself in midyawn. "There's something sinful about taking a nap before noon," she said.

"In that case, let's hear it for sin," said Rafe, smiling crookedly. Then, softly, "Go ahead. You didn't get enough sleep last night, or a lot of nights before that." He unbuttoned his flannel shirt, revealing a dark blue T-shirt beneath. With a few quick motions, he shaped the thick flannel shirt into a pillow. "Here. I don't need it."

Alana tried to object, but couldn't get any words past the sudden dryness in her mouth. Even in her dreams, Rafe had not looked so overwhelmingly male. The T-shirt defined rather than concealed the slide and coil of muscles with every movement Rafe made, every breath he took, his tanned skin stretched tightly over a body whose latent power both shocked and fascinated her. Suddenly she wanted to touch him, to trace every ridge and swell of flesh, to know again the compelling male textures of his body. She closed her eyes but still she saw Rafe, sunlight sliding over his skin, sunlight caressing him, sunlight burning in his eyes and her blood.

"Alana?" Rafe's voice was sharp with concern.

"You're right," Alana said in a shaky voice. "I haven't been getting enough sleep."

Rafe watched as she stretched out on the tarp, her cheek against the shirt he had rolled up for her. He would rather she had used his lap as a pillow but was afraid that if he had suggested it, the relaxed line of her lips would tighten with tension and fear. Yet for a moment, when she had looked at him as though she had never seen him before, he had hoped . . .

"Better?" he asked, watching Alana's body relax into deep, even breathing.

"Yes."

"Then sleep, Wildflower. I'm here."

Alana sighed and felt herself spiraling down into a sleep where no nightmares waited.

When Alana woke up, the sun was on the other side of noon. She rolled over sleepily and realized that she was alone.

"Rafe?"

No one answered.

She sat up and looked around. Through the screen of evergreens and aspens she saw Rafe outlined against blue water. He had found another rock shelf leading out into the lake. He was standing at the end of the granite finger. The fly rod was in his hands and line was curling across the sky. For a few moments Alana watched, captured by the grace of the man and the moment when line drifted soundlessly down to lie upon still water.

Except that Alana couldn't actually see the line touch the surface of the lake, because the screen of trees blocked her view. She stood up and started toward the shoreline, then realized that once Rafe saw her, he would probably stop fishing and start teaching her once again. She wasn't ready for that. She felt too relaxed, too at peace—too lazy—to attempt anything that required concentration. What she really wanted to do was to sit quietly, watching Rafe and the lyric sweep of line against the high-country sky.

Alana looked back down the lakeshore to where she and Rafe had been earlier, but she saw no place to sit and watch that wouldn't immediately bring her into Rafe's view. She looked left, to the cascade dancing whitely down rocks turned black by water. Rafe was facing away from the cascade, looking down the lake toward the cabins. That position gave him a hundred feet in front of the fly rod and an equal amount in back without anything to obstruct the motion of the line.

And he was using every bit of that two hundred feet.

On tiptoe, Alana peered through the wind-twisted branches of a fir, holding her breath as the curve of the fly line grew and grew, expanding silently, magically. Rafe's left arm worked in perfect counterpoint to his right as he stripped line off the reel, almost throwing fly line up through the guides as his right arm pumped smoothly, sending energy coursing through the rod.

"How are you doing that?" muttered Alana, knowing Rafe couldn't hear her. "You aren't a magician, are you?"

She stepped further to her left, but still couldn't see exactly what Rafe was doing to make the line lengthen so effortlessly. With a small, exasperated sound, she worked her way along the increasingly rugged shoreline, trying to find a spot that would allow her to see Rafe without attracting his attention to her presence. She leaped from stone to stone, avoiding the small boggy spots where coarse grass and tiny flowers grew, until she found herself confronted by the barrier of the cascade.

She turned around and looked back at Rafe, who was

about sixty yards away from her by now. Unfortunately, she still couldn't see what he was doing with his hands. Nor could she go any further forward without coming up against the cascade. She could either go back, or she could go up the boulder-tumbled slope.

With a muttered word, Alana looked at the jumble of stone rising on either side of the frothing water. She wouldn't have to go very far up the cascade to get the view she wanted. Just far enough to allow her to look over Rafe's shoulder, as it were. If she didn't get too close to the water, the climb wouldn't be too hard. Besides, she had been raised hiking and scrambling along mountain rivers and up steep slopes.

Alana turned and began climbing over the lichen-studded boulders. Twenty feet away, the cascade churned and boiled, making both mist and a cool rushing thunder. She avoided the slippery rocks, seeking the dry ones. Within a few minutes she was breathless, gaining two feet in height for every foot forward. She persisted anyway, scrambling and balancing precariously, until she stood on a ledge of granite that was barely eighteen inches deep. She stopped there because there was no other choice. In front of her rose a slick outcropping of rock six feet high, and not a handhold in sight.

"Well, this had better be far enough," she said, turning her head to look over her shoulder.

The earth seemed to drop away beneath Alana's feet.

Unexpected, overwhelming, a fear of heights froze Alana, shattering her. Twenty feet away, the cascade frothed down the steep mountainside, water seething and racing, white and thunder, and wind whipping drops of water across her face like icy rain. Thunder and ice and the world falling away, leaving her helpless, spinning, darkness reaching up for her.

Alana clung to the rough face of the granite and closed her eyes. The feeling of falling didn't stop. The boom of water over rock became remembered thunder. Drifting spray became ice-tipped winds and her screams were lightning as memory and nightmare and reality overlapped, surrounding her.

Cold.

God, it was cold, cold all the way to the center of the earth. Jack with anger twisting his face. Jack cursing her, grabbing her, hitting her and the storm breaking, trees bending and snapping like glass beneath the wind. Like her. She wasn't strong enough. She would break and the pieces would be scattered over the cold rocks.

Running. Scrambling. Breath like a knife in her side. Throat on fire with screams and the storm chasing her, catching her, yanking her backward while rocks like fists hit her, bruising her and she screamed, clawing and fighting. But she was swept up, lifted high, helpless, nothing beneath her feet, and she was falling

screaming

and Rafe was calling her name.

"You're safe, Wildflower. I've come to take you home."

Alana realized that she had heard the words before, over and over, Rafe's voice reaching out to her, peeling away layers of nightmare until only reality remained. Shaking like an aspen in a storm, she clung to the rock face. She sensed someone behind her, heard a male voice, felt the warmth of a man's body along her back, a man standing between her and the drop-off at the end of the rocky ledge.

"R-Rafe?" she said shakily, although she knew that it was Rafe; even with her eyes closed she knew. But his name was the only word she could say.

"I'm here, Wildflower. You're safe," he murmured,

his words and the tone of his voice soothing her. "You're safe."

Alana let out a breath that was more a sob. "Rafe? I'm so s-scared."

She couldn't see the darkness in his eyes or his savage expression so at odds with the reassurance of his voice. "I know. You had a bad time up along the lakes, even if you don't remember it. Or," softly, "have you remembered?"

Alana shook her head.

"Then why are you frightened?" he coaxed. "Is it because I'm close to you? Are you afraid of me?"

She shook her head again. "No." Though weak, her voice was positive. It wasn't Rafe she feared.

For an instant, Rafe closed his eyes. A strange mixture of emotions crossed his face. Then his eyes opened. Relief eased the tightness of his mouth and brought light to his eyes again.

"What is it, then?" he asked. "Can you tell me?"

"Height," said Alana in a trembling voice. "I'm afraid of heights now and I never was before, not until Jack fell and I guess I fell, too," she said, her words tumbling over each other like water in the cascade. She made a ragged sound. "Oh, Rafe, I felt so good when I woke up a few minutes ago. All morning I hadn't thought about Jack or the mountain or the missing days. I hadn't thought about anything since breakfast but fly-fishing and sunshine and you being so patient and gentle with me."

"I'm glad you enjoyed the morning," said Rafe, his voice low and husky. "I know that I haven't enjoyed anything so much for years."

"Do you mean that?" Alana asked. "Even though I ruined your line and scared every fish away?"

Rafe's lips brushed against Alana's shoulder in a caress so light that she didn't feel it. "I'll buy a hundred miles of leader and let you tie knots in every inch of it."

Alana let out her breath in a rush, then took another breath. She almost felt brave enough to open her eyes. Almost.

"Don't make any rash promises," she said shakily, trying to make a joke even though her voice wouldn't cooperate. "I'll hold you to every one of them."

"Wildflower," whispered Rafe, brushing his cheek against her glossy hair, "brave and beautiful. I'd carry away Broken Mountain stone by stone if that would allow you to come to me again with a smile on your lips."

The words were a warmth unfolding in the center of cold fear. As fear melted away, some of Alana's strength returned. She opened her eyes. The rough granite textures of rock were only inches from her face. On either side of her shoulders, close but not touching her, were Rafe's arms. His hands were flattened on the rock as he stood behind her, his legs braced, his feet wide apart on the narrow ledge, his body between her and any danger of falling.

Slowly, Alana put one of her hands over his. "But I'm not brave," she said, her voice tight with anger at herself.

Rafe's laughter was as harsh as it was unexpected. "Bravery isn't a square jaw and a thick head," he said. "Bravery is standing toe to toe with fear every minute of every hour, never knowing if you're going to get through this second and afraid the next one might be one too many. And the worst of it is that you're strong, so you survive when others would have broken and gone free, crazy free, but you survive day after day no matter how bad it gets. And it gets very bad, doesn't it?" he asked, but there was no question in his voice or in the grim lines of his face. "Some of those days are endless, and the nights are . . . unspeakable."

"How did you know?" whispered Alana, her grip on Rafe's hand so tight that her nails left marks on his skin.

"I've been there, Alana. Like you, I've served my time in hell."

She whispered Rafe's name as tears slid from her eyelashes down her cheeks, tears for him and for herself. His lips brushed her neck very lightly. She wouldn't have felt it if she hadn't been so sensitized to him, his emotions and his physical presence, Rafe like a fire burning between her and the freezing blackness that came to her in nightmares. She bent her head until her lips touched the back of his hand. She kissed him gently, not withdrawing even when his hand turned over and cradled her cheek in his palm.

Slowly, Rafe leaned down, unable to resist the lure of Alana's tears. He murmured her name as his lips touched her eyelashes, catching the silver drops. He expected her to stiffen at the caress, at the knowledge that she was trapped between his strength and the granite face of the mountain. But she turned her cheek to his lips, leaning lightly against him, her eyes luminous with emotion. He kissed the corner of her mouth, delicately stealing the tears that had gathered there.

"Are you ready to climb down now?" murmured Rafe.

Alana blinked away her tears, then looked beneath Rafe's arm to the rocks tumbling away to the lake. Everything spun for an instant. She closed her eyes and hung on to him.

Rafe saw the color leave Alana's face even before he felt her nails digging into his arms and the shaking of her legs against his. Quickly he leaned inward, bracing Alana against the rock with his body so that she wouldn't fall if her legs gave way.

"Don't be afraid," said Rafe softly, urgently. "I'm not going to hold you or hurt you in any way."

There was an instant of stiffness; then Alana sighed and nodded her head, unable to speak.

When Alana accepted his presence, his reassurance, relief came in a wave that for an instant left Rafe almost as weak as she was. And with relief came hunger for her, the hunger that had haunted the years since he had come back to find the woman he loved married to another man, desire and rage turning in Rafe when he saw a picture of her with Jack, Country's Perfect Couple, happiness condensed into two smiling faces on millions of album covers.

Ruthlessly, Rafe suppressed both desire and corrosive memories. He ignored the sweet warmth of Alana's body pressed along the length of his as he braced her against the cold granite. "I'll support you until you aren't dizzy," he said, his voice even, casual. "Tell me when you can stand again."

Eyes closed, Alana savored the sound of Rafe's deep voice, his warmth and reassurance, and his patience. If he didn't condemn her for being foolish, for being afraid, she wouldn't condemn herself, either.

"Alana?" asked Rafe, unable to see her face. Concern made his voice almost harsh.

"It's all right," said Alana. And as she spoke, she realized that it really was all right. When she stopped being disgusted with herself, when she stopped being afraid of fear, she was able to react more rationally. Rafe's strength and closeness made her feel protected rather than threatened. She sighed and felt the shaking in her legs diminish.

"You didn't frighten me, Rafael. I looked down the mountain, that's all."

He let out his breath in an explosive sigh. "That wasn't a bright thing to do, sweetheart."

Alana's mouth formed a smile that was gone as swiftly as it had come. "I figured that out real fast. Now maybe you can figure out how I'm going to climb off this damned ledge with my eyes closed."

"Gracefully, smoothly and quickly," murmured Rafe, brushing Alana's neck with his lips, not caring if she felt the caress, "like you do everything else."

"Including tie knots in your leader," retorted Alana, her voice almost steady but her eyes still tightly closed.

"Most especially tying knots in my leader," he answered, laughing softly against her hair. "Ready?"

"To tie knots? I was born ready for that, obviously. No practice needed. Perfect tangle on the first try." Then Alana took a deep breath. "Rafe," softly, "I really don't want to open my eyes."

"How else can you admire the gorgeous tangles you make?"

"Braille," she said succinctly.

"Okay. Braille it is." He hesitated. "For that to work, I'll have to be very close to you, Alana. Sometimes I'll have to take your foot and place it, or hold you, even lift you."

"*No.*" Then, quickly, "Don't lift me, Rafe. Please. That's my worst nightmare, my body being lifted high and then falling and falling and Jack—" She shuddered. "Oh, God. Jack. He fell. He fell into the darkness and rocks and the water was like thunder and he died and—"

Alana's throat closed around screams and her eyes opened dark and wild, dilated with terror and memories that faded in and out like a nightmare.

"Hush, Wildflower," said Rafe, aching to hold Alana but afraid of triggering the terror that he sensed seething beneath her words. "I won't lift you. Do you hear me? I won't lift you. You're safe with me."

Slowly, Alana's eyes focused on the strong hands braced on either side of her. She made a despairing sound. "Oh, Rafe, each time I come closer to remembering, but never close enough. And each time I'm so afraid. Does it ever end?"

"It will end," Rafe said, his voice a curious mixture of reassurance and shared pain. "It will end. And you'll survive. Like the wildflowers survive ice and darkness, sure of the summer to come. You're strong, Alana. I know you don't believe that now, but you are. If you didn't go under before, you won't go under now. Believe me. I know. I've been there too, remember?"

Alana put her forehead against Rafe's hand and fought to control her breathing. After a few minutes, she succeeded.

Only then did Rafe say quietly, "We're going to climb down, now. You'll have to help me, Alana."

"H-How?"

"You'll have to trust me," he said simply. "If you don't, you'll panic and then I'll have to knock you out and carry you down. I don't want to do that, Alana, even though I could do it and never leave a bruise on your body. Your mind, though—" Rafe looked at Alana intently. "Being knocked out and carried down the mountain would be your worst nightmare come true, wouldn't it?"

The words went through Alana's mind like a shock wave. Was that her nightmare? Being knocked out and carried?

Slowly, hardly even realizing it, Alana shook her head. "No, that's not my nightmare, Rafe. My nightmare is being lifted and then thrown, something throwing me away and then I'm falling, falling forever, ice and darkness and death.''

Rafe's voice was calm, but his eyes were burning with the rage that came to him every time he thought of Alana hurt, frightened, screaming his name. None of his emotions showed in his voice, however. ''Then you won't panic if I have to hold you?''

''I don't know,'' said Alana starkly. ''I guess we'll just have to find out, won't we?''

Chapter 8

WHEN ALANA FELT RAFE MOVE AWAY, FELT THE COOL wind on her back where his warmth had been, she wanted to cry out in protest. For a moment she simply stood, eyes closed, hands pressed against cold stone.

"About one foot below and slightly to your left is a flat stone," said Rafe. He watched while Alana crouched slightly and felt around with the toe of her walking shoe, trying to find the surface he had described. "Another inch down. That's it. Good." Legs braced, arms outstretched but not touching her, Rafe followed Alana's progress. "Now your right foot. Straight down, more, just another few inches. There. Feel it?"

Alana's answer was a drawn-out "Yes" as she felt the rock take her weight. She thought of opening her eyes but didn't trust herself not to freeze. Rafe described the next step, then the next, his hands always hovering just beyond

Alana without touching her. He talked constantly, encouraging her. Slowly, Alana backed down the steepest part of the slope.

"Now, use your left foot," said Rafe. "This is a tricky one. There are two rocks close together. You want the one on the left. No, not that one, the—Alana!"

The rock turned beneath Alana's foot, throwing her off-balance. Rafe grabbed her and held her in a hard grip, but only for an instant. Carefully, he put her back on her feet. Other than a choked cry when the stone slid out from beneath her foot, Alana had made no protest, even when Rafe's hands had closed around her arms. Yet she was very pale, and her hands shook noticeably as she searched for support among the tall boulders. Shudders rippled through her body.

Rafe sensed that Alana had fallen into nightmare again. Gently, he turned her until she was facing him. He kept his hands on her shoulders, more to give her contact with the world than to support her. "Alana, open your eyes. Look at me, not at the lake or the rocks. Just at me."

Slowly, Alana's black eyelashes parted. Rafe was only inches from her, his amber eyes narrowed and intent. His moustache was a deep, rich brown shot through with metallic highlights of bronze and gold. The pulse in his neck beat strongly, hinting at the heat and life beneath his tanned skin.

"It's daylight, not night," said Rafe softly. "It's warm, not icy. Jack is dead. You're alive and safe with me."

Mutely, Alana nodded. Then she sighed and leaned against Rafe. He wanted very much to put his arms around her, to hold her against his body and rock her until both of them felt only the other, knew only the other, comfort replacing fear. But, like Alana, he was afraid that if he held her there would be only fear and no comfort at all.

"I'm sorry you were frightened," murmured Rafe, smoothing his cheek against her hair.

"I was—but I wasn't. Not really." Alana took another long breath. "I knew after I called your name that you wouldn't let me fall."

And Rafe knew that Alana hadn't called his name. Not this time. She was still caught between the past and the present, a hostage to fear. Yet she had trusted him not to let her fall. That, at least, hadn't changed.

After a few moments, Alana straightened. "Let's finish it," she said, her voice flat.

"Aren't you going to close your eyes?"

"I don't think so. It's not as steep here, is it?"

"No. If you're going to take a look, though, do it now, when I'm close enough to catch you if you get dizzy."

Alana's mouth relaxed into a tiny smile. "I can't see through you, Rafe."

He turned partially, just enough to give her a brief view of the tumbled slope behind him. As he turned, he watched her face, ready to grab her if vertigo struck again. Other than a flattening of her mouth, she showed no reaction. Even so, Rafe stayed very close for the first few steps.

Alana glanced at him and tried to smile. "I'm all right."

Rafe nodded, but he remained within reach of her. Together they worked their way down the last of the slope. When there was only lake in front of them, they stopped. With a sense of triumph, Alana turned and looked back. She shook her head as she realized that the slope, which had seemed so steep and deadly from above, didn't look like much at all from the bottom.

"Fear always looks like that from the other side," said Rafe softly, knowing what Alana was thinking.

Alana looked from the mountainside to the man beside

her. Rafe's understanding of what she had been through, and his acceptance of her fear, untied knots deep inside her as surely as he had untied the snarls of fly line she had created. She put the palm of her hand against his cheek, savoring his warmth and the masculine texture of his skin.

"Rafael," she murmured, making music of his name. "You make me believe that some day I may even sing again."

Rafe turned his head until he could kiss the slender palm that had rested against his cheek. He whispered her name against her hand and smiled as her fingers curled up to caress his lips. Slowly, Alana's other hand crept up to Rafe's head, hungry for his warmth and the smooth thickness of his hair between her fingers.

Moving as slowly as Alana did, Rafe tilted his head down until his lips could slant across hers. The kiss was so gentle that it was impossible to tell the exact instant that it began. Alana neither hesitated nor pulled back when she felt Rafe's mouth caress hers. Instead, she whispered his name again and again, lost in the sensations that came as his lips brushed slowly against hers, his mouth moving from side to side with gentle pressures that made her fingers tighten in his hair, pulling his head closer in silent demand.

The tip of Rafe's tongue slid lightly over Alana's lower lip, then traced the curves of her mouth until she sighed and her fingers kneaded down his neck to his shoulders, seeking the long, powerful muscles of his back. Her mouth softened, fitting itself to his. When her tongue touched first his lips, then his teeth, Rafe made a sound deep in his chest. His hands clenched at his sides as he fought not to give in to his hunger to hold her, to feel her body soften and flow over his as surely as her mouth had. Hesitantly, Rafe caught the warmth and sweetness of her tongue with his own. Even then she didn't retreat. The kiss deepened until the sound of his own blood beating inside him drowned out the cascade's rushing thunder.

Rafe heard Alana call his name with hunger and need, a sound out of his dreams. As gently as a sigh, his fingers dared to touch her face, the smooth curve of her neck, the slenderness and feminine strength of her arms. When she showed no fear, he rubbed his palms lightly from her shoulders to her hands and back again. She murmured and moved closer to him, letting his heat radiate through her. He shifted his stance, fitting her against him, touching her very gently with his hands while the sweet heaviness of desire swelled between them.

Alana forgot the past, forgot the nightmare, forgot everything but the taste of Rafe and the rough velvet of his tongue sliding over hers. Fire shimmered through her, called by his hunger and her own; fire melting her until she sagged against him, giving herself to his strength. His arms circled her, holding her as she held him, molding her against the heat and hunger of his body. She responded with a movement that brought her even closer, standing on tiptoe, trying to become a part of him. And then she moved sinuously, caressingly, stroking his body with her own.

With a ragged sound, Rafe let his arms close around Alana. As his arms tightened, they tilted Alana's hips against his thighs. The movement lifted her just enough that for an instant her toes lost contact with the ground. In that instant, Alana went from passion to panic. Her whole body stiffened. Even as she tried to wrench free of his embrace, Rafe realized what had happened. Cursing himself, he released Alana.

"I'm sorry." They both spoke quickly, as one, identical words and emotions.

"It's not your fault." Again their words tangled, each hurrying to reassure the other.

When Alana would have spoken, Rafe gently put his fingers across her mouth. "No," he said in a husky voice. "It's not your fault. I should have known better than to hold you. I thought I could trust myself. But I'd forgotten how sweet and wild you are. Even in my dreams, I'd forgotten . . ."

Alana's black lashes closed and she tilted her face down so that Rafe couldn't see her expression for a moment. When she looked up at him again, there was no fear in the dark clarity of her eyes, only apology and the luminous residue of passion.

"Did you really dream of me, Rafael?" asked Alana, music and emotion making her voice as beautiful as her eyes.

"Yes," he said quietly. "It was all that kept me sane in hell."

Alana's breath caught at the honesty and pain in Rafe's voice. "What happened?" she asked, her voice soft, her eyes searching his expression.

Rafe hesitated. "It's not a pretty story. I'm not sure it's something you want to know."

"If you can stand to tell me," said Alana, "I can stand to hear it." When Rafe still hesitated, she took his hand and started back down along the lakeshore, leading him with a gentle pressure of her fingers. "Never mind, Rafael. We'll eat lunch and then we'll lie in the sun and count aspen leaves. Remember?"

The darkness left Rafe's eyes. His lips curved into an off-center smile. "I remember. The first one who blinks has to start all over again."

"After paying a forfeit," amended Alana.

"Of course," he said in a husky voice. "I remember that part very well."

A single sideways look into brilliant whiskey eyes told Alana that Rafe indeed hadn't forgotten. Her fingers tightened in his as he brought her hand up to his lips. He rubbed his moustache teasingly over her sensitive fingertips and nibbled on the soft pad of flesh at the base of her thumb.

"What's that for?" asked Alana breathlessly.

"I blinked," admitted Rafe. "Didn't you see me?"

"No. I must have blinked, too."

"That's one you owe me."

"But we haven't started counting aspen leaves yet," Alana pointed out reasonably.

"Well, if you're going to go all technical on me, I guess I won't start keeping score until after lunch."

Smiling, Alana led Rafe to the hollow where they had left their backpacks. While he retrieved the fishing gear he'd abandoned when he heard her scream, Alana set out a lunch of sandwiches and fruit. They ate slowly, letting the sun and silence dissolve away the last residue of fear and nightmare.

When Rafe had finished eating, he stretched out on his back with his hands linked behind his head. After a few moments he said lazily, "Twenty-three."

"What?"

"I counted twenty-three aspen leaves before I blinked."

"You can't even see any aspens from where you are."

"Sure I can," he said, his voice low and soft. "Just over your shoulder."

Alana turned and looked. Sure enough, a golden crown of aspen leaves rose above a thick screen of dark evergreen needles.

"You blinked," said Rafe. "How many?"

"Eleven," admitted Alana.

"That's two you owe me," he said complacently. Then he stared over her shoulder.

"Aren't you ever going to blink?" said Alana finally.

"Nope." Then, "Damn. Got me. Thirty-seven."

Alana shifted until she could look at the aspen without twisting around. She counted swiftly, then groaned when she blinked. "It's coming back to me now. I used to lose this game all the time."

Rafe smiled. "Yeah. I remember that best of all. That's three you owe me." He settled into counting again. After a long pause he said, "Forty. It's coming back to me now. The trick is not to stare too hard—and be sure the wind isn't in your face."

Alana got as far as thirty-five before she blinked. She groaned again.

"That's four," said Rafe.

"Aren't you worried about collecting?" she asked, piqued that he had made no move to kiss her.

Rafe's glance shifted. "Are you?" he countered in a soft voice, watching her.

Alana's breath shortened, then sighed out. "I don't know," she admitted, remembering both the pleasure and the panic she had felt by the lakeshore.

"Then I'll wait until you know," he said simply.

Alana propped herself on her elbow and rolled over to face Rafe. He ignored her, counting quickly, aspen leaves reflected in his amber eyes. She looked at the grace and strength of him as he lay at ease, legs crossed at the ankles, jeans snug over his muscular thighs and lean hips. The dark blue T-shirt had pulled free of his pants, revealing a narrow band of skin the color of dark honey. A line of hair so deeply brown that it was almost black showed above the low-riding jeans. Where the shirt still covered him, it fit like a shadow, smooth, sliding, moving when he did, a cotton so soft that it had felt better than velvet against her palms when she had touched him by the lake.

"Seven thousand six hundred and ninety-two," said Rafe.

"What?"

"Seven thousand six hundred and ninety-two."

"You can't have counted that many leaves without blinking," she protested.

Rafe smiled. For the last few minutes, he had been watching Alana rather than aspen leaves, but she hadn't noticed because she had been watching every part of him except his eyes. "Would you believe two thousand?" he asked innocently.

She shook her head so hard that the motion sent her silky cap of hair flying.

"Two hundred?" asked Rafe.

"Nope."

"Fifty?"

"Well . . ."

"Sold," said Rafe smoothly. "That's five you owe me."

"But I haven't had my turn yet."

"Think it will do any good?"

Alana sighed and stared very hard at an aspen, but all she saw was Rafe. She blinked to drive away his image, then groaned when she realized that single blink had cost her the contest.

"Fifteen," she said in disgust.

Rafe smiled and turned his attention back to aspen leaves quivering in the breeze. When Alana's fingers touched his cheek, his counting paused, then resumed. When her hand slid up the arm that was pillowing his head, his counting slowed. When her fingertip traced the supple veins showing beneath his skin, her touch sliding slowly up and down the sensitive inner side of his arm, Rafe stopped counting altogether.

"You're cheating, Wildflower," he said in a husky voice.

"I finally remembered."

"What did you remember?"

"How I used to win at this game."

"Funny," he said. "I remember us both winning. Every time."

"I wish—" Alana's voice broke. "I wish that it could be like that again. I wish you had never gone away that last time." She took a ragged breath and asked the question that she had asked herself a thousand times since she had learned that Rafe was alive. "What happened, Rafe? What did I do to deserve your silence?"

Rafe didn't answer for so long that Alana was afraid he would refuse to answer at all. Finally, he asked, "Do you mean the letter I returned to you?"

"Yes, but even before that. Why did you let me believe you were dead? Other people knew you were alive, but not me. I didn't find out until a year ago."

"I thought you were happily married," said Rafe.

"How could you believe that?" she asked, searching his expression with eyes that were too dark, remembering too much of pain and not enough of happiness. "I loved you. I thought you loved me."

"I did."

"Then how could you believe I loved Jack?"

Rafe's lips flattened into a grim line. "It happens all the time to soldiers. The Dear John syndrome. One man goes off to war and another man stays to comfort the girl who was left behind."

"It wasn't like that," whispered Alana. "I married Jack

because singing was all I had left after they told me you were dead. It was a business marriage. A convenience for all the time we spent on the road. He never touched me, Rafe. I wouldn't let him. I couldn't bear to be touched by any man but you.''

Rafe closed his eyes. When they opened again, they were hard, focused on the past, a past that had nearly destroyed him. ''I didn't know. All I knew was that six weeks after I 'died,' the woman who had said she loved me became one-half of Country's Perfect Couple. Everywhere I turned I saw Jack 'n' Jilly, America's favorite lovers, singing songs to each other, love songs that were beautiful enough to make Broken Mountain weep.''

''Rafael . . .'' Alana said in a frayed voice.

''No, let me finish,'' Rafe said tightly. ''I may never talk about it again. God knows I'd just as soon forget it, every second of it.''

''Like I did?'' she asked, her voice flat, all music gone. ''That wouldn't make it better. Believe me, Rafe. Forgetting, the way I did, just makes it worse in the long run. I can't imagine anything more awful than my nightmares.''

He closed his eyes and let out a long, harsh breath. ''I know. I learned the hard way that forgetting or ignoring doesn't make anything go away. So I'm going to tell you something that's buried in filing cabinets in the Pentagon and in the minds of the very few men who survived. Something that never happened at all, officially.''

Alana said nothing, afraid to move, straining to hear Rafe's low voice.

''I told you I was in the army. Well, I was, but in a very special branch of it,'' he continued. ''I was trained in counterinsurrection, with special attention to rural areas.'' He smiled grimly. ''Really rural. God, but I learned to hate jungles.''

After the silence had stretched for several moments, Alana touched Rafe's arm with gentle fingers. "What happened?" she asked, her voice soft.

"Four years ago, I'd just about decided that I'd rather fight lost causes with my stubborn father in Wyoming than fight lost causes in the jungles of Central America. I owed the army some more time, though."

Alana waited, remembering. When Rafe had asked her to marry him, he had also told her that they would be separated a lot of the time for two more years. Then he would quit the army and come back to marry her.

"Just before I left Wyoming the last time, some of our men were taken prisoner along with a native guerrilla leader. There was no chance of getting our men back through regular diplomatic means because the men weren't officially there in the first place. The records had them posted to Chile or West Germany or Indochina, anyplace but Central America. We couldn't just write off the men, even though the word was that nobody survived prison for long. And we needed that native leader. My group was asked to volunteer for a rescue attempt."

Alana's eyes closed, knowing what was coming next. "You volunteered," she said, her voice barely a thread of sound.

"I knew the men who had been caught, Alana. One of them was a very good friend. Besides," added Rafe matter-of-factly, "I was good at what I did. With me leading the raid, it had a better chance of succeeding."

She took a deep breath and nodded. For the first time, some of the agony she had gone through four years ago began to make sense. "I understand," she said quietly.

"Do you?" asked Rafe, looking directly at Alana for the first time since he had begun to speak of the past. "Do you really understand why I left you? Why I *volunteered* to leave you?''

"You couldn't have lived with yourself if you had stayed safe and the other men had died. That's the kind of man you are, Rafe," she said, stroking the hard line of his jaw with a gentle fingertip. "You'd never buy your own comfort with another person's life.''

Rafe kissed the finger that had moved to caress his moustache. "Most women wouldn't understand.''

"Most women never know a man like you.''

"Don't kid yourself," he said harshly. "I'm no hero. I scream just as loud as the next guy when the rubber hose brigade goes to work.''

Alana's eyes widened darkly at the implications of Rafe's words. She touched his face with gentle fingers, smoothing away the lines of rage that had come when he remembered the past. "You're a man of honor, Rafael. That's all anyone can ask.''

For long moments Rafe said nothing, responding to her with neither look nor words. Then he let out his breath and said quietly, "I'm glad you think so, Alana. There were times I didn't think much of myself. Men died. I was their leader. I was responsible for their lives.''

"They were soldiers. Volunteers. Like you.''

"And I led them right into hell.''

Alana's fingers smoothed the grim lines bracketing Rafe's mouth. "Was there another way you could have done it?''

"No," he said bitterly. "That's how I knew I'd led them into hell. The road there is paved with the best intentions. The better the intentions, the deeper you go. And all the way down you know that there was nothing you could have done differently, that if you were put in the same position

again you'd do the same thing again, the honorable thing
. . . and in doing so you'd take the same good people
down with you.

"And that," he whispered, "is my definition of *hell*."

Words crowded Alana's throat, all but choking her. She
spoke none of them, sensing that the only words that could
help Rafe right now were his own. Instead, she caressed
him gently, her fingers smoothing his skin in undemanding
touches that told him that she was there, listening, sharing
as much as she could of his pain.

"I've thought about that mission a lot," he continued,
"but I've never said anything to anyone since I was
debriefed. It wasn't so much the security regulations that
kept me quiet. I just never found anyone I thought would
understand what it was like to be scared every second of
every day, to be scared and fight not to show it, to face each
dawn knowing that it probably wouldn't be better than
yesterday and often would be worse. Serving an indetermi-
nate sentence in hell, listening to the screams as the damned
were tortured, listening and knowing that soon you'd be
screaming too."

Alana made a stifled sound and turned very pale. Yet
after a brief hesitation, her hand never stopped touching
Rafe, giving him what comfort she could while he relived a
nightmare she could barely imagine but could understand all
too well. The man she loved had been imprisoned and
tortured until he screamed. Whatever memories she had
hidden in her nightmares, his must be worse, memory and
nightmare alike. Yet he had survived. He was here, strong
despite the cruelly destructive past, patient with her despite
her weakness, gentle with her despite the brutality that he
had known.

As Rafe continued talking, low-voiced and intense,

Alana took his hand and pressed it against her cheek as though simple touch could take the agony and bitterness from his past and her own.

"I went into the jungle alone, about three days ahead of the others. They needed someone to get inside the prison for a fast recon so we'd know how many of the men were alive and able to walk on their own. It was too dangerous a job to ask anyone to volunteer for," said Rafe, his eyes unfocused, remembering. Yet even then his fingers moved lightly against Alana's cheek, telling her that her presence helped him as much as anything could.

"I got into the prison without any problem," said Rafe quietly. "Wire fences and a few perimeter guards. They were counting on the jungle and the prison's reputation as a hellhole to keep people away." His fingers tensed on her cheek. "It was a hellhole, all right. What I saw there made me want to execute every guard, every government officer, everyone I could get my hands on. And then I wanted to burn that prison with a fire so hot it would melt through to the center of the earth."

Rafe closed his eyes, afraid that if they were open, Alana would see what he was seeing. Men chained and tortured, maimed and slowly murdered for no better reason than the entertainment of guards who were too brutal to be called men and too inventive in their viciousness to be called animals. Grinning devils ruling over a green hell.

"I got the information I needed and I got out. The next day I led my men back in." Rafe's eyes opened. They were clear and hard as topaz, the eyes of a stranger. "As soon as we'd pulled out the men we came for, I went back to that prison. Three of my men came with me, against my orders. They were the three who had seen the wing where prisoners were tortured. The four of us freed every prisoner and then we blew that building straight back to the hell that had spawned it."

Alana held Rafe's hand against her lips, trying to comfort him and herself, rocking slowly.

"One of the men who had come with me was injured. The other two carried him to the rendezvous while I stayed behind to cover them. Some of the guards had survived the blast. I held them off until my gun jammed. They caught me, shot me, and left me for dead in the clearing. The helicopter got away, though. I heard it lift just after I was shot."

Alana made a low sound, but Rafe didn't hear. He kept speaking quietly, relentlessly, getting rid of the heaped memories from the past.

"I survived. I don't remember much about it. Some of the peasants hid me out, did what they could for my wounds. Then the government soldiers came back. I was too weak to escape. They took me to another prison just like the one I'd blown to hell. I knew there was no hope of rescue. My men had seen me shot. They would assume I was dead. Besides, you don't risk twenty men to save one, unless that one is damned important. I wasn't."

Wanting to speak, yet afraid to stop the flow of Rafe's words, Alana murmured softly against his palm and tried not to cry aloud. Her hands smoothed his arm and shoulder again and again, as though to convince herself that he really was alive and she was with him, touching him.

"I spent a long time in that prison. I don't know why I didn't die. A lot of men did and were happy to." Then Rafe turned and looked at Alana. "That's not true. I know why I survived. I had something to live for. You. I dreamed of you, of playing the harmonica while you sang, of touching you, making love to you, hearing you laugh, feeling and seeing your love for me in every touch, every smile. The dreams kept me sane. Knowing that you were waiting for me, loving me as much as I loved you, gave me the strength to escape and to live like an animal in the jungle until I crossed into a country where I wouldn't be shot on sight.''

Alana bent over to kiss Rafe, no longer caring if he saw her tears.

"And then," said Rafe, his voice flat, "I came home to find that the woman I'd loved enough to live for didn't love me enough to wait."

"That's not true!" Alana said, her voice a low cry of pain.

"I know. Now. I didn't know then. All I knew was what the papers told me. Jack 'n' Jilly. Perfect marriage. Perfect love. No one told me any different."

"No one knew," said Alana raggedly. "Jack and I worked very hard to keep the truth of our marriage a secret."

"You succeeded." Rafe looked at Alana for a long moment, seeing his pain and unhappiness reflected in her dark eyes and pale face. He touched her lips with his fingertip, loosening the tight line of her mouth. "I left the army as soon as my time was up. My father was dead by then. I came back to the ranch as bitter a man as has ever watched the sun rise over Broken Mountain. Until a year ago, I ran the ranch through my lawyers and lived out of the Broken Mountain fishing camp. Alone. You see," he said softly, "I wasn't sure that I was alive, not really. No one on this side of the mountain even knew that I hadn't died—except Sam, and he wouldn't tell anyone."

"Sam?" asked Alana, startled out of her silence.

"He took some training in Panama," said Rafe. "Different outfit. Civilian, not military. We worked together once, just before I left the army. He's a good man, if a bit hardheaded. And that's all I have to say on the subject of Sam Burdette.''

Alana started to object, then realized that it would do no good. Rafe might share his own secrets with her, but her brother's secrets were not Rafe's to share. ''When did you decide to tell people that you were alive?'' she asked, watching Rafe with eyes that were as dark as midnight, as dark as her nightmares.

''I didn't. It just happened.'' Rafe shook his head slowly, remembering his rage and bitterness at life and at the woman who had married another man just six weeks after her fiancé had been declared dead. ''I ran into Bob one day in the high country, fishing that crazy fly he favors. And he went straight down the mountain to you.''

Without realizing it, Alana's fingers clenched on Rafe's arm as she remembered the moment that Bob had burst into the house talking about Rafe Winter, a man come back from the dead—and looking like it. Hard and bitter, eyes as cold as a February dawn.

Rafe. Alive.

And she was married to a man she didn't love.

''A day later,'' continued Rafe, watching Alana, ''Bob brought me a letter. I recognized your handwriting on the envelope. I looked at it for a long, long time. And then I knew I couldn't open my own Dear John letter, couldn't force myself to read the words describing your perfect marriage, perfect career, perfect man, perfect lover. I couldn't read the death of my dream written in your own hand, the dream that had kept me alive when most of me hurt so much that death looked very good.''

Alana shook her head as tears fell from her tightly closed eyes. With a ragged sound, she put her head on Rafe's chest and held him until her arms ached. She couldn't bear the thought of Rafe being tortured, dreaming of her, surviving because he loved her; and then coming home to find her married.

"What was in the letter?" asked Rafe softly, so softly that it barely penetrated the sound of Alana's tears.

"The truth," said Alana hoarsely. "I was going to leave Jack. When I was free, I was going to write to you again if you wanted me."

"But you didn't leave Jack."

"No." She drew a ragged breath. "When I lost you a second time I thought nothing mattered. I went back to Jack. It was wrong. Knowing you were alive, I simply could not stay with Jack. Not even to save our singing career. So we lived separately, but very discreetly. It wasn't good enough. Even though you didn't want me, hadn't even cared for me enough to tell me you were alive, I had to be free. I had lived with lies too long. When you were dead, the lies hadn't mattered to me. Nothing had mattered except singing. That's how I survived, Rafe. I sang to the memory of the man I loved, not to Jack."

"And I wrote your death sentence on an envelope and sent it back to you," said Rafe bitterly.

"What?"

Rafe swore softly, savagely. Alana trembled, not knowing why he was so angry with himself. Then he was silent for a long time.

"What did you mean?" asked Alana, her voice shaking as she looked at Rafe's narrowed eyes. "Why was the envelope my death sentence?"

"It sent you back to Jack Reeves."

"What—"

"The answer is in your nightmares," said Rafe, cutting off Alana's question.

Alana's eyes searched Rafe's, looking for answers but

seeing only herself reflected in clear amber. "How do you know?"

"That, too, is in your nightmares." His hands came up to frame her face. "There's something else in those lost days, Wildflower," Rafe murmured, kissing her lips gently. "There's the moment you saw me, knew me, turned to me." He kissed her again, more deeply.

"Rafe—"

"No," he said softly, firmly. "I've told you more than the good doctor wanted me to. But I thought it might help you to know that something other than horror is buried with those six missing days."

Chapter 9

FOR A LONG TIME THERE WAS ONLY SILENCE AND THE
rushing sound of the distant cascade. Alana took one look at
Rafe's expression and knew that questioning him would be
futile. He had the same closed look that he had had when
he'd talked about leading his men into hell. But it angered
her that Rafe knew something about her six lost days and
wouldn't tell her.

"Why?" she asked finally, her voice harsh. "Why won't
you help me?"

"People told you Jack was dead," said Rafe bluntly.
"How much help was that?"

Alana searched Rafe's topaz eyes. "But—" she began.

"But nothing. Did knowing Jack was dead help you
remember anything?" asked Rafe in a flat voice.

Alana clenched her hands. "No."

"Did waking up in that hospital beaten and bloody tell
you how you got hurt?"

Silence. Then, tightly, "No."

"Did reading about Jack's death in every newspaper help?"

"How did you know?" she whispered.

"In some ways, you're a lot like me," said Rafe simply.

"But if you'd tell me what you know, it would help me sort out reality from nightmare."

"Would it?" Rafe asked, his voice soft. "The doctors don't think so. I might tell you something you don't want to know. I might tell you that your nightmares are pieces of the truth."

Rock and ice and wind, something lifting her, throwing her out into the darkness, falling, she was falling and rocks waited below, waited to break her, hatred breaking her—

Alana made a small sound and went pale. She wrapped her arms around herself as she felt the cold of her nightmares congeal inside her, fear and truth freezing her. She closed her eyes as though that would shut out the fragments of nightmare. Or was it true memory that she was shutting out, reality chasing her through her nightmares, truth saying to her *remember me.*

Rafe reached for Alana, wanting to gather her into his arms and comfort her. When his hands touched her, she gasped and flinched away. Rafe withdrew instantly, but the cost of controlling himself made muscles stand out rigidly along his jaw. He looked at Alana's pale skin and black lashes, her mouth shaped for smiling but forced by fear into a thin line, the pulse beating too quickly in her throat.

With a soundless curse, Rafe closed his eyes. The doctors were right. Telling her wouldn't help; even worse, it could hurt her. At first he had been afraid that she would remember too soon, before he had a chance to win her love again. Now he was afraid that she wouldn't remember soon enough, that she would lose faith in herself and then tear herself apart, hating herself. Yet Rafe couldn't bring back Alana's memory for her, no matter how much he wanted to. The bitterness of that knowledge made the brackets around his mouth deeper, harder.

"If telling you everything I know about those six days would stop you from freezing when I touch you, I'd shout the truth from the top of Broken Mountain," said Rafe, his voice thick with suppressed emotion. "My God, don't you know that I'd do anything to have you in my arms again? I want you so badly. I want to hold you, comfort you, love you . . . and I can't. All I can do is hurt you again and again."

Rafe's hands became fists. With a quick movement, he rolled aside until his back was to Alana. "It's like Central America all over again," he said harshly, "only it's worse because this time it's you I'm leading into hell, knowing with every step that there's no other way, knowing and hating myself just the same." His laugh was a short, savage sound. "Christ, I don't blame you for shrinking away every time I touch you."

The raw emotion in Rafe's voice called Alana out of the depths of nightmare as nothing else could have. She knew what it was like to feel snarled and helpless, hating yourself, feeling as though everything you did made the snarl worse, not better. The thought of Rafe feeling that way because of her made Alana ache with tears she couldn't shed. Rafe had given so much to her in just the last day, laughter and protection, patience and companionship, subtle passion and, above all, acceptance.

She might rail against herself for being weak, she might be angry and disgusted with herself . . . but Rafe was not. When she was close to hating herself, he had told her about strength and weakness and survival, torture and the breaking point every human being has. He had told her about his own time in hell, and in doing so he had coaxed her out of the depths of her own self-disgust. Rafe had given her hope when all she'd had was nightmare.

And for that, she flinched when he touched her.

"Rafael," murmured Alana, touching his arm.

She shifted her position until she was on her knees. She leaned over him, stroking him from the thick silk of his hair down to the corded tension of his neck. She repeated his name again and again, a soft litany that was nearly a song. Her hand moved down, trying to loosen the rigid muscles of his shoulders and back. The dark cotton of his T-shirt felt like warm velvet to her. Her fingers kneaded the hard flesh beneath. He felt so good to her, heat and smoothness and strength.

With a sigh, Alana bent over until she could put her lips just below the dark brown of his hair. Rafe's neck was warm and firm, tanned skin stretched tautly over tendons, tempting her tongue to taste and trace each subtle change in texture. She kissed him lightly, lingeringly, then gave in to temptation and touched his skin with the tip of her tongue. He tasted of salt and heat and man, slightly rough where his beard began and amazingly smooth just below his hairline at the back of his neck.

Delicately, Alana's teeth closed on Rafe's neck, testing the resilience of the muscle beneath. He moved his head and shoulders slowly, increasing the pressure of her teeth on his flesh, making her hand slide over the muscles of his back. He tasted good, felt good, and she wanted to touch and savor more of him. Her fingers dug into the bunched muscle beneath her hand as her teeth tested the male power of his shoulders. Rafe arched against her touch like a hungry cat.

The honesty of his response made an equal hunger sweep through Alana, a hunger that only Rafe had ever called from her. She wanted to lie down next to him, to fit her body along his, to feel his passion surround her as she surrounded him. Yet even as fire licked through her, melting her, Alana knew that if Rafe's arms closed around her she would freeze. And in freezing, she would hate herself and hurt him cruelly.

"Oh, Rafe," she said, her voice breaking over his name, "what are we going to do?"

"What we're doing right now feels wonderful."

"But I'm afraid I'll freeze," Alana admitted, and the words trembled with fear and the beginning of anger at herself.

"Does touching me frighten you?"

Alana made an odd sound that could have been laughter. "Touching you is like singing, Rafael. Only better."

She heard his breath come in sharply and felt the fine tremor that went through his body.

"Then touch me as much as you want," Rafe said simply.

"That isn't fair to you."

Rafe's back shifted beneath Alana's hand, urging her to explore him, telling her more clearly than words that he wanted to be touched by her. "Remember when you were nineteen?" he asked.

Alana's hand hesitated, then slid up Rafe's back to his hair. Eagerly, her fingers sought the warmth of him beneath the thick pelt. "Yes."

"You didn't object then."

"I didn't know what I was doing to you. Not really. Virgins can be very cruel."

"Did I complain?" asked Rafe, laughter and memories curling just beneath his words.

"No," she said softly.

"Did I ask for more than you wanted to give?"

"No. Never, Rafael."

"I never will." With a smooth motion, Rafe rolled onto his back and looked at her with eyes that were clear amber, brilliant with emotion and desire. "Do you believe me?"

"Yes."

"Then touch me."

"Even though I can't—?" Alana's voice faltered.

"Yes," said Rafe swiftly, almost fiercely. "However much or little you want. Everything. Anything." Then, whispering, "I've dreamed of you for so long. Touch me, Wildflower."

Hesitantly, Alana's hands came up to frame Rafe's face. Her lips brushed across his even as her fingers again sought the silky brown depths of his hair. With a sigh, her breath mingled with his and she knew again the heat and textures of his mouth. She made a throaty sound of pleasure as his taste spread across her tongue. Forgotten sensations stirred, wakening. The kiss deepened into a timeless sensual joining as they gave themselves to each other, knowing only each other. Finally, Alana lifted her mouth and looked at Rafe with eyes that remembered passion.

"The first time you kissed me like that," whispered Alana, "I thought I would faint. I think I could faint now," she admitted, trembling. "You take the world out from under me."

"Are you frightened?" asked Rafe quietly, watching Alana with smoky amber eyes.

She smiled slowly and shook her head. "With you, there's no danger of falling. With you, I'm as weightless as heat balanced on fire."

Alana bent her head and kissed Rafe again, savoring every instant, every changing pressure of tongue on tongue, the heat and pleasure of his mouth joined with hers. Her hands slid from his hair, caressing him with each tiny movement of her fingers. One hand curved around his neck just beneath his ear, her palm fitting perfectly against the slide and play of muscle as he moved his mouth across hers. The other hand slid down his arm, only to return as her fingers sought the warmth of his skin beneath the short sleeve of his T-shirt. She stroked him, murmuring her pleasure as she felt him flex against her touch.

Alana's hand slid higher until her palm rubbed Rafe's shoulder under his soft T-shirt. Catlike, he arched into her caress, telling her how much he liked having her hand on his bare skin. When her mouth left his and she began to nibble on his moustache and his neck and finally, delicately, his ear, Rafe made a sound deep in his throat. Alana responded by tracing the outline of his ear with her mouth, then caressing him with slow, probing touches of her tongue that made his breath quicken.

"I remember how I shivered the first time you did that to me," whispered Alana, her breath warm against Rafe. "Do you remember?"

"Yes," he said, his voice husky. "You had goose bumps all the way up and down your arms."

"Like you, now."

"Yes. Like me, now."

Alana's tongue touched Rafe's neck just as her teeth closed on his skin. Rafe moved his head, urging her to touch more deeply, to bite harder. Her teeth pressed into his flesh and she felt the male power in the tendon sliding beneath her mouth. He had caressed her like that when the storm had chased them to the Broken Mountain cabin. His bite had been just short of pain and had brought a pleasure that had left her weak.

With a small sound, Alana caressed Rafe's neck down to his shoulder until her teeth closed on the T-shirt. Her hands kneaded down his chest to the warm band of skin where his shirt had pulled free of his jeans. As her fingers touched his naked skin, Rafe's breath came in sharply. His weight shifted as his arms moved. Alana waited, frozen, anticipating his embrace.

"It's all right," said Rafe softly. "See? No hands."

And it was true. Rafe had moved, but only to put his hands behind his head, fingers tightly laced against the nearly overpowering temptation to touch Alana as she was touching him.

Alana smiled and relaxed against his side. "Does that mean I can still touch you?" she asked.

Rafe smiled just enough to show the tip of his tongue between the serrations of his teeth. "What do you think?" he asked in a deep voice.

"I think," said Alana, her glance moving from the rich pelt of Rafe's hair down the hard, masculine length of him, "that it's a wonder I kept my hands off you until I was twenty."

"And here I thought that I was the one who deserved a medal."

"That's probably true," Alana admitted, her eyes brilliant with memories of a storm and a cabin loft. "I didn't know what I was missing. You did."

"Not really," Rafe said softly. "You were unique, sweet and wild, as generous as summer. You gave yourself to me so completely that you made me realize that I'd never made love with a woman until you. Not completely. And I've never made love since. Not completely."

"Rafael," said Alana softly, pleasure and pain and regret in a single word.

"I'm not asking you for anything," Rafe said. "The fact that you're not ready to give yourself again doesn't mean that I've forgotten how it was between us once—and how it will be again. But not now, this instant,'' he added, regret and certainty evenly balanced in his deep voice. ''I don't expect that now. It's enough that you're touching me, that you're here with me, that you're alive.''

Alana felt the heat of Rafe's skin beneath her fingers, the tempting, silky line of hair curling down below his navel, and the sharp, involuntary movement of his body as her fingers slid beneath the soft T-shirt and traced the long muscles of his torso from his waist to his ribs. Eyes closed, smiling, Alana let her hands savor Rafe's strength and stillness and the changing, compelling textures of his body beneath her palms. Her fingers searched among the crisp hairs on his chest, alive to the feel of him, the silk and the hardness and the heat of him.

And he watched her, wanting her.

Without stopping to think, Alana tugged at Rafe's T-shirt, impatient with even the soft cotton restricting the freedom of her touch. She had the T-shirt bunched up beneath his arms before she realized what she was doing.

''I'm sorry,'' said Alana raggedly, her eyes still closed. ''I wasn't thinking.''

''I was,'' said Rafe, his voice deep, caressing.

''What were you thinking?'' she asked in a small voice. ''That I'm a tease?''

''Open your eyes and I'll tell you.'' His voice was gentle, coaxing, an intangible caress that made her shiver.

Alana's eyes opened slowly. She saw her hands against Rafe's chest, his nearly black hair curling up over her slender fingers. Her hands flexed sensuously, pressing her nails against his skin. ''What were you thinking?'' she asked, watching his eyes as her nails bit gently into his flesh with tiny sensual rhythms.

''I was thinking of the first time we made love,'' Rafe

said. "When I unbuttoned my shirt, you looked at me as though you'd never seen a man before, but I knew damn well that you lived with three brothers. And now," added Rafe softly, "you're looking at me like that again."

"Am I?" asked Alana, her voice barely a breath of sound.

"Do you want to take off my shirt?" murmured Rafe, his eyes watching her with hungry intensity.

"Yes," said Alana, bending to brush her lips across Rafe's mouth, loving the feel of him, firm and sweet, answering his heat with her own. She felt his lips smile beneath her caress; then his tongue moved teasingly over her mouth until she smiled.

"Then what are you waiting for?" asked Rafe, unlocking his hands and stretching his arms above his head.

Alana's hands moved up Rafe's body, pushing the soft folds of T-shirt over his chest, his head, his arms until the shirt fell aside, forgotten. Her breath came in, then went out in a long sigh as she ran her hands freely from Rafe's fingertips to his waist. His breath sounded more like a groan as he laced his hands behind his head once more.

For an instant, Alana hesitated. Then Rafe's body twisted sinuously beneath her hands, asking to be touched. She whispered his name as she bent down and kissed him, hungry for the feel of his tongue against hers. Her palms rubbed slowly over his chest, stroking him, enjoying him. When her nails scraped gently over his nipples, she felt him shiver. Her fingertips circled him caressingly, then tugged at the small, hard nubs. His tongue moved sensually in her mouth, stealing her breath until she was dizzy.

With a ragged sound, Alana shifted her position and sought the powerful contours of Rafe's shoulders, tasting and biting and kissing him until her mouth slid down and found the hard male nipples her fingers had teased. Her teeth closed lightly over him. She felt the tension in him, felt his body flexing, felt the powerful muscles of his arms harden beneath her palms. Memories raced through her.

"I never thought of you as really strong," Alana murmured, rubbing her cheek over his chest, "until the storm and the cabin loft."

Rafe smiled, though his fingers were so tightly laced around each other that his hands ached. "Thought I was a weakling, did you?" he said, his voice soft but almost rough, hungry and laughing at the same time.

"Weakling?" asked Alana. She laughed against Rafe's ribs, then turned her head and began caressing the long muscles of his torso with slow movements of her cheek and hand. "No, but Dad was six feet five, and my brothers were all over six feet tall when they were twelve. Bob was six feet six and weighed two-twenty when he was fourteen."

"Whatever attracted you to a shrimp like me?" asked Rafe, but the question ended in a groan when the hard tip of Alana's tongue teased his navel.

"First it was your eyes," she said, her voice blurred as she caressed the taut skin of Rafe's stomach. "Like a cougar, clear amber and more than a little untamed."

"And that made you want to tame me?" asked Rafe.

"No. It made me want to be wild with you."

Rafe's hands clenched until his fingers went numb. He tried to speak, but Alana's fingers had gone from his waist down to the hard muscles of his thigh. He could think of nothing except her touch and the fierce ache of hunger swelling so close to her hand.

"But I didn't know it then," continued Alana, kneading the long muscles that flexed and shifted beneath her fingers, "not in so many words. I just knew I got a funny, quivery feeling deep inside whenever you looked at me a certain way.''

''What way?'' said Rafe, fighting to keep his voice even despite the waves of hunger that hammered through his blood, his fingers twisting against each other until bone ground over bone.

''The way you looked at me when you took off my wet blouse and hung it by the fire,'' said Alana, her breath a warm flow across the naked skin above Rafe's waist. ''The way you looked at me when you peeled off that soaking, lacy bra . . . and then you touched me until I couldn't stand by myself. Do you remember?''

''Yes,'' said Rafe, closing his eyes, remembering. ''You were barefoot. Your jeans were black with rain and outlined you perfectly, those beautiful legs and hips. . . . Did you know that my hands were shaking when I took off your blouse?''

''Yes,'' said Alana, her fingers clenching for an instant on Rafe's leg. ''I was trembling, too.''

''You were cold.''

''Was I?'' she asked, her voice almost breathless as she caressed Rafe's navel again, biting him gently. ''I burned when you touched me. Your hands were so warm on my skin.''

''I didn't mean to undress you,'' whispered Rafe, ''not at first. But once I started . . . you were so beautiful, wearing only firelight. I couldn't stop looking at you, touching you.''

''I didn't want you to stop. I felt like the most exquisite woman ever born when you looked at me, when you kissed me, touched me. And your body fascinated me,'' Alana said, tracing the line of skin just above Rafe's jeans with her tongue. Her hand smoothed his thigh, enjoying the feel of his strength, remembering. "When I finally touched you, every bit of you tightened until each muscle on your body stood out," she murmured, shaping her hand to the heat and hardness of him. "You felt like warm steel. You feel like that now."

"Alana—"

"I knew how strong you were then," she said over Rafe's single, involuntary calling of her name when her hand had found him. "You lifted me high, then let me slide slowly, slowly down your body. So strong, yet so gentle. The eyes of a mountain cat and the hands of a poet."

Alana's mouth caressed Rafe's skin as her fingers unfastened his jeans, seeking him beneath layers of cloth, finding him. Her breath came out raggedly. "And the rest of you so very male." She rubbed her cheek across his stomach, then turned her mouth to his skin and kissed him quickly, fiercely.

"Alana," Rafe said, his voice hoarse as he moved reflexively, sensually against her hand. "I can't take much more of this."

"Then don't," she said simply, tracing the rigid muscles of his arm with one hand, feeling the mist of passion and restraint that covered his body. "You've given me so much. Let me give you something. It's not as much as either of us wants, but it's all I have right now."

Rafe closed his eyes for a moment, knowing that if he looked at Alana right then he wouldn't be able to keep his fingers locked behind his head. Her hand moved again in a devastating, sensual glide of flesh over flesh. Fire thickened in his veins, fire pooling heavily beneath her hand until he could only twist against the sweet agony of her touch. He groaned aloud, his breath hissing between clenched teeth. "Oh God . . . don't."

"Rafael, please understand," said Alana, her voice husky and urgent as she rubbed her cheek against his hot chest. "I can't give myself to you now, but you can give yourself to me. Please, give yourself to me. Let me know that I've been able to bring you some pleasure. I need to know that."

Rafe's eyes opened, an amber hot enough to burn. "Look at me."

Alana lifted her head. He saw the plea in her dark eyes, saw the fire and the fierce pleasure when he moved against her hand, and knew that she had been utterly honest with him. Slowly, he unlocked his fingers; but he moved only one hand, and then only to hold it out to her. When her lips pressed against his palm, his hand shifted, gently bringing her mouth up to his. What began as a simple brush of lips deepened with each heartbeat until it became a kiss of shattering hunger and sensuality.

And then he gave himself to her as freely and generously as she had given herself to him four years ago, in a cabin warmed by firelight and love.

Alana pulled the bubbling, spicy apple pie out of the oven, using the oversized potholders that felt as soft to her touch as Rafe's T-shirt had. She smiled to herself as she set the second pie on the wooden counter to cool, feeling more at peace than she had in a long time. Notes of music kept gliding through her mind, chased by lyrics that hadn't yet condensed into songs.

"What is that marvelous smell?" asked Janice from the doorway.

"Pie," said Alana, turning and smiling over her shoulder at the tall, slender woman.

"A miracle," said Janice.

"Actually, its just dried apples, sugar and spices," Alana said, her lips curving.

"In this wilderness, on that stove, those pies are a miracle," said Janice firmly. She looked at Alana with blue eyes that missed nothing. "Anything I can do to help?"

"I've got everything under control, but thanks anyway."

Janice smiled. "Must be a wonderful feeling."

"What?"

"Having everything under control."

Alana looked startled for an instant; then she nodded slowly. It was true. Since she had awakened in the hospital, she had felt as though her life was out of her control, as though she were a victim instead of a person. Fear had eroded her self-respect and confidence. But today she had been able to talk and laugh with Rafe. Today she had taken the first steps toward overcoming her fear of heights. Today she had realized that Rafe respected and cared for her despite her amnesia and irrational fears. Rafe had accepted her as she was, imperfect, and then he had given himself to her instead of demanding that she give herself to him.

"Yes," said Alana quietly. "It's an incredibly good feeling."

Janice's eyes narrowed in an instant of intelligent scrutiny that Alana didn't notice. "I'm glad," said Janice, unmistakable satisfaction in her voice.

Alana looked up quickly, seeing for the first time the compassion in the other woman. "Rafe told you about my husband, didn't he?"

Janice hesitated while her shrewd blue eyes measured the emotions apparent on Alana's face. "Don't be angry with him," said Janice. "Rafe just wanted to be sure that Stan and I wouldn't accidentally hurt you."

Frowning, Alana wiped her hands on the enormous white

apron that she wore. "It's not fair to ask you to walk on eggs so I won't be upset. This trip is for your pleasure, not mine."

Janice smiled. "Don't worry. We're having a ball."

Alana looked at her with skeptical dark eyes. "Uh-huh. When I'm not screaming at Stan or stealing your fishing guide."

"Stan's a big boy," said Janice dryly. "And as for Rafe, he showed us the water and we caught our limit. Besides, he cleans the trout for us and you whip up hot apple pies. What more could we ask?"

Laughing and shaking her head, Alana said, "You two are very special dudes. If your clients are half as easy to be around, Bob will think he's died and gone to heaven. Most dudes can't find their way downhill without directions and a hard push."

From the next room came the sound of cupboard doors being opened and closed briskly. "Hey, sis," called Bob from the dining room, "where did I put the dishes last night after I washed them?"

Janice and Alana exchanged a look and burst out laughing. Bob stuck his head in the kitchen. "What's so funny?"

"You wouldn't understand," said Alana. "But that's all right. I love you anyway."

She stood on tiptoe and kissed Bob's cheek quickly. He looked surprised, then very pleased. He started to hug Alana in return, then stopped, remembering. He patted her shoulder with unexpected gentleness, then put his blunt index finger on the tip of her nose.

"You look better, sis. Rafe was right. You needed to be home." Bob shook his head and smiled, giving her a somewhat baffled look. "How did you get to be so small, anyway?" he asked in a rueful voice, still not used to perceiving his sister as a contemporary rather than a substitute mother.

"You grew up," said Alana.

He smiled. "Yeah, guess so. Why don't you go get dressed? I'll whip up the potatoes and get everything on the table."

Alana blinked, startled by the offer. Then she blinked again, several times, fighting back sudden tears. Bob was being as protective of her as he was of Merry. "Thanks, big brother," she said, her voice husky. "I'd like that."

Alana showered quickly, then climbed into the loft wrapped in Bob's oversized velvet robe, which she had found hanging from a peg in the downstairs bathroom. She stood in front of the closet and tried to choose from the array of clothes that Bob had packed for her. She finally selected a pair of heavy silk slacks that were a rich, glowing chocolate color. The blouse she chose was long sleeved and the color of fire, its sensuous texture and folds in direct contrast to its businesslike cut.

Automatically, Alana began to button up the blouse so that the chain she always wore was concealed. Then she stopped, realizing that she no longer had to hide Rafe's engagement gift; it no longer mattered if people asked her about the unusual design of the necklace. Jack was dead. She no longer had to conceal the fact that one-half of Country's Perfect Couple wore another man's gift in the vulnerable hollow of her throat.

Alana smoothed the collar open. The elegant symbol of infinity shifted and gleamed with each movement of her head. She touched the symbol with her fingertip and felt another tiny increment of peace settling inside her, another step on the way to rebuilding her strength. For the first time since she had awakened in the hospital, she began to believe that she would not only survive, but would be able to love again.

Even if her nightmares were true.

"Alana?" Rafe's voice came from the bottom of the steep stairway. "Are you ready?"

"Almost," she whispered, too softly for Rafe to hear. "Almost."

Chapter 10

RAFE SLICED AND SERVED THE WARM APPLE PIE TO THE accompaniment of good-natured complaints as to which person was or wasn't getting the biggest piece. Bob and Stan swapped pieces with each other several times before Rafe gave in and put the last piece of pie between them. Even after a dinner of trout, potatoes, green beans and biscuits, everyone found room for a piece of pie. Even Alana. Rafe smiled approvingly as she ate the last bite of the generous slice he had cut for her. When she threw back her head and sighed that she was too full to move, he saw the gleam of gold in the hollow of her throat. With a fingertip, he traced the length of the chain and its elegant symbol.

"You still wear this," he said softly.

"I've never taken it off since you gave it to me," Alana said, watching his eyes. They were tawny in the late-afternoon light that was streaming through the window, tawny and very intent.

"Not even after I sent back your letter?" he asked, searching her eyes.

"Never. It was all I had left of you."

The back of Rafe's finger caressed Alana's throat. "I wish we were alone," he whispered. "I would like very much to kiss you. Many times. Many places. Would you like that, Wildflower?"

A suggestion of color bloomed beneath Alana's skin. She smiled and smoothed her cheek against Rafe's finger. "Yes," she murmured. "I'd like that."

Then she looked across the table and saw Stan watching her closely, his eyes so blue that they were almost black, his fair hair shimmering in a shaft of sunlight that came through the cabin window and fell across his thick shoulders. She looked away quickly, knowing that she was being rude but still not able to accept Stan's unnerving physical resemblance to Jack. When Stan asked Rafe about a particular kind of dry fly, Alana turned to Janice and asked the first question that came to mind.

"Somehow you aren't what I'd expect a travel agent to be. How did you choose that career?"

There was a sudden silence, then a determined resumption of the casual conversation taking place around the two women. Alana looked at Rafe suddenly, wondering if she had done something wrong. Rafe ignored her, apparently caught up in his talk with Stan.

"I'm sorry," said Alana. "Did I ask the wrong question?"

Janice's smile had a wry twist as she glanced sideways at Rafe. "I'd say you asked just the right one," she said.

Rafe looked up sharply, but said nothing.

"I used to be a psychiatrist," continued Janice. "After ten years, I burned out. So many problems. So few solutions." Her voice was light but her eyes were narrowed against memories that still had the power to hurt her. "So I became a special kind of travel agent. I match people with the kind of vacation that will do the most for them."

"Solutions," said Alana.

"Yes," said Janice simply.

Alana wanted to ask more. She was suddenly very curious about Janice's past, about the pressures that had driven her to change careers. And about Rafe, who had known Janice before.

"Would you like to hear about what happened?" asked Janice.

"If you don't mind," said Alana.

Janice and Rafe exchanged a quick look. He raised his dark eyebrows slightly, then shrugged. Janice turned back to Alana.

"I used to work for the government, like Rafe," said Janice.

Though she spoke quietly, at her first words Stan and Rafe's conversation died. Stan gave Janice a hard look, then looked questioningly at Rafe. Rafe ignored him. Stan seemed about to speak, when a gesture from Rafe cut him off.

"Men and women who work under impossible conditions," said Janice in a matter-of-fact tone, "often have trouble living with themselves. If something goes wrong and people die, or if nothing goes wrong and people die anyway, the person in charge has to live with it. The key words are *in charge*. These are intelligent people who care about the world. They are the actors, not the audience. They are in control of themselves and of life."

Janice smiled wryly and took a sip of her coffee. "At

least," she added softly, "they think they're in control. Then it all goes from sugar to sawdust and they're left wondering what hit them. My job was to explain that it was reality that ran over them and left them flat."

Stan made a sound halfway between protest and laughter. When Janice looked at him, he winked. Alana sensed the nearly tangible currents of affection and respect that flowed between the two people.

"People come in all kinds," continued Janice, "but those I dealt with usually fell into three categories. The first category contained people who couldn't cope with an unpredictable, unforgiving reality and simply fell apart. The second category contained people who survived by stuffing down their feelings of inadequacy, bewilderment and fear; these people did exactly what they had been trained to do and did it magnificently. The third category was made up of people who simply had so little imagination or such great faith in 'going by the book' that they had the same untouchable serenity that religion gives to some people."

Janice picked up her coffee cup, sighed, and put it down again without tasting the dark brew. "People in the first category, the ones who couldn't cope, didn't last long as operatives. The third type, the ones who did it by the book, did very poorly in the fluid world of field work. We tended to put them in office positions as quickly as they were discovered. Those in the second category did most of the work. They were the survivors, the people who got the job done.

"Unfortunately," said Janice, glancing quickly at Rafe, "sooner or later, the survivors paid a high psychic price when faced with the randomness of reality and the fact that Superman exists only in the comics. Real men bleed and make mistakes. If, once the crisis is past, the survivors can't deal with their feelings of weakness, can't accept that all any person can do is their best . . . well, then they begin to hate themselves. If they can't accept the fact that they can be afraid, be hurt, even be broken and *still* be damned fine, brave, effective human beings, then they tear themselves apart.''

Janice stared out over the table, seeing something from the past. ''My job was to help the survivors accept their own limitations, their humanity. I was supposed to help them accept themselves.'' She shook her head slowly. ''Because if they couldn't accept their humanity, I lost them. I—lost—them.'' Janice's hand clenched into a fist, softly pounding the table with each word.

Impulsively, Alana put her hand over the other woman's. ''It wasn't your fault,'' said Alana. ''You couldn't open up their hearts and make them believe in their own worth. All you could do was care, and you did.''

Janice looked at Alana for a long moment. Then Janice's lips shaped a sad smile. ''But when you love them, and you lose them, it hurts like hell. After a while there was one too many, and I quit.''

Alana looked quickly at Rafe, wondering if he had been the ''one too many'' for Janice.

''You did all anyone could,'' said Rafe quietly, ''and that was a lot more than most.''

''So did you.'' Janice's blue eyes measured Rafe. ''Did you think that was enough?''

''No,'' he admitted, meeting her eyes without flinching, ''but I'm learning to live with it. Finally.''

Janice looked at Rafe for a long moment, then smiled gently. ''Good for you, Rafe Winter. Very good. It was a near thing, wasn't it?'' Janice turned and looked at Alana. ''The strongest ones,'' Janice said quietly, ''have the hardest time. They go the longest before they come up against human limitations. And then they blame themselves. They reach a state where they are, in effect, at war with themselves. Some survive even that. A lot don't. For the strong ones, it's a case of the sooner they accept their own limitations, the better. There are very few ways to win a war with yourself, and a whole lot of ugly ways to lose.''

There was silence, and then Janice set down her coffee cup and said briskly, ''Enough of my past. Who's going to catch the biggest fish tonight?''

''I am,'' said Bob and Stan at the same moment.

The two big men looked at each other, grinned and began placing bets on the outcome. Rafe and Janice exchanged knowing glances and shook their heads. Alana stood and began to clear the table. Immediately, Rafe took the plates out of her hands.

''You look too elelgant to handle dirty dishes,'' said Rafe. ''Come sit in the kitchen and talk to me.''

Alana looked at him. He was wearing black wool slacks and a tailored black shirt of a wool so fine it felt like silk. The supple fabric fit him like a shadow, outlining the power of his arms and shoulders.

''You look too elegant, too,'' she said, touching the black fabric where it pulled lightly across his chest.

The warmth of Rafe radiated through the shirt to Alana's hand, making her want to rub her palm against him, to curl up next to him like a cat by a fire. And, oddly, she wanted simply to hold him, to comfort him, to take away whatever hurt she could from his past; for she had no doubt that he was one of the very strong ones whom Janice had talked about, the ones who had the hardest time accepting their own limitations.

''What are you thinking?'' asked Rafe, his voice deep.

''That you're one of the strong ones,'' Alana said, watching his eyes, amber and shadows.

"So are you."

The thought startled Alana. She didn't feel strong. She felt weak, useless, foolish, hiding from herself and reality behind a wall of amnesia and irrational fears.

Before she could protest, Rafe spoke, his voice quick and sure. "You are strong, Alana. You were only a child, yet you held your family together after your mother died. When you thought I was dead, you saw your best chance of emotional survival in a singing career, and you took it. And when another crisis came, you fought for life. You fought as bravely and fiercely as anyone ever has."

"Then why am I afraid?" whispered Alana.

"Because it wasn't enough," said Rafe grimly. "You came flat up against the fact that Wonder Woman, like Superman, doesn't exist in the real world."

"I didn't think that I was Wonder Woman."

"Didn't you? Who was the strongest Burdette, the one everyone came to when dreams and favorite puppies died? Your dad? No way. It was years before he was worth a damn after your mother's death. As for Jack—" Rafe made a cutting, dismissive gesture. "If it hadn't been for your discipline, your intelligence, your sheer talent at taking apart a song and putting it back together in a new, vital way, Jack would have been just another beer hall tenor. He knew it. He used you to make the world more comfortable for himself. And," grimly, "he acted as though using you was his God-given right."

Alana closed her eyes, hearing her own unwanted thoughts coming from Rafe's lips. "I used him, too," she whispered. "I used him to survive after they told me you were dead."

"Were you the one who demanded marriage?"

Alana shook her head. "I just wanted to sing."

"That's what Bob said. He remembered Jack hounding

you and then finally telling you that if you wouldn't marry him, he wouldn't sing with you. Jack knew exactly what he wanted, and he knew how to get it. When it came to his own comforts, he was as selfish as any man I've ever known.''

''But he didn't want me, not as a wife, not as a woman.''

Rafe laughed harshly. ''Wrong, Alana. You didn't want *him*. He could have your singing talent but he couldn't have you. Easy Street was more important to Jack than sex, so he accepted your conditions.''

''I didn't want him to want me,'' said Alana, her voice strained, her eyes tightly closed. ''I think—'' Her voice broke, then came back so harshly that it sounded like a stranger's. She shivered despite the warmth of the cabin, for she was feeling again the cold afternoon before the storm, hearing fragments of words, *Jack cursing, reaching for her*. ''I think Jack wanted me on Broken Mountain. I think we fought about it.''

From the front porch came the sound of Stan's laughter as he and Bob shouldered each other to see who would be first through the door. Alana swayed alarmingly. Her eyes opened, black with memories. She didn't hear the clatter of plates as Rafe put them on the table and stood close to her, not touching her, prepared to catch her if she fainted. Her skin was as pale and translucent as fine china, her pupils dilated to the point that only a small rim of brown remained.

''Jack was laughing,'' she whispered. ''The lake was so cold and he was laughing at me. All my clothes, my sleeping bag, me—soaked and so cold. He said I could sleep in his sleeping bag—for a price. He said he'd be glad to warm me up.''

Rafe's expression changed, pulled by hatred into savage lines of rage, the face of a man who had once gone through a jungle hell like an avenging angel. Alana didn't see. Her wide eyes were blinded by the past that she had hidden from herself, but not well enough.

"At first, I didn't believe him. Then I tried to ride out. He grabbed my braids and yanked me out of the saddle and kicked Sid until she bolted down the trail. He—he hit me. I couldn't get away. He wrapped my braids around his hand, holding me, and he hit me again and again. Then he tied me and dumped me on a rock ledge by the lake. He said he'd turn me loose when I changed my mind. He said we wouldn't go down the mountain until I'd changed my mind. 'When we come down off this damned mountain, you're going to heel for me like a bird dog.' And then he laughed and laughed. But—" Alana's head moved in a negative gesture—"He didn't want me. He just wanted to—to break me. I think he must have hated me."

Alana's eyes closed slowly. She made an odd sound and covered her mouth with her hand. "It was so cold. The lake and the rock and the night. Cold."

The words were muffled, but Rafe heard them. Silently, he cursed the fact that Jack Reeves had died quickly, painlessly, a hundred feet of darkness and then the deadly impact of granite.

Alana drew a deep, shuddering breath. When her eyes opened, they were focused on the present. She ran shaking fingers through her hair, short hair that couldn't be used as a weapon against her, chaining her. "That's why I cut off my braids," she said, relief and pain mixed in her voice. "I'm not crazy after all."

"No," said Rafe, his voice soft and yet harsh with the effort of holding his emotions in check, "you're not crazy."

"Are you sure?" she asked, trying to smile. "Because I have a really crazy thing to ask you."

"Anything," said Rafe simply. "Anything at all."

"Run your fingers through my hair," Alana said. "Take away the feel of Jack's hands."

Rafe brought his hands up to Alana's head, ready to retreat at the first sign of returning fear. Gently, he eased his fingers through her soft hair. Alana closed her eyes and concentrated on the sensation of Rafe's strong fingers moving through her hair. Chills of pleasure chased through her.

"More," she murmured, tilting her head against his palms.

Rafe's fingers slid deeper into the midnight silk of her hair, rubbing lightly over her scalp, caressing her.

"Yes," sighed Alana, moving against his hands, increasing the contact, deepening the intimacy until the heat of his hands surrounded her, taking away memories, warming her.

She opened her eyes and saw Rafe's face very near, his concentration as great as hers, and his pleasure. By quarter inches he lowered his mouth to hers, waiting for the least sign of fear when Alana realized she was caught between his hands and his lips. Her only answer was a smile and a sigh as her lips parted, welcoming him. He kissed her very gently, not wanting to frighten her. Then her arms stole around his waist.

"You feel so good," Alana whispered against Rafe's lips. "So warm, so alive. And you want me. Not to break, but to cherish." She kissed him slowly, savoring the heat of him, shaping herself to him, absorbing him like a flower absorbing sunlight. "So warm," she murmured.

Rafe felt Alana's breasts press against him as her arms tightened around him. Hunger swept through him, a fierce surge of fire. "Very warm," he agreed, smiling, nibbling on the corner of her mouth.

One of Rafe's hands slid from Alana's hair to her

shoulder, then to her ribs. Instead of retreating, she moved closer. Her scent and sweetness made the breath stop in Rafe's throat. Slowly, he moved his hand away from the soft temptation of her breast. With light touches, he ran his right hand over her back, enjoying the resilience of her body. His left hand rubbed through her hair, then stroked her neck. Finally, slowly, he moved his left hand to her back until he held her loosely in his arms.

"I'm not frightening you, am I?" asked Rafe.

Alana shook her head and burrowed closer to Rafe. "I love your warmth, Rafael," she murmured. "When I'm close to you like this, I can't even imagine ever being cold again."

The front door slammed open. "Hey, sis, where did I put the—oops, sorry."

Rafe glanced up over Alana's black cap of hair. Stan, who had followed Bob inside, gave Rafe a long, enigmatic look.

"Lose something?" asked Rafe mildly, keeping his arms around Alana.

"My net," admitted Bob. "I had it when I came in for dinner, but I can't find it."

"Last time I saw your net," said Rafe, "it was leaning against the back door of the lodge."

"Thanks," said Bob. He walked quickly around the dining room table to the kitchen and out the back door. When he realized Stan wasn't following, Bob called over his shoulder, "Come on, Stan. Don't you know a losing cause when you see one?"

The instant Alana knew that Bob hadn't been alone, she had stiffened and turned to face the living room. Stan walked toward her. Instantly she spun around, holding on to

Rafe's arm as though he were all that stood between her and a long, deadly fall.

"The trout are rising, Stan," said Rafe quietly. "Why don't you try that dark moth I tied for you? The one we both agreed on."

"You sure it will get the job done?" asked Stan. "You have to be real careful with trout. If they get away, they're even harder to lure the next time."

"What I've made matches the environment almost perfectly," said Rafe, choosing each word with care. "That, and patience, will get the job done. Ask Janice."

Stan paused, then nodded. "I'll do that, Winter. I'll do just that."

Without another word, Stan brushed past Rafe and Alana. In a few seconds, the back door banged shut.

"Two bulls in a china shop," muttered Rafe, resting his cheek against Alana's hair.

Alana shifted in Rafe's embrace. Immediately, he loosened his arms. She moved closer, kissed him and then stepped back.

"I'm going to change clothes and then do the dishes. You should get into fishing gear and help Stan win his bet with Bob." When Rafe would have objected, Alana said, "I'm all right, Rafe. Really. Stan startled me. He looks so much like Jack."

"Are you afraid that Stan is going to pick you up and throw you in the lake?" asked Rafe, his voice easy, casual.

Alana stood very still for an instant, then slowly shook her head. "No. I don't think—" Her voice died and her eyes were very dark.

"What?" asked Rafe softly, coaxingly.

"I don't think that was the worst of it," she answered in a bleak voice.

"Alana—"

She stepped away from Rafe. "I need to think, but when you're near, all I can think about is how good you feel, how patient you are with me, how much I want to reach back four years and touch love again." She took a breath and let it out slowly. "I'll catch up with you at sunset, when it's too dark to fish."

"That's two hours from now," protested Rafe. "You won't even know where Stan and I are fishing."

"Sound carries in this country," said Alana. "And Stan has the kind of voice that carries, period. I'll find you."

"We'll be fishing just below the cascade. If you don't show up before sunset, I'm going to stuff Stan into his own net and come looking for you," said Rafe, only half-joking. Then, softly, "I wanted to fish with you tonight."

"Oh no," Alana said, shaking her head. "I can hear your fly line whimpering for mercy right now. But," she added, running her fingertips across his moustache, "I'd love to watch you fish."

Rafe watched Alana walk across the living room to the loft stair. His skin tingled where she had touched him, her scent was still sweet in his nostrils, and he wanted her so much that he hurt. Abruptly, he went to the downstairs bedroom and changed into his fishing clothes. He let himself out of the cabin quietly, knowing that if he saw Alana again, he wouldn't leave her.

Alana changed into jeans and a sweater and had the kitchen cleaned long before sunset. Her mind was working as swiftly as her hands. She reviewed what she remembered about the six missing days, and what she didn't. She remembered parts of the ride up the trail with Jack. The first night—was it the first night that she and Jack had fought?

She frowned as she stacked wood in the stove for the morning fire. Three days in the hospital, of which she remembered only one. That left three days unaccounted for. No, two. She and Jack must have spent one day traveling to Wyoming and one night at the ranch house. So it must have been the first night on Broken Mountain, up by the lake, that Jack had thrown her and her clothes and her sleeping bag into the lake, and then slapped her all but senseless when she tried to run from him. That was the night she had spent curled around herself on a piece of ice-polished granite, shivering. That was why she was so cold in her nightmares.

But the wind hadn't been blowing that night. It hadn't been storming. No lightning. No ground-shaking thunder. If it had been the ice-tipped storm of her nightmare, she would have died of exposure before morning. Yet wind and thunder and ice were a part of her nightmares. The storm must have come the second night on Broken Mountain. The night she fell. The night Jack died.

Why had Jack untied her? Had she given in, gone to him, traded her self-respect for a dry sleeping bag and Jack's unwanted body? Was that what she couldn't remember? Did she hate herself because she had survived by prostituting herself? Or had Jack gotten impatient, untied her, raped or beaten her?

Alana waited, forgetting to breathe, anticipating the return of nightmare as her waking thoughts closed in on the truth. But nothing came. When she remembered Jack hitting her, her stomach turned and her breath came shallowly. When she thought of submitting to him, there was . . . nothing. When she thought of being raped, there was . . . nothing. No fear, no desire to scream, no sickness, no cold, no hammering heart or cold sweat. None of the physiological signals that had warned her in the past when she was approaching the truth.

Abruptly, Alana pulled off her apron and went to find

Rafe. The path to the lake was overgrown, clearly showing the bruised grass that marked the passage of at least two people. Alana walked quickly, barely noticing the crimson cloud streamers stretched across the sky. Nor did she see the deep amethyst mountain slopes crowned by luminous ramparts of stone, or the fragrant shadows flowing out of the forest around her.

The path approached the lake at an oblique angle in order to avoid what was a bog in the early summer and an uneven, rough meadow in the fall. Winding through trees, giving only occasional glimpses of water, the path kept to the forest until the last possible moment. She heard Rafe and Stan before she could see them. At least, she heard Stan, his voice pitched to carry above the exuberant thunder of the cascade.

"No, you listen to me for a change, Captain Winter, sir," said Stan sardonically. "I've got a nasty mind for situations like this. I was trained to have a nasty mind."

There was a pause. Whatever Rafe replied was lost in the sound of the cascade. Alana hesitated, then continued toward the lake, screened by spruce and aspen.

"Try this scenario on for size," said Stan. "There's a woman you've wanted for years. Another man's woman. It grinds on you real hard. So the woman you want and the man you hate come up here for a little camping trip."

Alana froze in place, suddenly cold. She didn't want to hear any more, but she couldn't move.

"You wait around, see your chance, and chuck good old Jack over the nearest cliff," continued Stan. "Then you go collect the spoils. But she's not used to that kind of violence. She runs away, spends a night in the open, cold and exposed. And then she just shuts it all out, forgets. That leaves you with a real problem. If she remembers, it doesn't matter whose friend the sheriff is. Your butt is in a sling."

Like a sleepwalker, Alana stirred and continued down the trail, using her hands to push herself away from the rough-trunked trees that seemed to grow perversely in front of her feet, as though to hold her back.

". . . crock of . . ." Rafe's voice faded in and out of the cascade's throaty thunder.

"I'm not finished," cut in Stan, his voice very clear, carrying like a brass bell across the evening. "You can save yourself by marrying her. She won't go telling tales on her own husband. From what Bob tells me, good old Jack wasn't much of a loss to this world, so it's not like she's going to spend a year mourning the son of a bitch. Besides, it's plain enough that she likes you. You've got a little problem, though. If she remembers before you marry her, you're up that smelly creek without a paddle."

"Then why . . . helping her to remember?"

Alana leaned forward, straining to hear all of Rafe's words, but she couldn't. Unlike Stan, Rafe's voice became softer, not louder, with anger.

"Are you?" retorted Stan. "Then why in hell won't you let me off the leash?"

". . . Janice."

"Janice would do a Marine crawl through hot coals for you, Winter, and you damn well know it!"

"I'd . . . same for . . ."

Alana left the trees behind and began walking over the rocks and logs that were between her and the lake.

"And I'm supposed to just shut up and go along with the program," shot back Stan. "Well maybe, and maybe not. That's a damned good woman you're hunting, Winter. I'm not real sure she wants to be caught. I think she should remember, first. That's the only way her choice will have any meaning. That's the best chance she has of surviving."

"Is that what Janice thinks?" asked Rafe.

Rafe's voice carried easily to Alana now that she was out of the muffling evergreens. The men were about fifty feet in front of her, but they had their shoulders turned to her as they faced each other. Neither man noticed her slow progress across the margin between the lake and forest.

"I'm not sure Janice is able to think straight where you're involved," said Stan.

Alana stopped, held by the curious pain in Stan's voice.

"There's nothing between me and Janice," Rafe said. "There never was."

Stan hesitated, then made an odd gesture, turning his hands palms up as though to accept or hold something. "I'd like to believe that. I really would. But," he continued, cutting across Rafe's response, "it doesn't matter right now. It wouldn't matter at all, except that I don't want Alana trapped because Janice allowed emotion to louse up her judgment. If it all goes to hell, I don't want Janice blaming herself. She's been through enough on your account. But that doesn't matter, either. Not up here. Just like the bad old days. All that matters is the mission. You've got two more days, Winter. If your way doesn't work by then, I'll try mine."

"If you do anything that hurts Alana," said Rafe, the suppressed violence in his voice curling and cracking like a whip, making Stan flinch, "you'll go back down Broken Mountain the same way Jack Reeves did—in a green plastic bag. Do you read me, Corporal?"

"I'm not a corporal any more," said Stan. "And you're not a captain."

Stan turned slightly. At first, Alana thought he had spotted her, for she was directly in his line of sight. Suddenly, Stan made a swift feint toward Rafe. At the first hint of movement from the other man, Rafe swiftly assumed a fighting stance. Legs slightly bent, hands held slightly apart at chest level, Rafe waited for Stan to move again.

"You're as fast as ever," said Stan, something close to admiration in his voice. He moved again, very quickly, his big hands reaching for Rafe.

Rafe stepped into the attack, pivoted smoothly and let Stan slide by, not touching him except for the hand that closed around Stan's wrist. Rafe twisted and brought Stan's arm up behind his back, applying pressure until Stan was on his knees. Stan's blond hair shimmered palely in the twilight as Rafe bent over the larger man, his face a mask of cold rage.

"No!" screamed Alana.

Rafe's head snapped around. When he saw the frightened, hunted look on Alana's face, he released Stan and started toward her. "Alana—"

"No," she said raggedly. *"No!"*

Alana spun away from Rafe and ran back into the forest. Rafe started after her, then realized that chasing her would only increase her fear. With a soundless snarl, he turned on Stan.

"You knew she was there, didn't you?" demanded Rafe.

Stan nodded and smiled grimly. "I saw her out of the corner of my eye. That's when I jumped you. Think it reminded her of something, old buddy?"

"Get up," said Rafe, his voice soft and deadly.

"So you can take me apart? No way, Winter. I've seen what you can do when you're mad. I think I'll just sit out this dance."

"And I think," Rafe said, spacing each word carefully, showing how much his control cost, "that if you don't get out of my sight, I'll take you apart anyway."

Chapter 11

THE WIND FLEXED AND FLOWED AROUND THE LODGE, bringing with it the sound of laughter. Words without meaning, wind, more laughter. Alana rolled over in bed, tangling in the covers for the tenth time and wishing that everyone would enjoy the poker game a little less enthusiastically. She wondered if Rafe was with them. Then she remembered his fury at Stan. She doubted that Rafe was in the last cabin, laughing and drawing cards.

Stan's accusations turned and prowled inside Alana's mind like the wind. She wanted to reject them out of hand, completely, yet they kept finding weaknesses in her resolve, cracks in her wall of refusal, little doubts clinging tenaciously. From the moment she had seen Rafe at the airport, she had at some deep, utterly irrational level assumed that he still loved her. A groundless, even ridiculous assumption. A year ago he had returned her letter unopened. He must have hated her. He had believed her happily married six weeks after his "death" had been reported. Before yesterday, nothing had happened to make him believe any differently.

Why, then, had Rafe leaned on Bob to get his sister home? Why had Rafe been so very gentle, so understanding, from the moment he had met her at the airport? Had something happened on Broken Mountain, something that she couldn't remember, something that had made Rafe believe that her marriage to Jack had always been a desperate sham?

Or was the truth as brutal as Stan's accusation? Was Rafe pursuing Alana to save himself? Had Jack's death been less than accidental? Was that why Rafe refused to tell her what had happened on Broken Mountain?

Waves of coldness swept over Alana, roughening her skin. She lay very still, curled around herself, shivering despite the blankets heaped on top of her. She knew that Rafe was capable of deadly violence. He had been trained for it, was skilled in it, had lived with it for most of his adult life. But she couldn't believe that he was capable of such sly deception, that he would coolly plan to murder Jack and then seduce and marry her in order to ensure her silence. That didn't match with the Rafe she had known, the Rafe she had loved.

The Rafe she still loved.

If Stan had accused Jack of such vicious duplicity, she would have been sickened—*but she would have believed*. Jack had been a totally selfish man. Jack had been capable of smiling lies and chilling cruelties, whatever it took to bend the world to his comfort.

Alana's stomach moved uneasily. Cold sweat broke out over her body. Suddenly she couldn't bear the clammy sheets and useless heavy blankets any longer. She needed the lively warmth and flickering companionship of a fire. She sat up in bed and groped for her bathrobe. All she found was the thick velvet robe she had borrowed from the downstairs bathroom. She pulled on the indigo robe, letting the sleeves trail down over her knuckles and the hem brush over the tops of her toes.

Groping along the wall, she worked her way down the inky darkness of the stairway. The living room was empty and lightless. The fireplace ashes were as cold and pale as the moon. Rafe hadn't been in the lodge at all tonight. He hadn't seen or spoken to her since she had run from him through the forest. After her irrational panic had passed, she had waited for Rafe by the trail, but he hadn't come. Finally, when the moon had risen in pale brilliance over Broken Mountain, she had given up and gone inside, shivering with cold and loneliness.

Alana struck a wooden match on the fireplace stone. She peered into the woodbox. There was a handful of kindling and a few small chunks of stovewood. Not enough to warm the hearth, much less her. With a dispirited curse, she let the top of the woodbox fall back into place. She turned to go back to bed, then froze.

A subtle sound permeated the cabin, a distant keening that drifted on the shifting mountain wind. The strange, bittersweet music held Alana motionless, aching to hear more. She held her breath, listening with an intensity that made her tremble. Music curled around her lightly, tantalizing her at a threshold just below memory, music curving across the night like a fly line, lengthening in grace and beauty with each surge of energy, each magic, rhythmic pulse.

Blindly, Alana felt her way through the lodge to the front door, lured by the elusive music. She opened the door, shut it silently behind her, and held her breath, listening and looking.

There was laughter tumbled by wind, bright squares of light glowing out from the cabin at the end of the row. Silhouettes dark against one curtained window, wordless movement of hands and arms, more laughter. But no music. It wasn't somebody's transistor radio or tape recorder that had slid through Alana's defenses, calling to her in a language older and more potent than words. Yet where else could the music be coming from? Of the three cabins that stretched out east of the lodge, only one was lit, only one was brimming with laughter when people won or lost small bets. The other two cabins were empty, as black as night itself, blacker, for the cabins had neither moon nor stars to light their interior darkness.

The wind stirred, blowing across the back of Alana's neck, teasing her ears with half-remembered, half-imagined music. Slowly she turned around, facing west. The fourth cabin was several hundred feet away, wrapped in forest and darkness, not really part of the fishing camp. No light shone out of the cabin in welcome, no laughter, no sense of brimming life.

Yet music came to her, an immaterial, irresistible lure drawing her closer with each note.

Alana stood and listened for a moment more, her heart beating, her blood rushing so quickly that it overwhelmed the mixed murmur of music and wind. Before she stopped to think, she stepped off the porch onto the overgrown path to the fourth cabin. Pine needles and sharp stones smarted against her bare feet, but she noticed them only at a distance, small hurts that meant nothing, for she had recognized the source of music.

Rafe. Rafe and his harmonica, mournful chords lamenting love and loss. It was Alana's own song curling toward her across the night, drifting down on the seamless black surface of her despair, music shimmering with emotion. Once, she had sung this song with Rafe. Once, they had looked into each other's eyes and shared sad songs of death and broken dreams; and they had smiled, certain of the endurance of their own love.

> I heard a lark this morning
> Singing in the field.
> I heard a lark this morning
> Singing wild.
>
> It didn't know
> You had gone away.
> It didn't know
> Love had gone to yesterday.
>
> I heard a lark this morning
> Singing wild.
> I heard a lark this morning
> Singing free.
>
> Maybe tomorrow I'll know.
> Maybe tomorrow you'll tell me
> Why the lark sang.
> And maybe yesterday
> Never came.
>
> I heard a lark this morning
> Singing in the field.
> I heard a lark this morning
> Singing free.
> It did not sing for me.

The music Alana had once picked out on her guitar now came back to her in haunting chords sung by Rafe's harmonica. The words she had written ached in her throat and burned behind her eyes. Thick velvet folds wrapped around her legs, slowing her. She picked up the hem of the robe and began to run toward the cabin, not feeling the rough path or the tears running down her face, drawn by her music, and his.

The cabin stood alone in a small clearing. There was no flicker of candlelight, no yellow shine of kerosene lamps, nothing but moonlight pouring through the cabin windows in a soundless fall of silver radiance. Sad harmonies shivered through the clearing, shadows of despair braiding through the pale brilliance of moonlight. Slowly, like a sigh, the song dissipated into silence. The last, transparent notes were born away on a cold swirl of wind.

Alana stood at the edge of the clearing, transfixed by music, aching with silence. Only her face was visible, a ghostly oval above the textured darkness of her robe and the sliding black shadows of pines flexing beneath the wind. She hesitated, feeling the wind and tears cold on her cheeks. Then the mournful chords began all over, sorrow coming back again, unchanged.

I heard a lark this morning . . .

Alana couldn't bear to stand alone in the haunted, wind-filled forest and listen to her lonely song played by the only man she had ever loved. Slowly, she walked across the clearing, seeing only tears and moonlight, hearing only song and sadness. She went up the cabin steps like a ghost, soundless, wrapped in darkness. The front door stood open, for there was neither warmth nor light to keep inside.

The cabin had only one room. Rafe was stretched out on

the bed that doubled as a couch during the day. Only his face and hands were visible, lighter shades of darkness against the overwhelming night inside the cabin. Silently, without hesitating, Alana crossed the room. She didn't know if Rafe sensed her presence. He made no move toward her, neither gesture nor words nor silence. He simply poured himself into the harmonica, music twisting through her, chords of desolation shaking her.

Alana knelt by the bed, trying to see Rafe's face, his eyes. She could only see the pale shimmer of moonlight, for the sad strains of music had blinded her with tears.

> I heard a lark this morning
> Singing wild.

She swayed slightly, her body lost to the music, her mind floating, claimed by emotions that were as wary and elusive as trout shimmering deep within a river pool. With each familiar chord, each aching harmony of note with note, she felt the past sliding away, fear draining into song until she knew only music.

She didn't know how many times the song ended and began, notes curling and curving across her inner darkness, music drifting down, floating, calling to her, luring her up from the dark depths of her own mind. She only knew that at some point she began to sing.

At first Alana's song was wordless, a supple blending of her voice with the harmonica's smooth sounds, clear harmonies woven between instrument and singer. The melody line passed between them, changed by one and then the other, renewed and renewing each other by turns.

And then like a wild lark, Alana's voice flew free. It soared and turned on invisible currents, swept up emotions and transmuted them into pouring song, a beauty so transparent, so flawless that a shiver of awe rippled through Rafe. For an instant the harmonica hesitated; then he gave himself to the music as completely as Alana had, pursuing the brilliant clarity of her voice, soaring with it, sharing her ecstatic flight out of darkness, touching the sun. . . .

Then there was nothing left of the song but the last note shimmering in the darkness, sliding into moonlight and the soft whisper of wind. Alana put her head in her hands and wept soundlessly. Rafe stroked her hair slowly, gently, until her lips turned into his palm and he felt her tears slide between his fingers. With careful hands, he eased Alana onto the bed beside him, murmuring her name, feeling her shiver as she came close to him. Her hands were cool when she touched his face, and she shivered again.

Rafe shifted until he could free the sleeping bag he had been lying on. He unzipped it, spreading fragrant, smooth folds of warmth over Alana. When he started to get out of bed, she made an inarticulate sound of protest and sat up.

"Lie still," Rafe said, kissing Alana's cold hands. He slid out of bed and closed the cabin door, shutting out the wind. "I'll start a fire."

Rafe moved swiftly in the darkness. Alana heard the muted rustle of paper and kindling, then the muffled thump of cured wood being stacked in the fireplace. A match flared in the darkness. Alana blinked, then held her breath, shivering again. Rafe's face looked like a primitive mask cast in gold, and his eyes were incandescent topaz beneath the dense midnight of his hair. For long moments he and the fire watched one another, two entities made of heat and potent light.

With the silence and grace of flame, Rafe turned toward Alana, sensing her eyes watching him. He stood and came toward her, his expression concealed by shadows. The bed shifted beneath his weight as he sat and looked at her face illuminated by the gliding dance of flames. Her eyes were both dark and brilliant, her skin was flushed, and her lips were curved around a smile. Reflected fire turned and ran through her hair in liquid ribbons of light.

"You are even more beautiful than your song," whispered Rafe. His fingertip traced Alana's mouth and then the slender hand that rested on top of the sleeping bag. "You're cold," he said, taking her hand and rubbing it gently between his palms. "How long were you outside?"

Alana tried to remember how long she had stood in the clearing, but all that seemed real to her now was Rafe's heat flowing into her as he touched her. "I don't know," she said.

Silently, Rafe rubbed Alana's hands until they no longer felt cool to his touch. When his fingers went up her arm, he encountered the heavy velvet of the robe she wore. He made a startled sound, then laughed softly.

"So that's where it went," said Rafe.

"What?" asked Alana, her voice soft, almost husky.

"My bathrobe."

"Yours?" asked Alana weakly. "I thought it was Bob's. The sleeves come down over my knuckles and the hem drags on my toes and—"

"—I'm such a shrimp," finished Rafe, smiling.

"Rafael Winter," she said, exasperation and laughter competing in her voice, "you're six feet tall and must weigh at least a hundred and seventy pounds."

"Closer to one-ninety."

In startled reappraisal, Alana looked at the width of Rafe's shoulders outlined by firelight. "Those are hardly the dimensions of a shrimp," she pointed out.

"I know. You're the one who keeps thinking that my clothes belong to Bob." Rafe's weight shifted, sending a quiver through the bed. "You're such a tiny thing, I'll bet you got the hem all muddy. Unless you're wearing high-heeled slippers?"

"No. Twice."

Rafe looked at Alana. A smile made firelight glide and gleam over his moustache. "Twice?"

"I'm five feet five. Not a tiny thing at all. And I'm barefoot."

"Barefoot?" said Rafe, all amusement gone from his voice. He moved to the end of the bed and pulled aside the sleeping bag until he could see her feet. "There's glass on the path from here to the main cabin. Not to mention sharp rocks and—" His voice died abruptly as he saw thin, dark lines of blood on her feet. "You cut yourself."

Alana wiggled her toes. "Little scratches, that's all," she said, tucking her feet up beneath the warm sleeping bag.

Rafe got up, went to the stove and tested the water in the kettle. He had intended to make coffee, but when he had found the harmonica on the kitchen shelf, he had forgotten about everything else. Although the fire in the stove had long since died, the water was still warm. He poured some into a basin, pulled a clean cloth from a drawer, took a bar of soap from the sink and returned to Alana.

"Rafe," she protested, squirming slightly as he pulled her foot out from under the sleeping bag and began washing the abrasions with warm water.

"Rafe what?" he asked, sitting sideways on the end of the bed, resting her ankle on his thigh. "Am I hurting you?"

"No," she said softly.

"Tickling you?"

Alana shook her head, watching Rafe as he washed both

of her feet and rinsed them carefully. Then he examined the cuts with very gentle touches, making sure that all the dirt was out.

"Hurt?" he asked.

"No."

"I don't have any antiseptic in this cabin."

"I don't need it," said Alana quickly.

"Yes, you do," countered Rafe in a firm voice. "Dr. Gene made a big point of how run down you were, fair game for any bug that came along." Rafe stopped, then smiled crookedly. "I take it back. I do have some antiseptic here, after a fashion."

Alana watched while Rafe took rag, soap and basin back to the tiny corner kitchen. He opened a cupboard and pulled out a fifth of Scotch.

"I'll bet it stings," she said as Rafe knelt by the end of the bed.

"Bet you're right. Bet that next time you go walking you'll remember to wear your shoes, tenderfoot."

Alana's breath came in sharply as Rafe applied whiskey to her cuts, using the tip of his finger. He blew across the cut, taking away some of the sting. Then he went to work on the next scrape, applying Scotch, blowing quickly, his eyes and the whiskey glowing gold in the firelight. When Alana's breath hissed sharply over the last cut, Rafe's fingers tightened on her foot.

"Why am I always hurting you?" he whispered, pain turning in his voice, tightening it into a groan.

Rafe bent his head until he could kiss the delicate arch of Alana's foot. His lips lingered in silent apology for having caused her pain, no matter how necessary it might have been. One hand cradled the arch of her foot, warming her, while the other hand stroked from the smooth skin at the top of her foot to the graceful curve of her ankle. He caressed her warmly, hands and mouth moving over her, savoring the heady mixture of Scotch and her sweet skin.

"Rafael," cried Alana softly as her toes flexed and curled into his palm in an involuntary, sensual response.

Rafe's whole body tightened as he fought a short, savage battle with himself for control. With an invisible shiver of rebellion, his hands obeyed the commands of his mind. Swiftly, he put Alana's feet under the sleeping bag and tucked it around her.

"Rafe . . . ?"

Without answering, Rafe stood and went to the fire. Using swift, abrupt motions he added wood to the hearth until the flames rushed upward into the night with a sound like wind.

"Warm enough?" he said finally, turning from the savage leap of flames to face Alana.

"No," she answered honestly, shivering slightly, watching Rafe with dark eyes, wondering why he looked so hard, so angry.

Rafe crossed the room in three strides, grabbed the day bed and pulled it closer to the fire with an ease that shocked Alana. Because he was so gentle with her, she kept forgetting how powerful he was.

"How's that?" asked Rafe, turning away from her to watch the fire with eyes that also burned.

"Not as warm as your hands felt," she said softly. "Not nearly so warm as your mouth."

Rafe spun toward Alana as though she had struck him. "Don't," he said, his voice harsh.

Alana's eyes widened; then her eyelashes swept down, concealing her confusion and pain. But nothing concealed the change in her mouth from smiling softness to a thin line, happiness flattened by a single word. Rafe saw, and knew that he had hurt her once again. He swore silently, with a savagery that would have shaken her if she had been able to hear him.

"I'm sorry," she whispered. "I thought—" Alana's voice broke, then strengthened as she sat up and pushed aside the sleeping bag. "I thought you wanted me." She made a helpless gesture, then slid out from beneath the sleeping bag and stood up, pulling the robe tightly around her. His robe.

"That's the problem," Rafe said. "I want you so much I get hard just looking at you. I want you so much that I don't trust myself to be petted and then to let you go. I want you—too much. A thousand times I've dreamed of having you in my arms, loving you, touching you, tasting you and then burying myself in your softness, feeling you loving me deep inside your body until nothing is real but the two of us and then there is only one reality—*us*." Rafe looked away from Alana to the fire raging in the hearth. "I've dreamed too often, too much," he said harshly. "You'd better go, Wildflower. Go now."

Alana sank back onto the bed for the simple reason that her legs felt suddenly weak. Rafe's words had washed over her in a torrent of desire so consuming that she couldn't stand. She thought of Rafe holding her, her body helpless beneath his strength as he became a part of her; and she waited for fear to come, freezing her.

But fire came instead, freeing her.

Slowly, Alana stood. She walked soundlessly across the short distance separating her from Rafe. He stood with his back to her, his neck corded with tension. When her arms slid around his waist, his whole body stiffened.

"I'm yours, Rafael," she said softly.

She felt the tremor that went through him, felt the slide and flex of powerful muscles as he turned in her arms and looked down into her eyes. Watching her, waiting for the least sign of withdrawal, of fear, he closed his arms gently around her. And then his arms tightened slowly, inexorably, drawing her against his body, holding her with the power and the hunger that he had fought so long to conceal from her. She tilted back her head and watched him through half-closed eyes, lips parted and waiting for his kiss.

With a muffled groan, Rafe bent his head and took what she offered, searching the softness of Alana's mouth with hard, hungry movements of his tongue. The force of his kiss bent her back over his powerful arm, but she didn't protest. She clung to him with fierce joy, giving herself to his strength, knowing that he was testing her, trying to discover if she would freeze, trying to find out while he could still stop himself. He shifted her in his embrace, holding her head in the crook of one arm and bringing her hips against him with the other. She answered with a soft moan and a supple movement of her body that sent whips of fire licking over him.

Despite the passion and power of Rafe's embrace, he was careful not to lift Alana off her feet. He didn't want to test either of them to that extent, for he knew suddenly that he couldn't let her go. He had dreamed of her too long, and this was too much like his dreams, cabin and firelight and Alana's sweet abandon in his arms.

"You aren't afraid," Rafe murmured against Alana's lips, pleading and urging and asking at the same time.

"I'm not afraid of you, Rafael," said Alana, slowly turning her head from side to side, rubbing her moist lips over his. "It was never you that I was afraid of."

She felt his strong hand slide up to her neck, felt gentle fingers trace the gold chain he had given to her, felt the slight roughness of his fingertip resting on the rapid pulse beating beneath her soft skin. His head moved, lips sliding down to her neck, his tongue touching her pulse so delicately that he could count her rapid heartbeats. His hand shifted, sliding inside the robe until the firm curve of her breast fitted into his hand and her heartbeat accelerated wildly.

"Yes," Rafe said thickly, "this is my dream. Your response, your hunger, the way your nipple rises against my palm, wanting my touch."

Alana's body curved against Rafe, savoring the hard muscles of his thighs, the heat of him as he moved against her, the texture of his flannel shirt beneath her palms. With a small sound, she slid her hands up to his head, buried her fingers in his thick, soft hair.

"Winter mink," she sighed, flexing her fingers sensually, shivering as Rafe arched against the caress, his whole body tightening against her. "I'd like to feel you all over me."

"You're going to," said Rafe, biting Alana's neck in a caress that was neither wholly gentle nor wholly wild. "Every bit of you, every bit of me."

The knowledge that Alana wasn't going to run away brought a greater measure of control back to Rafe. He no longer felt driven to steal what he could in the instants before she became afraid. She wasn't retreating from his strength; she was coming closer to him with every breath, every heartbeat, every touch. He untied the velvet robe in slow motion, taking it from her with hands that savored the pleasure of the moment and the woman who turned toward him smiling.

When Rafe dropped the robe onto the bed, the indigo velvet shimmered invitingly in the firelight. He didn't notice. He saw only Alana and the soft, floor-length nightgown that was the color of a forest at dusk. Tiny, flat silver buttons flickered, reflecting the dance of flames, tempting Rafe's finger to trace the shining circles from

Alana's throat to her thighs. His hand lingered on the buttons, gently kneading the slight, resilient curve of her stomach before continuing down until she moaned and her fingernails dug into his shoulders.

Rafe laughed softly and retraced the line of tiny buttons until they ended just below the hollow of Alana's throat. His fingers moved over the first button, trying to open it. But the button was very small, very stubborn, and his hand was less than steady.

"This nightgown would try the patience of a saint," said Rafe, amusement and passion equally mixed in his voice.

"The neckline is wide enough that I don't bother with the buttons," Alana admitted, bending her head to brush her lips across Rafe's fingers.

"But I've dreamed so many times of undressing you slowly," Rafe said, smiling and very serious. "I'm going to enjoy each button, each new bit of you revealed. And then I'm going to look at you wearing nothing but firelight. I won't even touch you at first," he said, rubbing the backs of his fingers lightly across Alana's soft lips. "I'll just look at you and remember all the times I could see you only in my dreams. I've dreamed of that, too, a dream within a dream."

Alana trembled, caressed as much by Rafe's words as she was by his hands. Rafe saw her shiver, felt the warm outrush of her breath against his fingers. He moved both hands to the line of buttons but became distracted when Alana's breasts brushed against the sensitive skin of his inner arms. His arms moved lightly against her, her breasts changing as he stroked her until her nipples stood boldly against the tantalizing softness of her nightgown. He bent his head and caressed the tip of her breast with his teeth, taking deep pleasure in the response that shivered through her.

Reluctantly, Rafe's hands returned to the tiny buttons. One by one they came unfastened until Alana's skin glowed between dark green folds of cloth. He kissed the softness and warmth of her, following the yielding line of buttons with his mouth. Slowly, sensuously, his mouth slid down her body, pursuing the elusive buttons, pausing only to kiss one breast, then the other, caressing her with teeth and tongue until she moaned and her fingers tangled helplessly in his hair. Only then did he continue down, his hands less steady, his breathing quicker, the taste and feel of her consuming him as passion pooled thickly, urgently between his thighs.

Swiftly, smoothly, Rafe knelt in front of Alana, his fingers moving over the remaining buttons until they were undone. He tugged at the cloth until it reluctantly yielded the secrets of her body, soft folds clinging to each feminine curve for long moments before giving up and sliding to the floor. For the space of several breaths Rafe simply looked at Alana, her skin flushed by firelight and passion, the smooth rise of her breasts, the rich contrast of her dark nipples against her glowing skin, and the tempting, midnight gleam of hair below her narrow waist.

When the tip of Rafe's tongue teased Alana's navel and his hands found the taut swell of her hips, she swayed even closer to him, calling his name. Rafe closed his eyes, letting the sound and scent and feel of Alana sink into him, healing and inflaming him at the same time. He had dreamed of this so many times, of touching her until she was too weak to stand and then carrying her to the bed, caressing her intimately until she cried aloud her need for him.

But he was afraid to lift her, carry her, afraid to shatter both dream and reality with a single incautious motion.

Rafe brushed his mouth across Alana's stomach, savored again the sweetness of her buttocks taut beneath his hands.

Then he stood quickly, ignoring the hammer blows of desire in his blood, dream and reality condensed into a passion that raged at the restraint he imposed on himself. With impatient hands he pulled off his own clothing and threw it aside.

At the sound of Alana's swiftly drawn breath, Rafe turned toward her, suddenly afraid that she would flinch from the naked reality of his desire. And then Rafe stood, motionless. Alana was looking at him the same way he had looked at her, her eyes reflecting fire as she touched him with hands that shook, wanting him with a force that made her tremble like an aspen. Alana's fingers went from Rafe's shoulders to his thighs in a single, shivering caress that almost destroyed his control. For an instant he let her fingertips trace the outline of his desire, and then he caught her hands between his own.

"No," said Rafe hoarsely. "If you touch me again I'll lose control. This time, let me touch you. Next time you can tease me until I go crazy, but not this time. This time is too much like my dreams. This time it's all I can do not to pull you down and take you right here on the cabin floor."

Alana closed her eyes, knowing that if she looked at Rafe right now she would have to touch him. With a graceful motion she turned away and stretched out on the velvet robe. Only then did she open her eyes and look at the man standing beside the bed, Rafe with firelight licking over his powerful body, molten gold pooling in his eyes, the most beautiful thing she had ever seen. When she spoke, her voice was a soft, husky song. "Come dream with me, Rafael."

Rafe came down onto the bed next to Alana and gathered her into his arms in one continuous movement. He held her as though he expected something to wrench her from his embrace, ending the dream, leaving him to wake hungry and despairing, the past repeating itself endlessly, dream sliding into waking nightmare. Alana felt Rafe's mouth demand hers, felt his arms close powerfully around her, felt the bruising male strength of his body, the hardness and the hunger of him; and she returned the embrace, holding on to him with every bit of her strength. After a long time, Rafe drew a deep, shuddering breath and released her.

"I'm sorry. I didn't mean to hurt you," he said, kissing her gently, repeatedly, tasting her with each word, unable to stay away from her for more than a second at a time.

"You didn't hurt me," she said breathlessly.

Rafe touched Alana gently, his hand trembling as it moved from her temple to her lips. Eyes closed, Alana twisted blindly beneath Rafe, seeking to hold him again, to feel the heat and power of his body pressed against hers. Rafe groaned and trapped her restless hands. He kissed her palms, bit her fingertips and the flesh at the base of her thumb, sucked lightly on her wrist and the inside of her arm. She moved against his loving restraint, wanting more than his inciting, teasing caresses. He laughed softly and watched her with smoky golden eyes.

"At first," said Rafe, his voice deep, his hands stroking Alana's body almost soothingly, "after they tortured me, I dreamed only of revenge. Blood and death and the devil's laughter. Later"—Rafe's head bent until he could touch the tip of Alana's breast with his tongue—"hatred wasn't enough to keep me alive. It was for some men, but not for me. That's when I began to dream of you, deep dreams, dreaming all the way to the bottom of my mind, dreaming with everything in me." His teeth closed lightly, tugged, then he took her breast into his mouth and cherished her with changing pressures of his tongue until she cried his name again and again. "Yes," he whispered, smoothing his moustache across her taut nipple until she shivered, "I heard you calling for me when I wanted to die, calling for me and crying . . . and so I lived, and I dreamed.''

The words came to Alana like another kind of caress sinking into her soul, Rafe's voice dreaming her while his hands and mouth moved slowly over her, memorizing her as she burned beneath his touch. Strong fingers stroked down her stomach, her thighs, sensitizing her skin until her breath came raggedly. When his cheek slid up from her thigh and ruffled the blackness of her hair, she moaned his name. His hands smoothed the curve of her legs, pressing gently, asking silently. Her legs shifted beneath his touch, giving him another measure of his dream.

When Rafe felt the waiting heat and need of Alana, his hand shook. She was even softer than his dreams, more welcoming. Alana tried to say Rafe's name, but she could only moan while he caressed her deeply, telling her of his dream and her beauty as she moved sinuously, helplessly, clinging to his touch. When his mouth brushed over her, tasting and teasing her, she gave up trying to speak, to think. She cried for him with each ragged breath, each melting instant, fire spreading in rhythmic waves through her body. He moved over her slowly, covering her body with his own, filling her, and she came apart beneath him.

Motionless, rigid, Rafe listened to the song of Alana's ecstasy, better than dreams, wilder, hotter, sweeter, and then he could hold back no longer. He moved within her melting heat, sliding slowly, fiercely, then faster, giving himself to her and to the incandescent joy they had created. They moved together, wound tightly around one another, sharing each heartbeat, each rhythmic wave of pleasure; and finally they shared the shimmering silence and peace that followed ecstasy.

Chapter 12

WHEN ALANA STIRRED LANGUIDLY AND LOOKED UP AT Rafe, he was watching her with amber eyes that remembered every touch, every cry, every moment, everything. She smiled and smoothed his moustache with fingers that still trembled.

"I love you, Rafael Winter."

Rafe gathered Alana against his body a little fiercely, like a man hardly able to believe that he wasn't dreaming. "And I love you, Alana. You're part of me all the way to my soul." He kissed her eyelids and her cheeks and the corners of her smiling lips. "As soon as we get off the mountain, we'll be married. On second thought, the hell with waiting. I'll get on the radio and have Mitch fly in a justice of the peace."

Rafe felt the change in Alana, tension replacing the relaxed pressure of her body against his. He lifted his head and looked into her dark, troubled eyes. "What is it, little

216

lark? Your singing career? You can live with me and write songs, can't you? And if you want to do concert tours, we'll do concert tours. I'd like to have kids, though,'' Rafe added, smiling. ''Boys as clumsy as me and girls as graceful as you; but there's no rush. You can do whatever you want, so long as you marry me. I can't let you go again.''

''Rafael, my love.'' Alana's voice broke and tears glazed her eyes. ''I can't marry you yet.''

''Why?'' he asked, looking at her dark eyes, which were wide and haunted. ''Because Jack has been dead only a month? The marriage was a mistake,'' Rafe said bluntly. ''A pretended mourning period would be a farce.''

''Jack has nothing to do with it,'' said Alana, touching Rafe's moustache with gentle fingertips, silencing him. ''I want to be the woman who gives you children. I want to live with you and love you all the way to death and beyond, because I can't imagine ever being without you again.''

Rafe took Alana's hand and kissed her palm with lips that clung and lingered over her skin. He began to gather her gently into his arms, then stopped as she continued speaking softly, relentlessly.

''But I can't marry you until I can trust myself not to shatter into a thousand useless pieces with every thunderstorm,'' said Alana. ''I can't marry you until the sight of a big, blond stranger doesn't send me into a panic. I can't marry you until I can come to you whole, confident of myself, of my sanity.''

Alana felt Rafe's retreat in the withdrawal of his hand, saw it in the narrowing of his eyes and the expressionless mask that replaced the face that had been lit by love for her.

''Until you remember what happened on Broken Mountain?'' asked Rafe, his voice neutral.

''Yes. Before I marry you, I have to be able to trust

myself," she said urgently, pleading with him to understand.

"Trust yourself—or me?" retorted Rafe. The amber eyes that measured Alana were remote, as cool as his voice, showing nothing of the pain that his words cost him.

"Rafael," said Alana, her voice frayed, her eyes searching his face anxiously, "I trust you more than I trust myself."

"Then trust me to know what's best for us. Marry me."

Alana shook her head helplessly, wondering how she could make Rafe understand.

"So much for trust," said Rafe, his voice clipped. "Well, at least I know how long you were standing by the cascade today. Long enough to hear Stan. Long enough to believe him. Long enough to kill a dream."

"No!" said Alana quickly. "I don't believe Stan. You aren't like that. You couldn't kill Jack like that!"

Rafe's laugh was a harsh, nearly brutal sound that tore at Alana almost as much as it tore at him. With a savage curse he rolled off the bed and began pulling on his clothes. When he snatched up his shirt, the harmonica fell out of the pocket onto the floor. Firelight ran over the harmonica's polished silver surface, making it shine. Rafe scooped up the instrument, looked at it for a long moment, then tossed it onto the bed.

"Souvenir of a dream," said Rafe roughly, kicking into his boots. "I won't need it any more."

Alana picked up the harmonica, not understanding, not knowing what to say, afraid to say anything at all. But when Rafe pulled open the cabin door and started to walk into the night, Alana came off the bed in a rush and threw her arms around him, preventing him from leaving.

"Rafe, I love you," she said against the coiled muscles of his back, holding onto him with all her strength.

"Maybe you do. Maybe that's why you forgot."

Rafe started to move away, but Alana's arms tightened, refusing to let him go. The pain that had come with her refusal to marry him raged against Rafe's control, demanding release. He jerked free of Alana's arms and spun to face her, his pain naked in his expression—and his anger.

"I tried to be what you wanted, Wildflower," said Rafe, his voice so controlled that it lacked all inflection. "I tried everything I could think of to lure you out of your isolation. I reassured you in every way I could. And it wasn't enough," said Rafe, his voice getting rougher, sliding out from his control. To see Alana in front of him right now, so lovely, so unattainable, to lose her all over again—Rafe made a harsh sound and closed his eyes so that he wouldn't touch her, hold her, stir desperately among the ashes of impossible dreams.

"No matter how carefully I constructed my lures, you didn't want them enough, not quite. Finally, I even tried music," said Rafe. "I hadn't played the harmonica since the day I found out you were married. I had played it too often for you, loving you with music the way I never could with words. After you married Jack, even the thought of touching that harmonica made me blind with rage. But music had always been irresistible to you. So I picked up that beautiful, cruel instrument and I called to you with it.

"And you came to me. You sang with me. You made love with me more incredibly than in my dreams. But it wasn't enough to make you trust me," said Rafe, his eyes as shadowed with pain as his voice. "Nothing will be enough for that. You may never remember what happened on Broken Mountain, Alana. And even if you do—" He shrugged and said nothing more.

"Rafael," said Alana, tears and firelight washing gold down her cheeks, her hands reaching for him.

"No," he said gently, stepping away, out of reach of her slender hands. "I once said my hooks were barbless, Alana. I meant it. I can't bear hurting you any more. You're free."

Alana watched as Rafe turned and walked away from her, Rafe passing from silver moonlight into dense ebony shadows, Rafe moving as powerfully as the wind, leaving her alone with the echoes of her pain and his.

"Rafael . . . !"

Nothing answered, not even an echo riding on the wind. Alana stood for a long time in the cabin doorway staring into moonlight and darkness, unaware of the cold wind blowing over her naked skin. Finally, the convulsive shivering of her body brought Alana out of her daze. She closed the door and stumbled back into the cabin. With shaking hands she pulled on her nightgown, but her fingers were too numb to cope with all the tiny, mocking buttons. She kept remembering Rafe's long fingers unfastening the buttons one by one as his mouth touched her body with fire and love.

With a choked sound, Alana grabbed Rafe's heavy robe. The harmonica tumbled free of the indigo folds and fell gleaming to the floor. She hesitated, looking at the firelight caressing the harmonica's chased silver surface. She bent and picked up the instrument and put it deep in the robe's soft pocket. Then she pulled the robe tightly around her and sat at the edge of the broad granite hearth, staring at the hypnotic dance of flames with eyes that saw only night.

She awoke at the first touch of dawn. She was cold. The rock hearth she lay on was cold. She ached from the chill of unforgiving stone. Heart hammering, she tried to move but could not. She was chained by stiffness and memories called up by the cold touch of granite.

"Rafe—"

Alana's voice was hoarse, as though she had spent the night calling futilely for help that never came. But not last night. Nearly four weeks ago, when she had spent the night on the rock ledge by the lake. She hadn't called to Jack that night. She remembered now. She had called to Rafe, crying his name again and again, cries that had come from deep inside her.

Jack had laughed.

Cold, helpless, a prisoner tied to stone. It was devastating to be so helpless, to know that beyond the tiny, icy circle constricting her there was a world of heat and sunlight and laughter and love; and that none of those things could reach her.

Cold.

Ice raining down. Darkness and wind lifting her, tearing her from—

"No!" said Alana fiercely, denying the nightmare. "There's no ice here. I'm in a cabin. I'm not tied by that lake. I'm not waiting helplessly for Jack to come and either free or hurt me. I'm not a tiny, shivering aspen leaf at the mercy of cold winds. I'm Alana Jillian Burdette. I'm a human being."

Her body shivered convulsively, repeatedly. "Get up," Alana whispered hoarsely to herself. "Get up!"

Slowly, stiffly, she pulled herself to her feet. She moved awkwardly toward the cabin door. When she finally managed to open it, she saw that a new day was pouring down the stone ramparts in a thick tide of crimson light. She stared up at Broken Mountain's ruined peak, rocks shattered and tumbled, cliffs and miniature cirques sculpted by winters without end.

Alana climbed down the steps to the clearing. Her feet were too cold to feel the impact of sharp stones. She hurried to the main lodge, wanting only to get dressed before Bob got up and saw her and asked questions that she had no way to answer and no desire to answer. Stumbling in her haste, she went up the cabin steps. For an instant she was paralyzed by the thought that Rafe might be inside, that she would run to him and he would turn away from her again, leaving her freezing and alone. A nightmare. No, worse than that, for in her nightmares Rafe didn't turn away from her, he came to her and—

Alana froze in the act of opening the door. Rafe. In her nightmares. Like Jack.

Shaking suddenly, clammy, dizzy, Alana leaned against the closed door, wondering if it was memory or nightmare or a terrible combination of both that was breaking over her, drenching her in cold sweat. Rafe had been up on Broken Mountain. He had told her as much. He had told her that with the horror she had buried beneath a black pool of amnesia, there was an instant of beauty when she had turned to him. Had he told her that only to urge her into remembering, using that moment like a single perfect lure drifting down onto the blank surface of her amnesia, luring her beyond its dark depths?

Alana waited for memory or nightmare to come and answer her questions, freeing her. Nothing came but the too-fast beating of her heart, blood rushing in her ears like a waterfall, *ice and darkness and falling, she was falling*.

With a hoarse cry, Alana wrenched herself out of nightmare. She opened the lodge door and hurried up the loft's narrow stairway. She pulled on clothes at random, caring only for warmth. The fiery orange of her sweater heightened the transparent pallor of her face and the darkness below her eyes. She rubbed her cheeks fiercely, trying to bring color to her skin. It didn't help. Her eyes

were still too dark, too wide, almost feverish in their
intensity. She looked fragile and more than a little wild, as
though she would fly apart at a word or a touch.

Abruptly, Alana decided that she would have to find
Rafe. She would find him and then she would demand that
he tell her what he knew. To hell with what Dr. Gene had
said about what would or would not help her remember. To
hell with what everyone else thought was good for her or
right for her or necessary for her. *She had to know*. No
matter how horrible the truth, it could be no worse than
what she was enduring now . . . Rafael turning away from
her, sliding into night, nothing answering her cry, not even
an echo.

Alana heard someone in the kitchen. She went down the
stairs quickly, determination in every line of her body. She
would confront Rafe now. She was through running,
hiding, feeling screams and memories clawing at her throat.

But it wasn't Rafe in the kitchen.

"Morning, sis," said Bob as she walked into the kitchen.
His back was to her as he finished filling the coffee pot with
water, but he had recognized her step. "You're late, but so
are the rest of us. Poker game didn't break up until after
three." Still talking, he turned toward her as he set the
coffee pot on the hot stove. "Janice is the luckiest—my
God, Alana. What's wrong?"

"Nothing that coffee won't cure," she said, controlling
her voice carefully.

Bob crossed the room in two long strides. He reached for
Alana, then remembered Rafe's very explicit instructions
about touching her. "I'm going to see if you're running a
fever," said Bob, slowly raising his hand to her forehead.

"I'm not," said Alana, but she didn't step away from her
brother's touch.

Bob's big palm pressed against Alana's forehead with surprising gentleness. "You're cold," he said, disconcerted by the coolness of her skin.

"Right. Not a bit of fever." Alana's voice was as clipped as the smile she gave her brother. "Have you seen Rafe?"

Bob's dark eyes narrowed. "He left."

"Left?" said Alana.

"He told me he'd gotten a holler on the radio from the ranch. Something needed his attention right away. Said he'd radio us as soon as he got home."

"When?"

"It's a long ride to his ranch house, even on that spotted mountain horse of his. Tonight, probably."

"When did he leave?"

"About an hour ago. Why?"

"No reason," said Alana, her voice dry and tight as her throat. "Just curious."

"Did something happen between you two? Rafe looked as rocky as you do."

Alana laughed strangely. "Did you know that Rafe was on the mountain four weeks ago?" Then, at Bob's odd look, she said in a fierce voice, "Rafe was on Broken Mountain when Jack died."

"Sure," said Bob in a matter-of-fact tone. "How do you think you got off the mountain after you were hurt?"

"What?" whispered Alana.

"C'mon, sis," said Bob, smiling despite his worry. "Even you can't walk down three miles of icy mountain switchbacks on a badly wrenched ankle. The storm spooked all the horses, so Rafe carried you out on his back. If he hadn't, you'd have died up there same as Jack did."

"I don't remember," Alana said. "I don't remember!"

"Of course not. You were out of your head with shock. Hell, I'll bet you don't even remember Sheriff Mitchell landing on the lake and flying you out of here in the middle of a storm. Mitch told me it was the fanciest piece of flying he'd ever done, too."

Then, smiling and patting Alana's shoulder gently, Bob added, "Don't look so amazed, sis. Nobody expects you to remember anything about the rescue. When I got to the hospital, you didn't even recognize me. Hypothermia does that to you. Turns your brain to suet every time. Remember when we went after that crazy rock climber way up on the mountain? By the time we found him, he had less sense than a chicken. He did fine after we thawed him out, though."

Alana looked at Bob's very dark eyes, eyes like night, only brighter, warmer. Eyes like her own before she had forgotten. But Bob remembered and she didn't. Even when he told her, she could hardly believe. It was like reading about something in the newspaper. Distant. Not quite real.

Rafe had carried her down Broken Mountain.

She didn't remember it.

No wonder Rafe hadn't told her what had happened. Telling her did no good. Being told wasn't the same as remembering, as *knowing*. He had saved her life and she didn't even know it. He had carried her down a treacherous trail, ice and darkness all around, risked his own life for her; and it was as though it had never happened. He must have waited for her to remember after she had fled to Portland, but she hadn't remembered, hadn't called, hadn't even known that he was waiting back on Broken Mountain for her.

So Rafe had worked on Bob until her brother had asked her to come home. Once home, Rafe had treated her with gentleness and understanding, asking nothing of her, giving everything. When being in the mountains had frightened her, he had apologized, shared her pain to a degree that she wouldn't have thought possible, given her all the reassurance he could. And never once had he shown how much she was hurting him. He had loved her, cherished her, done everything possible for her except remember. No one could remember for her.

That she must do for herself.

"Alana?" asked Bob, his voice worried. "You better sit down, sis. You look like death warmed over."

"Thanks a lot." Alana's voice was thin, as thin as the smile she gave him. She forced her throat to relax, using the discipline she had learned as a singer. It was important that Bob not worry about her. It was important that he not hover or watch over her, preventing her from doing what must be done. It was important that she act natural, as though there were nothing wrong with her that breakfast and a day lazing around the lake wouldn't cure. Nothing wrong. Absolutely normal.

"Check the box in the kitchen, okay? I don't want to run out of wood halfway through the eggs." Alana's voice sounded calm, if a little flat. The smile she gave Bob echoed her voice precisely.

"Why don't you let me do breakfast?" said Bob, a worried frown creasing his forehead. "You go sit and—"

"I'll sit later, while you and the dudes are out fishing. I have a place all picked out for me. Grass and sunshine and a perfect view of aspen leaves." Alana's throat constricted as she remembered counting aspen leaves with Rafe while he lay quietly with his hands locked behind his head, smiling and aching as she touched him. She closed her eyes and took a breath. "Get cracking on the woodbox, baby brother. I don't want to spend all day in the kitchen."

Bob hesitated, then went out the back door of the cabin. A few minutes later the clear, sharp sounds of an ax biting into cured wood rang through the dawn. Carefully thinking of nothing at all, Alana moved around the kitchen, letting the routine of cooking and setting the table claim her attention. Whenever her mind veered to Rafe, she dragged it back. First she had to get through breakfast. When everyone was safely caught up in fishing, when she was alone with only her erratic memory, then she would think of Rafe. Thinking of him would give her the courage to do what had to be done.

The thought sent a moment of panic through Alana. A piece of silverware slipped from her hands and landed with a clatter on the table. With fingers that trembled, she retrieved the fork and put it in its proper place. She finished setting the table just as Janice came in.

"Good morning, Alana," said Janice cheerfully.

"Morning," responded Alana. "Coffee's ready."

"Sounds like heaven. Is Rafe up yet?"

"Yes. I'll get you some coffee," said Alana quickly, avoiding the scrutiny of the other woman's eyes. The former psychiatrist was entirely too perceptive for Alana's comfort right now.

"Is that Rafe chopping wood?" asked Janice, falling into step beside Alana.

In an instant of memory that almost destroyed her control, Alana's mind gave her a picture of Rafe working by the woodpile four years ago. His long legs had been braced, his shirt off, the powerful muscles of his back coiling and relaxing rhythmically as he worked with the ax beneath the July sun chopping stovewood. She could see him so clearly, the heat and the life of him so vivid she could almost touch him. Yearning went through her like lightning, hunger and love and loss turning in her, cutting her until she could feel her life bleeding away.

"No," whispered Alana, desperately pushing away the memory. If she thought of Rafe right now she would go crazy. Or crazier. Then, before Janice could ask any more,

Alana said quickly, "Bob drew the short straw this morning."

Despite Alana's efforts to keep her voice normal, Janice looked at her sharply. "You look a bit feverish. Are you feeling all right?"

"Fine. Just fine," said Alana, pouring coffee. Her hand shook, but not enough to spill the coffee. "Tired, that's all. Altitude, you know. I'm not used to it. That and the cold nights. God, but the nights are cold on Broken Mountain."
And I'm babbling, added Alana silently, handing Janice her coffee and saying, "Breakfast will be ready in about twenty minutes."

Janice took the cup and sipped thoughtfully, watching Alana's too-quick, almost erratic movements around the kitchen. "I thought I heard a horse ride by earlier this morning," said Janice. "Before dawn."

"That must have been Rafe," said Alana very casually, concentrating on laying thick strips of bacon across the old stove's huge griddle. Fat hissed as it met the searing iron surface.

"Rafe left?" asked Janice, startled.

"He has to check on something at the ranch. He'll be back later."

And pigs will fly, thought Alana, remembering Rafe's pain and anger. He won't come back until I'm gone. I've used up my chances with him. Her hand shook, brushing against the griddle. She took a steadying breath and thought only about getting through breakfast. One thing at a time. Now, this moment, that meant frying bacon without blistering herself through sheer stupidity. Later she would think about Rafe's leaving, about what she must do, about remembering. Later. Not now.

"I hope everyone likes scrambled eggs," said Alana, turning toward the refrigerator. No light came on as she opened the door; Rafe had forgotten to start up the generator. She pulled out a bowl of fresh eggs, then went to the back door and called to Bob. "Do you know how to start up the generator?"

The ax sank cleanly into wood as Bob called, "Sure thing." Then, gesturing toward a pile of split wood with the ax, "How much wood do you need?"

"Enough for the fireplace, too," she said, remembering the night before, when she had found the living room woodbox all but empty. "You'll want a nice fire tonight."

"What about you?" asked Bob dryly, looking over his shoulder at Alana. "Don't you want a nice fire tonight too?"

I won't be here tonight. But the words were silent, existing only in Alana's mind. "Does that mean I have to chop it myself?" she retorted, her voice sounding rough.

"Just teasing, sis," answered Bob, swinging the ax again and burying its shining blade deep in the wood. "You never could chop wood worth a damn."

Alana turned back to the stove. She was relieved to see that Janice had gone. The woman's eyes were just too intent, too knowing.

Breakfast was an ordeal that Alana hoped never to have to repeat. Toast was impossible to chew, much less swallow. She forced herself to eat anyway, sensing that if she didn't, Bob would stick by her like a mother hen for the rest of the day, worrying over her. She couldn't allow that to happen. So she ate grimly, washing down eggs and bacon with coffee, eating as little as she thought she could get away with.

As soon as Bob finished, he looked at Alana, then at Stan and Janice. "I'm going to stay behind and help Alana with the dishes. Rafe thought you should try the water on the north side of the lake, where that little creek comes in. Some real big trout hang around there feeding on whatever washes down. Now, Rafe suggested using dark flies, or the grasshopper imitation he tied for each of you. Me, I'm going to use the Lively Lady.''

Alana got up, her plate and silverware in her hands. "I'll take care of the dishes, Bob," she said, grateful that her voice came out casual rather than almost desperate, the way she felt. "If you're doing dishes while Stan is fishing, he'll get the prize for the biggest fish.''

"What prize?" asked Bob.

"Apple pie," said Alana succinctly. "Winner takes all.''

In the end, everyone stayed and helped Alana with the dishes. When the last lunch had been packed and the last dish was draining on the counter, she turned and smiled rather fiercely at everyone. "Thank you and good-bye. The trout are rising. The best fishing time of the day is slipping away. Have fun. I'll see you for dinner.''

Stan and Janice exchanged glances, then left the kitchen. Alana looked expectantly at Bob.

"I'll leave in a while, sis," said Bob, smiling genially and reaching for an apron. "Stan needs a handicap in the trout sweepstakes. I'll help you with the pie.''

Alana looked at Bob in disbelief. Determination showed in every line of his face. He didn't know what was wrong, but he plainly was not going to leave her by herself until he did.

"You'll have a long wait," she said finally. "I'm going to take a bath. A very long, very hot bath." Then, smiling, "And no, baby brother, I don't need you to scrub my back.''

Bob had the grace to laugh. But the laugh faded quickly into concern. "You sure?" he asked softly.

"I've never been more sure of anything in my life.''

Alana's eyes held Bob's. "It's all right, Bob. Go fishing. Please."

Bob expelled a harsh breath and ran his hand through his black hair. "Alana, I'm worried. Rafe looked like hell. You look worse. I feel like the guy who grabbed for the brass ring and came up with a handful of garbage. I want to help you, but I'm damned if I know what to do."

"Go fishing," said Alana, her voice soft and certain.

In the end, Bob gave in. "I'll be at the north side of the lake if you need me. Why don't you come over for lunch?"

"I'll probably be asleep."

"Most sensible thing you've said today," retorted Bob, looking pointedly at the dark circles beneath his sister's eyes. Then he threw up his hands and walked out of the kitchen. "We'll be back for dinner about five," he called over his shoulder.

"Good luck," said Alana.

She held her breath until she heard the front door of the cabin close. Then she ran to the window and looked out. Bob had picked up his rod, net and fishing vest and was stalking over the lake trail with long, powerful strides.

"Take care, big brother," whispered Alana. "Don't be too mad at me. You did everything you could. Like Rafe. It's not your fault that it wasn't enough."

Alana pulled off her apron with shaking hands and hung it on a nail by the back door. Then she ran upstairs and began stuffing warm clothes into the backpack that she had found in her closet. Broken Mountain could be cold, brutally cold. She of all people should know that.

Alana went down the stairs, listening to her racing heart and the harsh thump of her hiking boots on the wooden stairs. She ran to the kitchen and began throwing food into the backpack. Cheese, raisins, granola, chocolate. Then she closed the flap.

For an instant Alana stood and looked uncertainly around the kitchen. A note. She had to leave a note. She scrambled frantically through the drawers, looking for paper and a pencil. When she found them, she couldn't think of anything to say. How could she explain in words something that she barely understood herself? Yet she had to write something. She owed Bob that much. She bent over and wrote quickly:

> When Rafe calls, tell him I've gone
> to find the lark.
> <u>This time it will sing for me.</u>

Chapter 13

ALANA WALKED ALONG THE TRAIL, GRATEFUL FOR THE trees screening her from the lake. Through the breaks in the forest, she could see three people spaced out along the north side of the lake. Bob looked no bigger than her palm. Bits of sound floated across the lake to her, fragments without meaning.

When she came to a fork in the trail, she hesitated for a moment. The right-hand path wound back to the lake, coming out just in front of the cascade where she had overheard Stan and Rafe arguing. The left-hand path skirted the worst of the rock jumble that formed the basis of the cascade. Alana adjusted the backpack and turned onto the left fork of the trail.

Once past the fork, the trail began in earnest the long climb to the top of Broken Mountain. The first part of the climb consisted of long switchbacks looping through the

forest. Before Alana had gone half a mile, she wished she
had Sid to do the work for her. But taking the horse would
have been too great a risk. Sid would have spent the first
mile neighing to the horses hobbled in the meadow behind
the main cabin. Short of a siren, nothing carried better in
the high mountains than the neigh of a lonely horse.

Sunlight quivered among aspen leaves and fell silently
through evergreen boughs. The air was crisp, fragrant with
resin, dry but for the occasional stirring of wind off the
lake. The cascade's distant mutter filtered through the
forest, telling Alana that she was approaching one of the
open, rocky sections of the trail. She would have to be
careful not to be spotted by the fishermen below.

The forest dwindled, then vanished as the trail crawled
over a steep talus slope. Broken stone in all sizes littered the
ridge. The thunder of the cascade came clearly across the
rocks. To the right of the trail the land fell away abruptly,
ending in the sapphire depths of the lake. Alana took one
look, then did not look again. Fixing her eyes on the rugged
ground just in front of her feet, she picked her way across
the talus slope. For the first hundred yards her breath came
shallowly, erratically. Then she regained control of her
breathing. Slowly her fear of heights diminished, giving
strength back to her legs.

Just before she dropped out of sight over a fold of Broken
Mountain, Alana turned and looked down at the lake.
Wisps of brilliant white cloud trailed iridescent shadows
over the water, emphasizing the clarity and depth of both
lake and air. Alana's heart beat faster and her palms felt
clammy, but she forced herself to look at the north shore.
There were three specks, dark against the gray granite of the
shoreline. Three fishermen. No one had spotted her and run
after her to bring her back. With luck, no one would even

notice that she was gone until dinnertime. And then it would be too late to come after her. No one rode or walked high mountain trails at night unless a life was at risk.

Besides, even when Bob discovered that she wasn't at the lodge, he wouldn't think that she had gone further up Broken Mountain, all the way up to the first and highest lake, up to the lip of the cliff where water leaped into darkness, until she could stand on the exact spot where Jack had died and she had lost her mind. Surely there, if anywhere, she would remember. Surely there, where conditions most exactly matched the environment of her nightmare, she would rise from the bleak, safe pool of amnesia into the transparent light of reality.

If she didn't remember right away, she would simply stay until she did, sleeping on a rock by the lake if she had to. She would do whatever she must to remember, and accept whatever came. For the truth was that there was little at stake that she was worried about losing. That's why she had come finally to Broken Mountain.

She had nothing left to lose.

Alana climbed steadily through the morning. Though the second lake was less than two miles from the cabins, it took Alana three hours to make the climb. Part of the problem was the altitude. Another part was the roughness of the trail. The hardest part, though, was her own fear. Every step closer to the first lake was like a pebble added to her backpack, weighing her down. By the time she scrambled up the saddle of land that concealed the second lake, Alana was sweating freely and almost dizzy. She stood and looked down on the tiny, marshy stretch of water. More pond than true lake, during the driest years the second lake existed only on maps. This year, though, the winter had been thick with snow and the summer ripe with storms. The water was a rich wealth of silver against the dense green of meadow and marsh plants.

The lake had been full the last time she was there. Clouds seething and wind bending the aspens, wind shaking the elegant spruce trees, wind moaning down the slopes. It hadn't rained, though. Not then. Just clouds and a few huge water drops hurled from the heights by the wind. Thunder had been distant, erratic. The peak next to Broken Mountain had been mantled in blue-black mist and lightning. But not Broken Mountain. Not then. There thunder hadn't come until the next night.

Alana stared sightlessly at the shining silver ribbon of water nestled in a green hollow between folds of granite. Remembering. They had rested the horses there. She had gone to the edge of the small meadow and leaned against a tree, listening to the distant song of water over rock. Jack had come up behind her and she had wanted to put her hands over her ears, shutting him out. . . .

"Jilly, don't be stupid about this. We won't be famous forever. A few more years, that's all I ask."

She wanted to scream with frustration. Jack simply wouldn't accept that she couldn't go on with the farce of Country's Perfect Couple. She had to be free.

"Jilly, you better listen."

"I'm listening," she said flatly. "I'm just not agreeing."

"Then you don't understand," he said confidently. "As soon as you understand, you'll agree."

"You're the one who doesn't understand. You're not getting your way this time, Jack. You shouldn't have demanded that I marry you in the first place. I shouldn't have given in." Alana ran her hand down the long black braid that fell between her breasts. "It was a mistake, Jack. A very bad mistake. It's time we faced it."

"You're wrong. Think about it, Jilly. You're wrong."

"I've thought about nothing else for several years. I've made up my mind."

"Then you'll just have to change it."

She had turned suddenly, catching the black look he gave her. Then Jack had shrugged and smiled charmingly.

"Aw, c'mon, Jilly. Let's stop arguing and enjoy ourselves for a change. That's why we're here, remember?" he asked. . . .

Yes, she was remembering.

But it was too late. Rafe was gone. She was remembering. And she was afraid.

Alana shuddered and shifted the weight of her backpack, letting echoes and memories of the past gather around her as she climbed. At first she remembered small things, a little at a time, minutes slowly building into whole memories. The closer she came, the higher she climbed on Broken Mountain, the thinner the veil of amnesia became—and the greater her mind's rebellion. She no longer told herself that her rapid heartbeat and breathing came from altitude or exertion. She was struggling against fear just as she had struggled against Jack's stubborn refusal to face the reality of her decision to leave him.

Suddenly Alana realized that she had stopped walking. She was braced against a rock, shaking, her eyes fixed on the last, steep ascent of the trail leading to the first, highest lake. Broken Mountain waited in front of her, granite rising to the sky. It waited for her, the cliff and talus slope where wind howled and water fell into blackness and exploded far below on unyielding stone. It waited for her, and she was terrified.

"Pull up your socks and get going, Alana Jillian," she said between gritted teeth. "Like Dad always said, you can't keep the mountain waiting. Besides, what do you have to lose that you haven't already lost?"

She fastened her eyes onto the trail just in front of her feet and began walking. She didn't look up, didn't stop, didn't think. One by one, memories came, wisps of cloud gathering over the blank pool of amnesia, clouds and memories condensing into columns of white seething over mountaintops, over her.

Alana stood at the edge of the tiny, hanging valley where the first lake lay beneath the sullen sky. Thunder rumbled distantly, forerunner of the storm to come. But not yet. The clouds hadn't met and wrapped around each other and the peaks. Only then would the storm begin, bringing darkness in the midst of day, black rain and white ice and thunder like mountains torn apart.

But not yet. She had a breathing space in the shelter of the stunted trees that grew in the lee of the mountaintop, Broken Mountain looming raggedly against the sky. At the base of the shattered gray peak lay the lake, mercury-colored water lapping at the very lip of the valley. She looked away from the white water leaping over the valley's edge, water falling and bouncing from rock to boulder, water exploding like thunder.

Jack flying out, turning and falling, white water and screams.

Alana slipped out of her backpack and went like a sleepwalker to the edge of the trail. Was it here Jack had fallen? She looked over the edge, suffered the wave of dizziness and looked again. No, it hadn't happened here. Where, then? The trail turned to the right, keeping to the trees. To the left was the end of the lake and the beginning of the waterfall, lake and rock and land falling away. Suddenly, nausea turned in Alana, and a fear so great that it brought her to her knees.

The lake. The lake lapping at the edge of space, water

churning, thunder bounding and rebounding, darkness and screams. She was screaming. No, it was the wind that screamed. The wind had come up at dawn and she had shivered until Jack came. . . .

"Change your mind yet, Jilly?"

She closed her eyes and said nothing, did nothing, helpless, tied to stone.

"That's okay, babe. We've got all the time in the world."

"Untie m-me." Her voice came at a distance, a stranger's voice, harsh as stone scraping over stone.

"You going to listen to me if I do?"

"Y-Yes."

"You going to stop crying for Winter?"

Silence.

"I heard you, Jilly. Last night. Lots of nights. I'm going to break you of loving Winter, Jilly. I'm going to break you, period. When we get down off this mountain, you'll come to heel and stay there."

Alana listened, all tears gone. She listened, and knew that Jack was crazy. She listened, and knew that she would die on Broken Mountain unless she stopped crying and started using her head. Her mind worked with eerie speed and clarity, time slowing down as she sorted through probabilities and possibilities, certainties and hopes. And then came understanding, a single brilliant fact: she must get Jack to untie her. And then the second fact: Jack's only weakness was his career; he needed her.

"If you l-leave me on this rock any longer, I'll be too s-sick to sing."

Jack put his hand on Alana's arm. It was cold enough to shock him. He frowned and fiddled with the zipper on his jacket. "Are you going to listen to me?"

"Y-Yes."

Jack untied her, but Alana was too stiff, too weak to move. He hauled her off the rock and set her on her feet. She fell and stayed down, helpless, tied by a pain that made her dizzy and nauseated. Finally, feeling began to come back to her strained joints and limbs, and she cried hoarsely, never having known such agony.

Jack half-dragged, half-carried Alana to the camp, jerking her along, her braids wound around his hand. He dropped her casually by the fire. She lay there without moving, her mind spinning with pain. Eventually the worst of it passed and she could think. She concealed the fact of her returning strength, afraid that Jack would tie her again. When he spoke to her, she tried pretending that she was too dazed to answer. He hit her with the back of his hand, knocking her away from the fire. She lay motionless, cold and aching and afraid.

"You listen to me, Jilly. I need you, but there are other ways, other women who can sing. I've been sleeping with one of them. You can sing circles around her, but," shrugging, "she heels a hell of a lot better than you do. Don't be more trouble than you're worth."

Alana shuddered and said nothing. It seemed hours before the moment came that she had been waiting for. Jack went to get more wood. She came up off the ground in a stumbling rush, running in the opposite direction, seeking the cover of the forest and boulders on the mountainside.

That was the beginning of a deadly game of hide-and-seek, Jack calling to her, threats and endearments, both equally obscene to Alana's ears as she dodged from tree to thicket to boulder, her heart as loud as thunder. Storm clouds opened, drenching the land with icy water mixed with sleet. Weakened by cold, her mind fading in and out of touch with reality, Alana knew she was running out of time and possibilities. Her only chance was to flee down the mountain. She had been working toward that from the first moment, leading Jack around the lake until he was no longer between her and escape.

Now only the margin of the lake lay between her and the trail down Broken Mountain, the lake where water lapped over boulders and then fell down, down, to the rocks below. There was no shelter there. No place to hide from Jack. Lightning and thunder shattering the world into black and white shards. Ice sleeting down, freezing her.

And then a rock rattled behind her, Jack coming, reaching for her.

Cold.

She was too cold but there was no warmth, only fear hammering on her, leaving her weak. She tried to scream but no sound came. She tried to run but her feet weighed as much as mountains and were as deeply rooted in the earth. Each step took an eternity. She had to try harder, move faster or she would be caught.

Something caught her braids, jerking her backward with stunning force. Jack loomed above her, *anger twisting his face. Jack cursing her, grabbing her, hitting her, and the storm breaking, trees bending and snapping like glass beneath the wind. Like her. She wasn't strong enough. She would break and the pieces would be scattered over the cold rocks.*

Jack slipped on the rocks, white pebbles of sleet gathering and turning beneath his boots. He let go of Alana's braids, breaking his fall with his hands.

Running. Scrambling. Breath like a knife in her side. Throat on fire with screams and the storm chasing her, catching her, yanking her backward while rocks like fists hit her. She was broken and bleeding, screaming down the night, running.

Caught. Her braids caught in Jack's fist, ice sliding beneath her feet, wind tearing at her, Jack lifting her as she screamed, lifting her high and when he let go she would fall as the water fell, down and down, exploding whitely on rocks far below.

Clawing and fighting. But she was swept up, lifted high, helpless, nothing beneath her feet, earth falling away and her body twisting, weightless, she was falling, falling, black rushing up to meet her and when it did she would be torn from life like an aspen leaf from its stem, spinning away helplessly over the void.

She called to Rafe then. Knowing that she was dead, she flung his name and her love for him like a talisman into the teeth of the waiting mountain.

And Rafe answered.

He came out of the storm and darkness like an avenging angel, his hands tearing her from Jack's deadly grasp. Rafe spun aside from the drop-off at the last instant, balanced on the brink of falling. With certain death in front of him and Alana at his feet, Rafe whirled around and launched himself in a low tackle that carried Jack away from Alana, helpless at the edge of the cliff. The two men grappled in the darkness, pale sleet rolling beneath their feet, the struggle bringing them closer to the brink with each second.

Rafe kicked away, freeing himself and coming to his feet in a single smooth motion. Jack staggered upright, his hair shining palely with each flash of lightning, his face dark with hatred. He leaped blindly for Rafe.

But Rafe wasn't there. He slipped the attack with a supple, disciplined movement of his body, leaving nothing but night between Jack and the lip of the cliff. Jack had an instant of surprise, a scream of fury and disbelief, and then he was falling, turning over slowly, screaming and falling into night.

Silence came, and then the sound of Alana's tearing screams.

"It's all right, Wildflower. I've come to take you home."

Alana shuddered, giving her mind and her body to the cold and blackness. . . .

Alana stirred and slowly surfaced from memories. She was surprised to find that it was day rather than evening, fair rather than stormy, and she was huddled on her knees rather than unconscious in Rafe's arms. She shook her head, hardly able to believe that she wasn't still dreaming. Rafe's words had sounded so real, so close. She opened her eyes and saw that she had walked to the treacherous margin of rock and water and cliff. With a shudder, she turned away from the edge; and then she saw a man silhouetted against the sun. She froze, fear squeezing her heart.

Rafe's face tightened into a mask of pain when he saw Alana's fear. She had remembered, and he had lost her.

"Stan was right," said Rafe, pain roughening his voice. "You were running from me, too. You didn't want to believe that the man you loved was a killer."

"No!" said Alana, her voice shaking, making a ragged cry out of a single word.

"Yes," said Rafe flatly. "I killed Jack Reeves. And you remembered it."

"It wasn't like that," said Alana, shaking her head. "Stan was wrong. You didn't come up the mountain planning to kill Jack and seduce me and—"

"But Jack's dead. I killed him."

"You were saving my life," said Alana, trying to understand why Rafe's face was so closed, so remote.

Rafe shrugged. "So it's manslaughter, not murder one. Jack's dead just the same."

"It was an accident!" she cried fiercely. "I saw it, Rafe! I know!"

"Technically, yes, it was an accident," said Rafe, his voice as controlled as his expression. "When I ducked, I didn't know that Jack would go over the cliff. But there's something about the fight that you still haven't faced, Alana." Rafe spoke slowly, clearly, leaving no room for evasion or misunderstanding. "When I saw Jack trying to kill you—after that instant, Jack Reeves was a dead man walking. There was no way I'd let him leave the mountain alive." Rafe's voice changed, harsh, aching with pain. "You knew that. Yet you couldn't stand knowing it. So you forgot. But not well enough. Somewhere, deep inside, you knew. You didn't trust me enough to marry me."

"That's not true," said Alana desperately. "You saved my life! You—"

"It's all right," said Rafe, cutting across Alana's urgent words. "You don't owe me anything. You gave it all back to me that night. When you thought you were going to die, you screamed, but not for mercy or for revenge. You called to me, telling me you loved me . . . *and you didn't even know I was there*. In those few seconds you wiped out all the bitterness that had been destroying me since I found out you were married. You don't owe me anything more. Certainly not trust."

Alana looked up at Rafe wildly. "But I do trust you!"

Rafe's mouth turned down in a sad travesty of a smile. "I don't think so, Wildflower." Then, before Alana could say anything more, he turned toward the trail where his horse stood patiently. "We'd better go. Bob has probably found your note by now, and mine. He'll be beside himself with worry."

Rafe began walking toward the big spotted stallion. After a few steps, Rafe realized that Alana wasn't following. He turned back and saw that she was still sitting on a rock near the edge of the cliff. "Alana?"

She sat motionless, watching Rafe, her eyes dark. "I'll need your help."

"Did you wrench your ankle again?" asked Rafe, reaching Alana in a few swift strides. He knelt in front of her and began running his hands from her knees to her feet. "Where does it hurt?"

"Everywhere," she said softly. "You'll have to carry me."

Rafe's head snapped up. He searched Alana's eyes and her expression, afraid to breathe, to hope. Even when she had given herself to him in the moonlit cabin, he had not dared to lift her, to hold her helpless above the ground.

Silently, Alana held out her arms to Rafe.

Rafe stood and looked down at Alana for a long moment. Then he bent and caught her beneath her arms. Slowly, he lifted her to her feet, waiting for the first sign of fear to tighten her body. He held her almost level with him, her toes just off the ground. She smiled and put her hands on his shoulders.

"Higher," said Alana huskily. "Lift me higher. Lift me over your head."

"Alana—"

"Lift me," she whispered against his lips. "I know you won't let me fall. I'm safe with you, Rafael. You aren't like Jack. You won't throw my life away. *Lift me.*"

Rafe lifted her as high as he could, held her, watched her smile, felt her trust in the complete relaxation of her body suspended between his hands. Then he let her slide slowly down his body until their lips met in a kiss that left both of them shaken, clinging to each other, whispering words of love and need.

They rode double down the mountain, Rafe's arms

wrapped around Alana and her hands over his as he guided the big stallion along the trail. Rafe was the first one to spot the plane bobbing quietly on the third lake.

"Sheriff Mitchell," said Rafe. "Bob must have hit the panic button."

Alana shrank against Rafe. For the rest of the ride she was silent, her hands clinging to his wrists, her mind racing as she tried to figure out ways to protect the man she loved. No matter what Rafe said, he wasn't at fault for Jack's death. Jack had brought it on himself. Rafe didn't deserve to be punished for Jack's selfishness, his murderous rage.

Sheriff Mitchell was sitting on the porch of the lodge, his feet propped against the rail. When he heard the big stallion's hoof strike a rock, Mitch looked up.

"I see you found her," said Mitch, satisfaction in his voice, "just like I told Bob you would."

Alana spoke before Rafe could. "My memory is back, Mitch. Jack's death was an accident, just like Rafe said. It was icy and Jack fell and I passed out from shock and cold."

Mitch looked at Alana oddly. His homely face creased into a frown. "That's not what Rafe told me. He said that Jack tried to kill you, they fought, and Jack ended up dead. Is that how you remember it?"

Alana had made a helpless sound and looked over her shoulder at Rafe. He kissed her lips. "I told Mitch everything when we rode back in to bring out Jack's body. When we came off the mountain, you were gone."

"But—but that's not how the newspapers explained Jack's death," said Alana, turning back to the sheriff, confused and afraid for Rafe.

Mitch shrugged. "Well, I didn't figure that justice would be any better served if we went to the hassle of arraigning and then acquitting Rafe on a clear-cut case of justifiable homicide. And then there would have been reporters hounding you for all the bloody details, what with Jack being such a famous s.o.b. and all. You didn't need that. You were having a hard enough time staying afloat as it was. So I told the reporters the only truth that mattered: In my opinion, Jack Reeves's death was legally an accident.'' Mitch paused and looked at Alana, his gray eyes intent. ''Unless you remember it different and want to change the record?''

''No,'' Alana said quickly. ''No. I just didn't want Rafe to be punished for saving my life.''

Mitch nodded. ''That's how I had it figured.'' He pulled out a pipe from his jacket pocket. ''Well then,'' said the sheriff, changing the subject with finality, ''what's the fishing been like?''

Rafe tilted his head and kissed the nape of Alana's neck. ''You're too late, Mitch. I just caught the most beautiful trout on the mountain.''

Mitch grinned around a cloud of pungent smoke. ''Keeper size?''

Rafe laughed softly as he slid off the big stallion and held his arms out to Alana. She smiled and let him lift her out of the saddle. He held her off the ground, enjoying the sensation of her pressed against the length of his body. ''Definitely keeper size,'' said Rafe. ''Unless,'' he whispered too softly for Mitch to hear, ''the trout doesn't want the fisherman?''

Alana kissed Rafe gently, brushing her lips across his mouth as her fingers slid deeply into his thick hair, dislodging his Stetson.

The front door of the cabin slammed open. ''Mitch, when in hell are you going to—Alana! Are you okay?''

Mitch laughed. ''Bob, are you blind? She's never been better.''

Reluctantly, Rafe released Alana so that she could reassure her brother.

"I've remembered," she said quietly, turning to face Bob. "And I'm fine. I'm sorry I worried you."

"Hell, sis, it was worth it!" He turned and yelled over his shoulder. "Stan! Janice! Alana's got her memory back!"

There was a triumphant whoop from the cabin; then Janice and Stan ran out onto the porch. Stan looked at Alana wrapped securely in Rafe's arms, relaxed and smiling, obviously not afraid. Then Stan turned and gave Janice a thorough, hungry kiss.

Bob looked startled. Rafe simply smiled. "I think I better make a complete introduction this time," said Rafe. "Bob, meet Mr. and Mrs. Stan Winston."

When Stan finally let go of Janice, she smiled and said, "Now we can wash out the blond highlights and get rid of the blue contacts. If I open my eyes, I feel like I'm kissing a stranger."

Alana watched, speechless, as Stan removed his dark blue contacts, revealing eyes that were light green. "Blond highlights?" asked Alana.

"Yes," said Janice, tugging on a lock of Stan's fair hair. "I'm used to my man being a sun-streaked brown, not a California blond."

"I don't understand," said Alana.

"I'm afraid you've been caught in a conspiracy," said Janice gently. "But it was a conspiracy of love. When Rafe told me what had happened to you, I told him to give you a few weeks to remember on your own. Then he called again and told me that you weren't sleeping, weren't eating, were having nightmares—"

"How did you know?" asked Alana, turning to Rafe.

"I told you, my love. You're a lot like me."

"In short," summarized Janice, "you were tearing yourself apart. Rafe thought that if you came back here, you would see him and know that you were safe, that it was all right to remember what had happened. I agreed, so long as you came willingly. If you came back it would mean that you wanted to remember. You wanted to be whole again."

"Some travel agent," said Alana. Then, "Oh. You're still a practicing psychiatrist, aren't you?"

"One of the best," said Rafe, his arms tightening around Alana. "Damn near every word we said in front of you was vetted by Janice first."

"Not every word," said Janice, looking sideways at Stan. "I nearly choked Stan when I found out about the fight by the lake."

Stan almost smiled. "Yeah, I know. I don't take orders worth a damn. We've argued about Rafe a lot," said Stan, flashing Alana a pale green glance. "I thought she was too gentle on Rafe after he got back from Central America. And then, when she couldn't put him back together, it took two years for me to coax her into marriage."

Janice looked surprised. "Two years! You only asked me out two months before we were married!"

"Yeah. So much for being subtle. I wasted twenty-two months tiptoeing around, thinking that you held it against me that I was the one who'd been wounded. If it weren't for me, Rafe would have flown out of the jungle with the rest of us."

Rafe started to say something, but Stan cut him off.

"No way, buddy. I'm not finished. I thought you were being too gentle with Alana to get any results. Hell, I didn't even know you had that much gentle in you! I'm still having a hard time believing you're the same man I worked with in Central America." Stan shrugged. "Anyway, I wanted to stir up Alana to make her think. I didn't believe you'd snuffed old Jack to get Alana. If you'd wanted to do that, you wouldn't have waited almost four years, and you sure as hell wouldn't have been caught after you'd done it. You're too smart for that.'' Stan smiled and fell silent.

''Thanks . . . I think,'' said Rafe dryly.

Alana looked from Stan to Janice to Rafe. Finally she gave her brother Bob a long, considering look. He flushed slightly. ''You aren't mad, are you, sis?''

''Mad?'' She shook her head. ''I'm . . . stunned. I can't believe that you knew about the whole conspiracy and kept it a secret. Old in-the-ear-and-out-the-mouth Bob. I'm impressed, big brother.''

''It wasn't easy. I thought I'd blown it more than once,'' admitted Bob.

''We didn't tell him everything,'' said Rafe dryly. ''Oh, he knew that he wasn't trying to start a dude ranch, but that's about it. He didn't know that I'd worked with Stan and Janice before. He didn't know that Stan was camouflaged as carefully as any lure I'd ever made. And he didn't know that Janice was a practicing psychiatrist.''

''Well,'' said Mitch, knocking his cold pipe against the bottom of his boot, ''I'd better get down the mountain before the light goes.''

''Can you fly back tomorrow?'' asked Rafe.

''Sure. Need something in particular?''

''Champagne. A justice of the peace.''

Mitch smiled. ''Somebody getting married?''

Rafe looked at Alana, a question in his amber eyes.

''Yes,'' she said, putting her arms tightly around Rafe, ''somebody is getting married. This time, the trout is landing the fisherman.''

Alana stood by the hearth in the small cabin, wearing only Rafe's velvet robe. She let the song fade from her lips, watching Rafe as he played soft notes on the silver harmonica. He was stretched out on the bed, eyes closed, sensitive fingers wrapped around the harmonica as his lips coaxed beautiful music from it. He wore nothing but firelight, which clung and shifted with each breath he took. His hair gleamed like winter mink, alive with the reflected dance of flames. He looked up, sensing her watching him.

"Happy, Mrs. Winter?" he asked, holding out his hand.

"Yes," said Alana, taking his hand and curling up beside him, enjoying the hard warmth of his flesh beneath her cheek.

"Even though you haven't remembered everything?"

She looked at Rafe's eyes, gold in the firelight, and wanted nothing more than to be loved by him. "I don't care."

"Good. I don't think you'll ever remember coming down the mountain," continued Rafe, his finger tracing the satin darkness of Alana's eyebrow. "You were bruised, bloody, out of your mind with cold and shock. Frankly," he said in a low voice, "I'd forget it if I could. I loved you so much and I thought you were dying, that I'd come too late."

"How did you know that I needed you? Why did you come to the first lake when I was there with Jack?" whispered Alana.

"I can't explain it," said Rafe, looking at the harmonica for a moment, then carefully setting it aside. "I was half-crazy the night before I rode up Broken Mountain. I kept thinking I heard you calling me again and again, but that was impossible. I was alone at the ranch. Nothing but the wind. Yet by morning, I was wild, sure that you needed me. I had no choice but to ride up the mountain and find you. It was crazy, but I had to do it."

"You weren't crazy," said Alana, trembling. "When

Jack tied me and left me by the lake, I called for you all night long. I couldn't help myself.''

Rafe's breath came in sharply. He rolled over and faced Alana, touching her as though she were a dream and he were afraid of awakening. "I should have come to you sooner," he whispered.

"It's a miracle that you came to me at all, Rafael. You hated me."

"No," he said, kissing Alana's eyebrow, her eyelid, the corner of her mouth. "I never hated you. I wanted to, but I couldn't. We were tied too deeply to each other, no matter how far apart we were. That's why I couldn't ride away from you after we made love, even though I thought you didn't trust me. Every time the wind blew down the canyon, I heard you calling me. I had to come back to you." Rafe's fingertip traced Alana's lips. "I love you more than you know, more than I have words to say."

With slow, caressing movements, Rafe unwrapped the velvet robe until Alana wore only firelight and the fine gold chain he had given to her. The elegant symbol of infinity gleamed in the hollow of her throat, speaking silently of love that knew no boundaries. He gathered Alana close to his body, kissing her gently at first, then with a passion that was both restrained and deeply wild. She gave herself to the kiss, to him, melting in his hands, wanting him, loving him. He listened to the soft sounds that came from her, and he smiled.

"Yes, Alana," he whispered, "sing a song of love for me."

If you enjoyed this book...

Thrill to 4 more Silhouette Intimate Moments novels (a $9.00 value)— ABSOLUTELY FREE!

If you want more passionate sensual romance, then Silhouette Intimate Moments novels are for you!

In every 256-page book, you'll find romance that's electrifying...involving... and intense. And now, these larger-than-life romances can come into your home every month!

4 FREE books as your introduction.

Act now and we'll send you four thrilling Silhouette Intimate Moments novels. They're our gift to introduce you to our convenient home subscription service. Every month, we'll send you four new Silhouette Intimate Moments books. Look them over for 15 days. If you keep them, pay just $9.00 for all four. Or return them at no charge.

We'll mail your books to you *as soon as they are published.* Plus, with every shipment, you'll receive the Silhouette Books Newsletter absolutely free. *And Silhouette Intimate Moments is delivered free.*

Mail the coupon today and start receiving Silhouette Intimate Moments. Romance novels for women...not girls.

Silhouette Intimate Moments

Silhouette
Intimate Moments

more romance, more excitement

─── $2.25 each ───

Silhouette
Intimate 💑 *Moments*
more romance, more excitement

Silhouette Intimate Moments